Annaliese Darr

Believe

Don't ask why—Just Believe

Believe in the magic
Annaliese

BELLASTORIA PRESS

Books that nurture the soul

ISBN: 978-1-942209-02-7

Cover design by WickedSmartDesigns.com

Bellastoria Press
P.O. Box 60341
Longmeadow, MA 01116
info@bellastoriapress.com
www.bellastoriapress.com

To Marie Darr Dodson

That old time religion must have made an impression.

Part One

The Alpha and
Omega of Innocence

Chapter 1

Atlanta - Present time

When I fell in love I knew that God had given me another swift kick in the butt. Obviously, that was the only way He could get my attention. From childhood on I've lived in a world of secrets and half-truths, but in a blinding epiphany, I realized that if I wanted a loving husband, a couple of kids and a minivan life, I had to conquer my demons.

That's how I ended up in an Atlanta rainstorm debating the pros and cons of keeping my appointment with a therapist. It was an interesting choreography of one-step forward and two-steps back– should I or shouldn't I? That question was pinging through my brain when a gorgeous woman in a silk raincoat strolled down the stairs with the panache of Heidi Klum on the runway.

"I've been watching you from my office window. Do you need some help?" A whiff of Versace perfume accompanied her inquiry.

"I have a meeting scheduled, but I'm not sure I want to keep it." Had I really shared that with a stranger?

"So, why do you want to leave?"

The logical explanation would be that I didn't feel comfortable revealing my secrets to anyone, but truth be told, I was a chicken. I could almost hear my sister Fiona making clucking noises. But when in doubt, I defaulted to the truth. "I'm not sure."

"I suspect you're my new patient. I'm Dr. Jill Martin, but everyone calls me Dr. Jill, or simply Jill. I answer to just about anything but 'hey, you.'"

I was so busted. "I'm Springen O'Flaherty, but please call me Spring. And right now I'm terribly embarrassed."

"Don't be." Her easy grin made me feel much better. "Folks are sometimes afraid to visit me. In fact," she said, adding a chuckle, "people occasionally avoid me in social situations. They think I can read minds, but that's not true. I simply ask a lot of questions." She pointed toward the front door. "Would you like to join me for a cup of tea?"

"Sure." I followed her into a converted 1930s mansion. It had originally been designed around a wide front hall with double parlors on one side and a library and dining room on the other. During the remodel from a home to an office complex, the developer had retained most of the charming architectural features, including the mahogany trim and crown molding.

That nod to historic restoration made Dr. Jill's suite feel more like a cozy library than a sterile therapist office. She indicated a matching pair of leather wing chairs. "Please make yourself at home while I put the kettle on. It's chilly today and the fireplace makes the place feel welcoming, but I can turn it off if it's too warm."

"It's fine, and your office is lovely." I sat down and tried not to fidget.

"Thanks," she said before disappearing into a back room. Several minutes later she returned and placed a tray laden with cups of tea and a plate of goodies on an antique butler's table. "I spend a lot of time here, so I want to make it feel like a home." She held out a plate of cookies. "I made them last night. I have a sweet tooth." Her laugh was so down-to-earth it reminded me of Mama.

We chatted for a few moments before Dr. Jill steered the conversation to the business at hand. "What can I do for you?"

My first reaction was to thank her for the tea and head back to my office, but I had too much at stake to bail. "I don't want you to think I'm crazy."

She smiled. "I hear that a lot. Let me assure you that assessing your mental health is not my job. I'm here to help you work through your issues."

"Okay." I took a deep breath and tried to organize my thoughts. "I suppose I should start at the beginning."

She didn't bother to stifle her grin. "That would be a good place."

Her bit of levity was enough to loosen my tongue. "I'm in love with a wonderful man, but I've been keeping secrets from him. And some of them are so awful they might send him running for the hills." That possibility sent cold chills up my spine.

"What's his name?" she asked as she refilled her teacup.

9

Thinking about Mr. Right put a smile on my face. "Jed Collinsworth. He's the District Attorney of Fulton County."

Dr. Jill nodded. "I've heard good things about his stand on crime."

"He is one of the good guys." I didn't mention that he's also funny, sexy and smart. And best of all, he's mine—that is, unless I screw it up.

"How did you meet Mr. Wonderful?"

That part of the story was easy. The rest would be more problematic. "I'm a junior partner in a boutique law firm specializing in taxes. Sam Pritchett is a senior partner. Plus, he's my mentor and friend. He asked me to go with him to a bar association reception. His wife was in Savannah for the birth of their new grandson, so I tagged along to keep him company. As a matter of fact, Sam referred me to you."

Dr. Jill nodded. "We've been pals for a long time, but we could talk about him for hours. So back to how you met Jed."

My preference would be to procrastinate. Instead I continued my story. "The minute we walked in the ballroom Sam told me there was someone he wanted me to meet. He's always pulling tricks, so I was leery. He towed me toward a group of people standing around a temporary bar. At first, I thought our target was a paunchy man with a receding hairline, but at the last second Sam made a right turn toward the most gorgeous guy I've ever seen." I took a deep breath trying to describe the man I loved. "Jed has Bradley Cooper's good looks and the body of an athlete. When I put my hand in his, there was an incredible attraction that I can't begin to describe. It almost felt as if I'd been hit by a jolt of electricity."

"Sam, that sly old fox, made sure we were seated at the same table. It had been at least a decade since anyone had piqued my interest, but everything about Jed Collinsworth, from his looks, to his voice, to his Southern manners, was incredibly appealing. It didn't hurt that he had dimples as deep as craters." I smiled thinking about that magical evening. "Under normal circumstances, the next two hours would have been excruciating, but with Jed sitting next to me, brushing my arm and talking to me in a voice meant only for my ears, the time flew by. Before the salad plates were removed I was smitten, and by the time dessert was served, I'd tumbled head over heels."

"After dinner we strolled to a neighborhood carnival in a park across the street. There was a cool late September breeze. We ate cotton candy and threw baseballs at targets that were impossible to knock over. Then we rode the Ferris wheel, and after that we gave the carousel a try. That evening changed my life."

"When Jed walked me back to my car, he asked if he could see me again. My gut reaction was to say 'of course' but my head was more hesitant. Fortunately, I decided to go with my gut, and that was the beginning of our romance."

"How long have you been dating?"

"We met six months ago. Now we see each

other, or talk, every day."

Dr. Jill nodded. "That sounds like you're going in the right direction. So let me summarize. You've found a man you love, but you're keeping secrets that if revealed could ruin your relationship. Is that right?"

"Yes."

"Would you like to tell me about those secrets? And remember, anything you say is privileged."

It took a leap of faith, but for some reason I felt as if I could trust her. "I'm psychic. In earlier times my powers would have earned me the noose, or worse. But even in the twenty-first century people fear what they don't understand, or can't rationalize." I shrugged trying to relieve the tension in my shoulders. "My powers are like a smorgasbord, a little of this and a whole lot of that. I've seen auras for as long as I can remember. But I also have precognitive and retrocognitive abilities. That means I can see things that will happen in the future, as well as what's occurred in the past." I decided to delay telling her that I can talk to dead people until later, much later, or hopefully never.

"According to family legend one female child in every generation has the gift, and I seem to have hit the jackpot." Dr. Jill's expression didn't change throughout my monologue.

"That's fascinating." Her voice was so comforting I could feel the tight coil that had been with me my entire life start to loosen.

"Please continue," she said.

I wasn't exactly sure where to start so I decided

to go back to the beginning. "The auras are my reality. As a child I felt like I lived in a box of six-ty-four crayons. The kids were bright and shiny, while the older folks at Daddy's church were pastel and fuzzy around the edges. It was my Popsicle world. Life seemed like Christmas and Easter and the Fourth of July all wrapped up in one delightful package."

"That's a lovely description." Dr. Jill tilted her head and then asked, "What's my color?"

"You're emerald green. That means you're a healer." I leaned back and sipped my tea, as much to soothe my nerves as to provide wetness for my dry mouth. "The colors are a part of me, so I'm comfortable with them. It's the other powers that have created havoc in my life. When I touch some-one I can see their past and their future. I know if their death is imminent. That's antithetical to juris-prudence. In my work I deal with numbers and laws. I want to dwell in a structured world, but my psychic abilities play havoc with that dream."

"So that's why you didn't shake my hand."

"True," I admitted. "A lot of people think I'm standoffish, but that's really not the case. I'm afraid to connect with people, both physically and emo-tionally." And that took me full circle back to Jed. How would he handle being in a relationship with a freak?

"I think you just zoned out," Dr. Jill said, draw-ing me back to the present.

"I'm sorry. I got lost in my thoughts." I took a deep breath in an attempt to calm my racing pulse.

"As a teen I helped the police solve a crime, and that experience didn't end well for me. As you know, Jed's job is to prosecute criminals. What if I was tempted to help him with his job? And even more important, what if he asked me for assistance?"

Dr. Jill was silent for a few seconds. "Just for my clarification, why did you shake hands with him when you two first met?"

That was a good question. "My precognitive powers have never extended to my family or dear friends. I can see their auras, but that's the extent of it. When I met Jed, I *knew* that he was meant to be a part of my life."

"Okay." She nodded. "So what do you want to get out of our talks?"

I thought carefully before answering. "I want to live a normal life, and I want to be completely honest with the man I love. In order to do that, I need to be comfortable with my unique abilities." I shrugged, pondering everything I had to gain...or lose...by confiding in Dr. Jill. "I don't want to be afraid of being me. In the long run, I need to make peace with God. We haven't been very good friends lately." I was surprised that I'd made that confession. "I suppose I also want to get some of my innocence back. From there, I'll throw the dice and see what happens."

Dr. Jill smiled. "That seems like a healthy goal. Why don't you start with your early childhood? That sounded like a happy time in your life."

"It was," I said. "I remember..."

Shenandoah Valley, Virginia
September 1984

"I'm going to kindergarten!" Mama didn't like noise while she was driving, but my inside voice didn't seem to be working. "It's going be so much fun and I'm gonna make lots of new friends. Will there be Popsicle people?" I asked, even though I knew that Mama didn't like it when I talked about the colors.

"I suspect that'll be the case." She didn't seem happy, but nothing was going to bother me today. I had on the new pink dress we'd ordered from the Penney's catalogue. It had ruffles down the front and a big satin bow in back. And best of all, it wasn't a hand-me-down from my sisters Maeve and Fiona. I even had pink hair ribbons and a brand new pair of socks with lace on the tops.

I felt all grown up, that is until my tummy started feeling icky like the time at the fair when I up-chucked my corndog on the Ferris wheel.

"What if I need to pee and I can't find the bathroom?"

"Please." Maeve did that silly eye thing she'd started during the summer. "Do you have to blabber all the time?" She thought she knew everything because she was in the third grade.

"Maeve, that's enough," Mama said, and then yelled at the twins. "Boys! Stop the caterwauling. You're making me nuts." Beau and Bubba were three years old, so they were strapped in their car seats in the back of Mama's VW van. The twins were a yellow color that made them look like a couple of baby chicks.

"Mama, do you think I'm really going to like school? It's so big and I'm afraid the twins will miss me."

"Sweetie. You've been to the school before. Remember last year when I took Fiona her lunch box and I showed you the cafeteria and the playground?"

"But I've never had to stay before. And I don't know if I can find those places again."

"Oh, boy!" Leave it to my middle sister, Fiona to pipe up.

I stuck out my tongue. "Just 'cause you're in the first grade doesn't mean you're smarter than me."

"Girls, please. We're almost there." We all knew that when Mama got impatient it was time to zip our lips.

"Yes, ma'am," Fiona said, and I nodded.

"Talk quietly until I get into this parking spot." Mama turned the car this way and that trying to get into a space not much bigger than the twin's stroller. The minute she turned off the engine, Maeve hopped out and went running across the playground.

"Don't even consider following your sister," Mama warned.

Fiona took my hand. "Don't worry. You're going to have tons of fun."

There was a question that had been bothering me for weeks. "I can read a little, but I can't do whole books. Will I look like a dummy?"

"You know your letters and numbers, so you're good."

Mama got out and opened the back door. "You girls stand on the sidewalk while I get the twins."

Beau jumped out, and almost made a getaway

before Mama snagged his shirt. She pulled her purse up on her shoulder and corralled the boys.

"Spring, hold your sister's hand. We'll walk Fi to her class. Then we'll go meet your teacher."

Kids of every size and shape filled the hall, and they all seemed to be making noise.

"What if I need to talk to you?" I shouted, hoping Mama could hear me. "What if I get sick? What if..."

"No more what ifs today. Come along," Mama said, making her way through the crowd.

I was tempted to plant my heels, but I knew that wasn't a good idea. "I really, really don't want to stay."

Mama didn't say a word, at least not until she stopped in front of Fiona's classroom. "Go on in, honey." She patted Fi's head.

"Love ya. I'll pick you up out front."

"Love ya, too." Fi skipped in the room without looking back.

"Now that Fiona's taken care of, let's get you settled."

"Okay." It wasn't really, but I didn't have a choice.

The smell of chalk dust, rubber erasers, crayons, paper and sweaty kids drifted from my new classroom. "In the summer when Beau and Bubba have been playing outside, they stink like dead fish," I said. "That's what this smells like."

"You're absolutely right." Mama had the prettiest smile. "Are you ready to go in?"

"I guess." I closed my eyes and asked God to help me be brave. I stepped inside the room and when I got enough courage to pop my eyes open, I found myself in a world of beautiful colors. My sisters and brothers were surrounded by color, but this seemed so much bigger and better.

Every kid in the room was swaddled—that's from the baby Jesus story—in a different color. The kids were a rainbow of orange, red, blue and green, with some really cool purples thrown in. I wanted to do happiness cartwheels. Never in my whole life had I seen anything so awesome.

"Mama. Mama!"

"Not now, baby."

Mama was a stickler for manners, but I couldn't wait to share. "Look at the colors." Why wasn't everyone squealing about the light show? Seriously, couldn't someone else see the party colors?

Paloma—that's Mama's name when she's not being our mom—was next in line to talk to my teacher.

"Sweetheart, why don't you run over and check out the books while I have a chat with Miss Monroe?"

I'm no dummy. Mama wanted to tell my teacher something she didn't want me to hear.

"Okay."

I tried to listen, but I only heard little bits of what they were saying. Miss Monroe told Mama that she loved my blonde curls. That made me feel special. But Mama said something about me having an imagination. I didn't know what that meant, but the way she said it, it didn't sound good. She had to be talking about the colors, so I decided not to tell any of the kids about what I could see. I didn't want my teacher or my new friends to think I was a trouble maker.

Those thought were tumbling through my head

when Miss Monroe called to me. "Spring, come here, please."

"Yes, ma'am."

"Let's go meet your seat mate."

I followed her to a desk in the middle of the room. "This is Tommy Herndon," she said. "And Tommy, this is Springen O'Flaherty."

Tommy's hair was fire-truck red and he was missing two front teeth. He looked like a big boy version of the twins, but what I liked best was the bright green light all around him. He was as pretty as a Christmas tree.

"How many crayons do you have?" he asked.

"Sixteen. I wanted the big box, but Mama said I had to make do."

"That's what my mom said, too. Do you want to see my school supplies?"

"Sure."

He pulled out a brand new backpack and laid out pencils, erasers, a new tablet and his box of sixteen colors.

"I have that stuff, too," I said, spilling my supplies out on the desk.

"Do you want to be my best friend?"

I'd never had a best friend, except for Fiona, and she didn't count because she's my sister. "I'd like that."

"Pinky swear?" He held his hand out, little finger held high.

"What does that mean?"

Tommy grinned.

"It means that if we lock fingers and make a promise, we can't ever break it."

"Oh, okay. I pinky swear." I held my hand out to my new best friend.

Present Day

Much to my surprise, it felt good to discuss that part of my past. But I wasn't being completely honest with Dr. Jill. I didn't tell her that after a childhood of being best friends, and later young lovers, Tommy died in my arms, and I couldn't do anything to prevent it. Why had my powers deserted me when I needed them most?

"How are you feeling?" she asked.

"I have to admit it was refreshing to talk about that experience" I said. "That part of my childhood was special, but when logic and the surreal collide, the story will become a lot more difficult to tell."

"I know," she said. "We're done for today. I think we should schedule several more sessions. In my professional opinion, verbalizing your concerns and fears about your unusual abilities will reduce their power over you. Our goal is for you to be comfortable sharing your *secrets* with your young man"

Even though I wanted to shake her hand, I avoided the social courtesy. "As you probably guessed, I was about to abort our appointment. But I need to do this sooner rather than later. I suspect that Jed's in the market for a ring."

"So let's advance the program."

Dr. Jill checked her tablet. "How does day after tomorrow at noon sound?"

"That works for me."

"We'll talk more about your early life. Most people are molded by childhood experiences, and I suspect that's particularly true in your case."

Chapter 2

I smiled as I pulled into the driveway of my Ardmore Park bungalow. My World War II-era home was more than a place to sleep, or eat or even entertain. It was my sanctuary in a world that at times seemed overwhelming. The neighborhood somehow managed to combine the convenience of city living with an environment of rolling hills and lush vegetation. It wasn't the Shenandoah Valley of my childhood, but it was perfect for me.

My cell rang seconds after I opened the back door.

"Are we still on for dinner?" Jed asked.

"Sure." After my session with Dr. Jill, I needed to decompress. "Where are we going?" I really didn't care where we went, or what we did, as long as I could be with the man I loved. I wanted to talk to him, and touch him, and just watch him smile.

"You might want to dress up. I have something special in mind."

That sounded suspicious. "Okay. What time?" I could hear voices in the background so I knew he was still at work.

"Just a minute," he mumbled, obviously speaking to someone else. Seconds later he came back on the line. "Our reservations are for seven, so I'll pick you up around six-thirty. I have to run. I'll see you soon."

Jed had his hands full trying to keep Fulton County safe, so the quick conversation didn't bother me. After we disconnected, I went to my closet in search of the perfect outfit for... whatever. A suit? Too professional. Slacks and a sweater? Not dressy enough. I finally decided on a blue silk wrap-dress that matched my eyes. I completed the outfit with high heels and pearls. When in doubt about the proper attire, I usually deferred to my Princess Grace persona.

Between dawdling and daydreaming, it took me longer to dress than I expected. I was in front of the mirror doing a last minute inspection when Jed showed up looking like he'd just left a board meeting in his charcoal gray suit and red power tie.

Did I mention I loved that man like crazy!

"Hey." I was about to ask him about his day when he pulled me into his arms and messed up my carefully applied make-up, not that I minded.

Ten minutes later, I reluctantly disengaged myself from the seduction of his hot, wet kisses. "If we want to make it to dinner on time, I need to do some repairs." I touched his mouth where a residual smear of lipstick lurked.

Jed laughed as he took a handkerchief from his pocket. He wiped his lips and then dabbed at mine.

"You look great," he said and then placed another soft kiss on my lips before we strolled out to his sports car.

I leaned back in the leather seats and enjoyed the ride. We'd been driving for several minutes before it dawned on me that we were heading out of town. "Are we going to the river?" One of our favorite places was a catfish joint on the Chattahoochee River. Dressed as I was, I'd stick out like a debutante in a redneck bar.

"Yes, ma'am," he said, adding a wink. "But not where you think." Despite my questions, he kept mum until we pulled into the parking lot of Serenity, one of the most expensive restaurants in the Atlanta area. The tranquil river provided a beautiful backdrop for the colorful gardens.

"What are we celebrating? It's not my birthday, and it's not your birthday, so what's the deal? Did you win a big case?"

The man was a prosecuting attorney. so he knew how to keep his cards close to the vest. Instead of answering he went for a distraction by kissing my neck. That happened to be one of my very best erogenous zones.

"Enough talking, let's go enjoy ourselves," he said as he helped me out of the car.

We'd finished a wonderful meal when the waiter arrived, carrying a dozen red roses. He placed the flowers on the table and discreetly slipped away. That was when Jed pulled a small velvet box from his pocket—a ring box. And the ring was an exquisite, humongous diamond. *Oh my God*! He was about to propose. I desperately wanted to marry him, but why hadn't he waited a week, or two, or even a couple of months?

At some point I had to trust him and tell him everything, but not quite yet. There were so many reasons we didn't suit, but love wasn't one of them.

We came from entirely different worlds. A marriage between us would be like a merger between Larry the Cable Guy and Donald Trump. The Collinsworth family was Atlanta's version of royalty. Jed grew up in a 1920s mansion in Ansley Park, one of Atlanta's premier neighborhoods. He spent his vacations at the family homes in Vail and Hilton Head.

My family tree was laden with bootleggers, subsistence farmers and itinerant preachers. Not to mention that I grew up in a two-hundred-year-old farmhouse in the mountains of Virginia. We were grateful we had not only one, but two working bathrooms. And most telling of all, the O'Flaherty clan summered in the Elvis bus. But none of that mattered when Jed and I were together.

I desperately wanted him to understand what I was about to tell him. "I love you so much that I can't imagine life without you."

He started to say something, but I put my hand up. "I can't marry you, at least not right now. There are some issues that I have to settle first."

Jed jerked back, almost as if I'd slapped him. "Like what? Do you have an ex-husband you haven't told me about? Or kids?"

"No, no." How could I explain? "I just need some time."

He ran his fingers through his hair, a clear indication he was frustrated. "Spring, please don't do this to us. I love you, and we're good together. Give us a chance."

All I could do was shake my head. "You're in politics," I said, trying to organize my thoughts. The District Attorney was an elected position, and my otherworldly abilities could be detrimental when it came to politics.

"If that's the problem, I can get a job in any law firm in town."

Avoidance had become a way of life, so I ignored his comment. "You're too good a prosecutor to jump to the other side."

"I'll do whatever it takes to have you in my life. We love each other." He held out the ring. "I'm going to put this on your finger. Wear it as a friendship ring until you can talk yourself into being happy." He took a deep breath as if girding himself for a confrontation. "I've known for a long time that you're keeping secrets. I don't know what they are, but I do realize they bother you. Share them with me so we can move on."

The facets of the diamond glittered in the light. "Love has never been a problem for us. And I'm working on my issues, really I am. Please believe that I'll figure this out. I just need some space. Please."

The next morning bright and early I called Dr. Jill. "I have a ring on my finger so we need to talk. Do you think you can find some time today for an extended session?"

"I'll pull up my calendar."

Several seconds elapsed before she came back on the line. "I have a couple of hours this afternoon starting at two o'clock. Does that work for you?"

"I'll see you then."

I skipped lunch and cleared my desk of paperwork. Then I headed to Dr. Jill's office. She met me at the door with a plate of peanut butter cookies.

"I thought you could use a treat," she said as she led me into her office. "I want to see that ring."

I held my hand out for her inspection.

"Wow! That's gorgeous. He certainly has good taste." She smiled. "Have you set a date?"

I blinked back the tears. This was not the time or place for the waterworks. "I told him I needed some time. He agreed, reluctantly, and said to call it a friendship ring."

"I suppose that's sufficient for the time being. I'll make some tea, and then we can get serious."

Her easy style of questioning, and the comfort of her office almost made it seem as if we were friends chatting. But that wasn't the case, so I prepared myself for a tell-all session.

"It sounded like your kindergarten experience was positive, but something happened to change all that. Would you like to tell me what it was?"

"Not really, but here goes..."

Shenandoah Valley
Late May 1985

"Would you girls like to go with me to Harley's Feed Store? I need to pick up some things." Harley's was one of our favorite places. We liked

27

to play in the hay bales while Daddy chewed the fat with Harley III. The feed store with its peeling paint and pot-holed gravel parking lot wasn't fancy, but I loved the smell of sweet horse feed, leather and freshly mowed hay.

Daddy let us play on the wooden dock out front where folks pulled up to load their trucks. He led us to a place where there weren't many people bustling around. "You girls stay right here and have fun with your dolls. I'll be inside. Don't get in anyone's way."

"Yes, Daddy." Fiona could be such a suck-up. I'd heard one of the big boys at school say that. I didn't know what it meant, but I was pretty sure it wasn't good.

"My Cabbage Patch baby is prettier than yours." Fi was using the sing-song voice that made me want to smack her.

"No, she's not." My doll was named Susie and she had blonde hair just like mine. Fiona's Cabbage Patch was a redhead. "And your baby has freckles," I said. Fiona hated the spots on her nose, so I knew that I was being tacky.

"I still say my baby is prettier than yours." Fiona's nose was pointed so far up that if it rained she'd drown.

I stuck out my tongue and plopped on the end of the bench to hug my doll. "You're mean and I'm not going to talk to you anymore." Mean sisters were just…mean.

I was trying to come up with another ugly comment when an old man in stained overalls strolled down the loading dock. He had a dirty gray beard, and his battered hat was ringed with sweat stains. Mama would say he was a mountain man, but

28

Daddy would call him a good old boy.

At first, I thought he was going to walk straight into the store, but when he saw me he stopped and touched my shoulder. That's when the weird stuff started happening. The colors faded, and everything from the sun, to the sky, to Fiona's bright green hair ribbon changed to brown like the herbal tea my Auntie Aurora drank. It felt like a giant had gotten mad and was holding his breath. I don't know how long it lasted, but it was really bad.

After he ambled on down the sidewalk, the colors came back. The flowers that had looked like the dead of winter were perky and colorful, the sun was shining and the sky was blue.

All I wanted to do was scream and run away, but Fiona acted as if she hadn't noticed anything. "Did you see that?"

"See what?" Fi asked. She must have known I was upset, so she scooted closer.

"Nothing." I didn't want her to think that I was nutty. But it had happened, hadn't it?

Then there was a lot of noise, and people started running toward the store. One man yelled for Doc Watson, our vet, to get his butt inside because someone was having a heart attack.

Daddy came out and scooped us up. "We'd better get home." he said as a siren sounded in the distance.

"That man is gonna die." I didn't know where that came, but I knew I was right.

"No, honey. He'll be fine." Daddy was a preacher, so he usually knew what he was talking about, but this time he was wrong.

It wasn't until later that I put on my worry hat—that's what Mama called it when we fretted. What if something was wrong with me? What if I could make people sick?

The Popsicle kids were neat, and even the Creamsicle® people at church were okay, but the man with the gray color gave me the willies. And the way everything had gone quiet, like a bad storm was coming, really scared me.

It wasn't until Mama was tucking me into bed that I got the courage to say anything.

"Mama, I need to tell you something."

"What is it, sweetie?"

"I saw something today."

She held up her finger. "Just a sec." She went to the door and called, "Micah, I need you in here."

He was grinning as he strolled up to my bed. "What's up?"

"Spring wants to talk to us."

"Okay."

Mama sat down on the edge of the bed and pulled me into her lap. "What's happening, punkin?"

Now that I had their attention, I didn't know what to say. "I, uh…"

Daddy sat down and scooted his chair over far enough to pat my leg. "Did the thing at the feed store scare you?"

"Um-huh." I wanted to plop my thumb in my mouth, but I hadn't done that since I'd become a big girl. "It was that man. He made me afraid."

"What man!" Daddy was halfway out of his chair before Mama put her hand on his arm.

He took a deep breath, and then asked, "What man are you talking about?"

"When Fi and I were playing, the old man that died walked by and touched me. That's when stuff got icky." I told them everything from the stillness, to the colors going muddy brown. Mama and Daddy didn't say a word. "Do you think I'm going to die?" Just the thought gave me goose bumps.

"No, baby, you're not going to die," Daddy said. "I think it's time we have a chat with God." He was good friends with God—him being a preacher and all—so that was good. And my folks seemed to believe me, so that made me happy. But I sure hoped this wouldn't happen again.

Present Day

"Do you want to take a break?" Dr. Jill looked almost as drained as I felt. Our survival instinct encourages humans to debunk the inexplicable.

"No, it feels good to talk about it. And the incident at the feed store is just the beginning. Ask me that question in about thirty minutes when my lawyer brain is telling me that it's time to go home."

The therapist nodded.

"Would you like a Coke, or some other cold drink? I think I could use something icy and sweet."

"A Coke would be wonderful." This story was about to become more and more complicated, and by rights, more traumatizing for me. But confiding in Dr. Jill might go a long way toward my healing.

Chapter 3

We chatted for a few minutes before Dr. Jill said, "I have another patient at five o'clock, but that gives us an hour. Are you up to it?"

"Sure. Jed's coming for dinner, so that still gives me time to go home and cook."

"I'm dying to hear more about the ring."

How could I explain putting off the catch of the century? "I told him that I had issues to resolve. He wanted to know if I had a secret ex-husband. No telling what else his imagination has dredged up, but he's being amazingly patient. That's why I have to resolve this as quickly as possible. I can't imagine my life without him."

Dr. Jill smiled. "I don't think I've ever had a patient as receptive as you are."

"I have a lot to lose, or gain."

"Then let's go for it. Continue wherever you'd like."

June 1985

"Mama, may I invite Tommy over for a play date?" I missed seeing my best friend. Plus I was itching to talk to someone outside the family.

"Give him a call and see if it's okay with his

32

mom. I can pick him up when I go to the grocery store."

Two hours later, Tommy hopped out of Mama's VW van and ran over to where my sisters and I were watching Daddy and Uncle Hiram paint a picture on the side of an old school bus.

"Hey!" I squealed so loud that Fi covered her ears. "I'm so glad you could come."

"Me, too." He waved at Fiona and Maeve. "What's happening with the bus?"

Before I could answer, Maeve piped up. "Daddy and Uncle Hiram are making a camper out of it. We're going to spend the summer taking the Word to mountain folks who don't have a church. Isn't that neat?"

"You're going to be doing revivals?" Tommy asked. He went to a town church that had choir robes and stained glass windows. They didn't set up tents and do baptisms in the river.

"It's so exciting." Fi waved her hand like she was leading a band. "We'll be doing gospel music. Did Spring tell you that we sing at Daddy's church?"

"Yeah, she did. I'll bet y'all are good." He turned to me. "Will you be gone all summer?"

"I don't know. Daddy hasn't told us, but probably so." Tommy didn't look happy. "But we can do lots of playing before we leave."

Fiona, the dweeb, didn't care about Tommy's feelings. "It'll be a blast. We're going to camp out and eat lots of hot dogs and marshmallows. The services will be so cool. Mama's bought us new dresses. We're going to be stars."

"That's good, I guess," he muttered.

"Does the picture on the bus look like Elvis?" Fiona asked, but didn't wait for an answer. "Or maybe that Beatles guy, what's him name," she paused before coming up with *John Lennon.*

"Don't be a silly toad," Maeve said. "Daddy wouldn't paint a picture of Elvis on our bus. That would be blas...blas, uh something or other. Anyway it wouldn't be good."

"It is too Elvis. I know Elvis when I see him," Fi said and then stomped her foot. "So there!"

I wanted to whack them both, but then Mama walked up.

"Mama, who's that?" The man in the mural was wearing a white bathrobe and had his hands in the air.

"That's Jesus. When we show up for a revival, the people will see Him and get energized about hearing the Word. They'll tell all their friends, and that way lots of people will come to your Daddy's services. Are you girls excited about our adventure?"

"Oh, yes!" I exclaimed. "Can we really sing songs around the campfire?"

"Certainly."

"And not take showers, eat junk food, and..."

Fiona interrupted me. "And bathe in the river and stay up late?"

"That's a lot of questions." Mama gave us a smile. "We'll see how things go, but I know you'll love singing at the services."

"Where are we going?" I asked because I wanted Tommy to hear her answer.

Mama sat down on the grass and we plopped next to her. "We're heading to towns in the mountains where they don't have churches, and where they don't often get a chance to hear the Word."

"Will we introduce them to God?" Fiona asked.

"Yes, honey. That's what we plan to do."

"Do they have TV?" That was more important to me than helping people I didn't know make friends with God.

Mama ruffled my hair. "Most of the time we'll be in small mining towns up in the hills, so they probably don't get TV. But you'll like it, I promise. And you girls can dress up and sing to your hearts' content."

"It sounds a whole lot better than weeding the garden and trying to keep Beau and Bubba out of our things." Maeve said, and I nodded.

"And it'll give you more time to work on your instrumentals." Mama was a stickler about our music lessons.

"Do we have to?" Fiona whined. She'd been playing the guitar since she ditched her piano lessons. I was still working on the second book of the piano series.

"Yes, you have to," Mama answered. "You don't believe it now, but one of these days you'll thank me."

"Mrs. O'Flaherty," Tommy said.

"Yes, Tommy."

"Could you teach me to play the guitar?"

"I certainly can. After we get back from our trip I'll talk to your mom to see if it's all right with her. Do you want to play at church?"

"Nope, I want to be in a rock band."

"Okay," Mama said. "That works for me."

We played a couple of games of Hide and Seek before Maeve and Fiona wandered back to the house.

"Tommy, would you like to go with me to the orchard?" I asked. There's a swing where we can sit.

I'd like to tell you something."

Tommy was my best friend, so he knew about the auras, but I wanted to see what he thought about what had happened at the feed store.

"Okay." He tossed rocks at imaginary targets as we walked through the orchard. "What's wrong?" he asked as he sat down in the swing.

I joined him and started pushing back and forth, wondering how much to tell him. "I'm scared." I was trying not to cry, but my eyes were starting to leak.

He took my hand. "It can't be that bad."

"It is. I think I can tell when people are about to die," I said, and then told him about the man at the feed store.

It took him a few seconds to say anything. "That's...uh, that's awful."

"Mama and Daddy said we should pray about it, but I've prayed and prayed, and God's not answering me." Once my tears dried up, I wiped my nose on my sleeve. "What do you think I should do?"

"Your daddy's a preacher, so he probably has an in with God. Prayer can't hurt, can it?"

"But God's not listening." I was tempted to pout. "I guess he has more important things to do than to worry about me."

"God loves us," Tommy said, and then he hugged me. It made me feel a lot better.

"Any time you need me, I'll be here. Always. I promise."

A couple of weeks later, the bus was ready. "Do you want to see what we've done?" Daddy asked. We hadn't been allowed inside the bus while they were working, so it was going to be a big surprise.

"Yes!" we exclaimed.

"Here you go," Daddy opened the door like he was Bob Barker on the *Price Is Right.* "This will be your home for the summer."

Fi and I scrambled up the steps and almost ran over Maeve when she stopped. "We're living here?" She touched one of the bunks. "Is this where I'll be sleeping?"

Daddy grinned. "Yep. You'll probably have to arm wrestle one of your sisters for a top spot."

"The twins are not bunking with me." Fiona stomped her foot for emphasis.

"Don't worry. The boys can either share one of the bunks, or we have sleeping bags," Mama said. "Your daddy and I have a tiny room in the back."

The bunk beds were located on one side of the bus. A tiny refrigerator and a small stove—with a table in-between—occupied the other side.

That looked okay, but then I panicked. "Where's the bathroom?" I hated outhouses!

Daddy pointed toward the back of the bus. "It's down there on the right. Go check it out."

Fiona raced me to the bathroom. "Oh, boy!" she exclaimed, and then muttered, "How's Daddy going to fit in there."

"You two worry too much. Everything's going to be great." When Mama put her arms around me, I believed every word.

Early the next morning we were packed and ready to go. Our housekeeper, Pearlie Jean, was staying home to take care of the pets and the farm. She'd been with us since...forever, and I loved her like another mom.

"Lordy mercy, I can't believe you're takin' my babies on that rattletrap."

She made the same tsking sound I'd heard a thousand times before.

Daddy hugged her. "Don't worry. We'll be fine."

Pearlie Jean jabbed him the ribs. "You'd better be. I'll be prayin' for ya."

"I'm counting on it," Daddy said. After we boarded the bus, he fired up the engine and off we went.

I spent most of that day playing games with Fiona and Maeve. The twins were being brats, trying to turn over our board game and making noise. Maeve finally slammed her hand down and grabbed Beau, giving him a not-very-friendly noogie. Mama must have heard the ruckus because she came back and corralled the twins.

"I love them, but they make me nuts," Maeve whispered. I wholeheartedly agreed.

Hours later, Daddy pulled into a town that Mama said looked like a wide spot in the road.

"Check that out." I pointed at a couple of gas pumps that looked like wind-up toys.

"Have you ever seen anything like it before?" Fiona asked.

Maeve shook her head, but before she could say anything Daddy spoke up. "The map says this is Barking Dog Creek."

As usual Fiona expressed an opinion. "That's silly."

"And look at the Coke machine." Maeve pointed at a cooler that looked like the deep freeze in our mud room.

"Oh, my." Mama was ignoring us and staring at two old men wearing bib overalls and playing dominoes. Occasionally one of the guys would hack up a chaw and spit it into an old coffee can.

"Micah O'Flaherty!" She was using her *don't give me no guff* voice. "I wasn't expecting this!"

Daddy was heading down the bus steps, but stopped and turned to Mama.

"Paloma, honey, it'll be okay." He looked kind of...funny. "Let's go in and get some milk and a couple of ice creams. Then we'll find the campground. Come on kids, chop, chop. Times a'wasting."

Fiona flew down the steps and I was right behind her. Maeve almost knocked me over on her way out. We were anxious to get off the bus before Mama worked up a real mad.

I tugged on Daddy's sleeve. "Are those houses?" I pointed at the tarpaper shacks perched on the side of the mountain.

"Considering the condition of this town, I suspect they are."

"Do you think kids live up there?"

Daddy shrugged. "Probably."

"I'll bet they don't get TV."

"I don't see any antennas, so you're probably right." Daddy put his hands in the air and that said it all—no TV, no radio, no five-and-dime, no movie, no nothing.

"How long are we going to be here?"

"Maybe less than a week. It depends on how the services go."

"I won't be able to see Love Boat, will I?"

"Nope, afraid not." Daddy always told the truth, even if it wasn't something we wanted to hear.

"I can't call Tommy, can I?"

"A long distance call would be expensive, so I'm afraid that's a no, too."

I couldn't believe it—no TV for a month. That

was downright uncivilized. As for not talking to my best friend, that seemed even worse.

"Did Daddy really say they don't have TV?" Maeve looked like she wanted to be sick. "No Gilligan?"

"Guess not." I was so busy thinking about TV that I hadn't noticed how close we were to the domino guys. "Fi, let's get out of here." The men reminded of the man from the feed store—old and kind of musty. I knew that if I touched one of them, things would get scary again.

Daddy strolled out carrying a handful of Popsicles. "What color do you girls want?" he asked. "They don't have Eskimo Pies, so I thought these would do."

Maeve picked a cherry and Fiona went for the orange. That left me with grape. It wasn't my favorite, but at least it was a Popsicle.

"Let's go find the campground," Daddy said after we piled on the bus.

"There'd better be a swimming pool," Fi muttered.

Maeve rolled her eyes. "Or at least a creek."

I really wanted a TV, but instead we found a campground on a river. As soon as Daddy stopped the bus, we scrambled out.

"You kids be careful. Don't get too close to the water until I'm with you," Mama yelled as we raced down the hill.

"The way the water sparkles looks like the rhinestones on Dolly Parton's dress," Fiona said. She loved TV shows with lots of singing and dancing.

Maeve pointed at a huge peak. "That mountain is a lot bigger than the ones we have at home,"

Mama walked up carrying Bubba. She put him

down, but kept a grip on his hand. "I love our mountains, but these are spectacular. They're so...big." She skipped a rock across the water. "And this river...oh, my goodness, it's beautiful."

She was in a better mood, and that was good, because if Mama wasn't happy, wasn't nobody happy, or at least that's what Daddy said.

"This is a perfect place for a baptism." Daddy put his arm around Mama's waist. "John the Baptist conducted his baptisms in a river similar to this one."

I'd heard that story so many times I could recite it from memory. Daddy never missed a chance for a Bible lesson, and Brother John was one of his favorites. I thought the parable was cool, that is until I found out that John's head had been lopped off, and then it wasn't so nice.

"Tell you what. Let's get unpacked and then we'll walk back to town to put our posters out," Daddy said. "Kids, you can pick the spots. Won't that be fun?"

Actually I'd rather be playing, but when Daddy was on a mission everyone had to help.

"Micah, you are going to find someone to help you put up the tent, aren't you?" Mama asked. "I have to keep track of the kids." She nodded toward the twins who were chasing Fiona with a frog.

"We'll find some strapping young men and get that tent up in two shakes of a lamb's tail. There are always guys hanging out around the gas station."

It took us a while to walk back to town. Mama stared at the two men leaning against a huge, black motorcycle. "The one with the scraggly ponytail looks like he belongs in the Hell's Angels," she whispered, although it was loud enough for me to hear. "I'm not so sure about this," she said to Daddy. "Can't we do something else?"

"Don't worry. The gas station owner said they're good guys. The mine closed down a couple of months ago and folks are desperate for work."

"That doesn't make me feel a whole lot better," she said. "But I guess we'll have to put it in God's hand."

"Mama." I tugged on her arm.

"What baby?"

"Their colors aren't bad. I think it's okay."

Mama knelt to give me a hug. "Oh, sweetie. Everything will be fine."

Two hours later, we were ready for the services. Daddy paid the men and invited them to attend the services.

"Sure enough, we plan to come." That came from the man with the scruffy beard. "But I've got a question." He was pointing at the bus. "I have a bet with my buddy, Leroy. He said the guy on the picture is Jesus. I think it's Elvis." He gave Daddy a wink. "The right answer is worth two bits to me."

"I'd like to help you out, but it is Jesus."

"Jesus, I'll be dad-gummed. Sure is the spittin' image of the king of rock and roll."

Leroy chuckled. "Actually, he looks like John Lennon, and I'm not talkin' about that picture where he's butt naked."

Fiona poked my arm. "I told you it was either Elvis or John Lennon."

I'd seen pictures of Elvis, but I didn't know who John Lennon was, so I kept stacking the hymnals. This revival stuff was turning out to be a whole lot of work. Nobody had bothered to tell me that.

"We're finished here," Daddy said. "What do you say we go to the diner for burgers?" When it came to work versus burgers, burgers won every time.

The next day the services were supposed to start at noon, but by eleven o'clock there was already a crowd. They'd come on foot, in junk cars and pickups, and a couple of people had even shown up on horseback. The ladies of the town had raided their gardens to decorate the tent. The flowers were pretty, but they weren't nearly as nice as the colors. It was so beautiful that it made me want to cry happy tears.

Mama had dressed us in ruffled sundresses and curled our hair in ringlets. "We look like princesses," Fiona fluffed her hair and patted her pinafore.

"Pretty is as pretty does." Maeve quoted one of Pearlie Jean's favorite sayings.

Fiona made a face.

"See what I mean," Maeve said, and mimicked Fi's gesture.

My sisters were about to get in a spat and I didn't want that to happen. "Come and look at the people." I pointed out the bus window. "That lady is gonna be a mommy. She's an Easter color. I'll bet she'll be a good mom."

"I wish I could see the colors," Maeve said.

"Me, too," Fiona agreed.

My tummy rumbled. "Oops, sorry."

"Are you hungry, or are you scared?"

"I don't know."

Truthfully, I was afraid, but I didn't want to admit it, especially not to Fiona. There wasn't any reason to have stage fright. We'd been singing for Daddy's congregation as long as I could remember. But I knew those folks.

"Girls, it's time to go." Mama interrupted my fretting. "People are standing because there aren't enough seats. Isn't that exciting?"

The revival turned out to be a big party with everyone singing and dancing to the music. At church we usually sang gospel songs, but sometimes we did folk music with Mama accompanying us on the fiddle.

"What other colors do you see?" Fiona asked after we'd finished a song that had people clapping and singing.

"See that woman with the frizzy hair." I was talking about a pudgy woman with a toothpaste grin sitting on the second row. "She's a light blue, and the guy next to her is green." I loved green because it was Tommy's color.

"Are there any purples?" That was Fiona's favorite color.

"The guy standing in the back is a dark purple. And the pretty girl on the end of the first row is a light purple."

"That's so neat."

"Sometimes it is." But most of the time being different wasn't any fun at all.

At the end of the service, Daddy issued an invitation for people to come to the pulpit and tell everyone how much they loved the Lord.

"My girls will lead us in singing an old favorite, 'Just As I Am.' Lift your voices to the heavens, God's listening."

My sisters and I were walking down the aisle singing the first verse when a lady in a pink hat grabbed my hand and it was the feed store, all over again. The colors faded and the singing went away.

"Fi, do you see what's happening?"

Please God, I wasn't the only one who noticed the colors change. The bright pink hat wasn't pink anymore. Fiona's green hair ribbon was light brown, and her pinafore looked like it had been soaked in weak coffee.

"It's happening again."

"What are you talking about?" Maeve got crabby when she thought we were doing something silly. "Keep singing."

I couldn't do anything but close my eyes and hope that it would all go away. But when the colors returned the lady in the hat was lying in the aisle, as still as death.

I squeezed my legs together. It was the only way I could keep from peeing my cute little panties with the ruffles around the legs. It was like a nightmare.

Present Day

"That was the end of my innocence." I took a deep breath hoping to regain my equilibrium.

"Are you all right?" Dr. Jill asked. "It seemed as if you *were* in another time and place."

"That's how it feels." My Coke wasn't cold, but taking a sip gave me time to get my thoughts together. "That story was fairly easy. The rest will be a lot more difficult."

"Are you positive you want to continue with our sessions?"

Believe

"Absolutely!   My future and my happiness are at stake."

Chapter 4

"Hey, Ms. O'Flaherty. Would you like your usual?" Leave it to my favorite coffee shop barista to point out the predictability of my everyday life.

"I think I'll live dangerously and go with a banana nut muffin instead of a scone."

"You got it." The cute twenty-something bagged the muffin. "How's it going?" he asked.

"So far, so good."

He handed me the pastry bag before grabbing a to-go cup for my coffee. "I hope you don't mind me saying this, but you look mighty pretty in that yellow dress."

That warranted a grin. "In my world a compliment is always welcome." Especially when it came from a Zac Efron look-alike. Girls all over Atlanta were probably smitten.

"You have a good day now, ya hear," I said, falling back on the speech patterns of my childhood.

"Yes, ma'am," he said, and then turned his attention to the next customer.

Ma'am! Had he really called me ma'am? I was still pondering that when Jed's ringtone sounded on my cell. "Are you already at work?" I asked, skipping the usual salutation.

"Yeah. I have some paperwork that's due to-day, so I came in early."

Trying to handle my briefcase, my cell, a hot cup of coffee and a pastry was unmanageable, so I sat down on a bench in front of the coffee shop. "How did your meeting go last night?" Jed had had dinner with his campaign committee to plan his re-election for District Attorney.

"Everything's looking good. The other party came up with a credible candidate, but I think I can beat him."

"That's great."

I took a bite of my muffin.

"Um…I have a favor to ask." My organized, super-efficient boyfriend was sounding a lot like a middle-school kid asking a girl for a date. What was going on?

"Of course, whatever you need, I'm yours." I took a sip of coffee. If something bad was about to go down, I'd probably need that shot of caffeine.

"It's uh…my parents want us to come over for dinner tonight."

Jed's folks were lovely people, but they lived in a foreign stratosphere. We'd had dinner together, but it had always been at a restaurant, not on their home turf.

I paused a little too long before answering. "Okay. What time?"

"Will this be a problem?"

"No, of course not." Did a white lie count?

"Good." Jed sounded relieved.

His parents made me nervous, but I suspected

that was my problem, not theirs. And it was something I needed to work on, right after I told their son about my psychic powers.

"Can you be ready around six?"

"That'll work." It should give me enough time to run home and worry about what to wear to dinner at a mansion.

"Dress casual. My dad's doing burgers."

Burgers? What happened to capers and foie gras?

My work was too hectic for me to obsess, and that was a good thing. Later that afternoon, with five minutes to spare, I was dressed and ready to go. I'd tried on every casual outfit in my closet and finally chose my only real option for a garden party/barbecue. The minute I'd spied the girly-girl dress on a sale rack at Neiman Marcus, I'd been hooked. I was admiring my early twentieth-century look when the doorbell rang. Show time!

"You look gorgeous," Jed said, holding me at arms' length. "I like that dress."

I couldn't resist doing a pirouette. "Thank you."

"Here we are," Jed said as he pulled into a brick drive that was guarded by an ornate wrought iron gate. The lawn looked like it had been manicured with scissors. The antebellum home with its white pillars and expansive porches could have been used as a set for *Gone With the Wind*.

You grew up here? Here? OMG! The Collinsworth family was *so* out of my league.

"Yes, I did. And I'm perfectly normal. So are my parents." He wasn't happy with me, and I couldn't blame him. I was being a snob. "I'm sorry. Of course, you're normal. And your parents are lovely."

"Do you really mean that?"

"I do."

"Okay, let's go enjoy my dad's cooking. He thinks he's the barbecue king of Atlanta. My mom and I don't have the heart to disabuse him of that notion," he said as he pulled up to the front door.

I was still gaping at the house. What was wrong with me? I was acting like a country bumpkin. By the time I snapped my mouth shut, Jed had come around to the passenger side of his Porsche.

"Are you okay?"

"Absolutely."

"Mom's really excited about this." Jed took my hand and helped me out of his low-slung sports car.

He didn't bother to ring the doorbell before ushering me into a foyer that was larger than my living room, dining room and kitchen combined. The white marble floors and twin semi-circular staircases almost took my breath away. People really lived like this?

"It's pretty easy to get lost in this place, so stay close. It was perfect for playing Hide and Seek when we were kids. My sister never could find me."

I knew that Jed's sister, Amy, and her family lived in Northern Virginia, but I hadn't met any of his extended family.

"This place is huge."

"Let's go to the kitchen." He took my hand and led me down a long corridor. The art on the walls looked like paintings I'd seen in art museums. "I'm sure that's where we'll find my mom."

The great room was almost as large as a hotel ballroom, and the kitchen looked like a set for the Food Network with an eight-burner Viking gas stove and an industrial sized Sub-Zero refrigerator.

"Is anyone home?" Jed didn't wait for an answer before he started foraging in the refrigerator. "Wine?" he asked, holding up a bottle of chilled white.

Before I could answer, Jed's mom strolled in and spied her son.

"Get yourself over here and give your mom a hug!"

As perverse as it might be, it was entertaining to see someone as masculine as Jed hop to it. Amelia Collinsworth was petite and blonde, with that classy Junior League look. She wasn't physically imposing, but her personality was an entirely different story.

"We haven't seen you in weeks," she scolded. "Don't tell me you need an engraved invitation to come home for dinner."

Watching the interplay between parent and grown child was entertaining.

"And Spring." She held her hands out to me. "You're stunning as usual."

I could tell that she intended to include me in the hug-fest. I glanced over Amelia's shoulder and noticed Jed's grimace. He instinctively realized that I didn't do hugs.

I prepared for the worst and was pleasantly surprised that all I felt was her genuine welcome. "Thanks for the invitation."

"Come with me, there are a couple of people I want you to meet."

I glanced at Jed for guidance, but all he did was grin.

The great room had a stone fireplace worthy of a castle, and the entertainment options included a huge TV and a pool table. I was so fixated on my surroundings that I almost missed the two geriatric ladies sitting at a round table. If the quibbling was any indication, they were laser focused on a cut-throat game of Scrabble.

"You're in for a treat," Jed whispered. "Mom, Aunt Daisy, our guest has arrived," Amelia yelled. In a more conversational tone she added, "When they play Scrabble, they sometimes don't turn up their hearing aids."

"Oh." What else could I say?

The ladies were almost identical in appearance. Except one of them had dyed her hair bright red and the other sported a white pixie haircut.

The woman with the pixie cut jumped up and grabbed Jed in a hug. "You haven't been home in a month of Sundays."

Seconds later, the redhead joined in the hugging, also chastising Jed for his absence.

"Grams, I was here for dinner two weeks ago."
"Still too long," she replied, and then turned her attention to me.

Before I could step back, she grabbed my hand. The woman had to be in her late eighties, so I really didn't want to see her future. Thank goodness my foresight was on the fritz, or perhaps it was similar to the psychic immunity I had with my family. Whatever, I breathed a sigh of relief.

"My, my, my." Grams gave me a head-to-toe inspection. "You look like an angel. She's absolutely gorgeous, isn't she sister?"

The redhead nodded with obvious enthusiasm.

"We're forgetting our manners," Amelia said. "Mom, this is Jed's friend, Spring. And Spring, this lady," she indicated the woman with the pixie cut, "is my mother, Zinnia, otherwise known as Zinnie Collinsworth. And," she motioned toward the redhead, "this is my Aunt Daisy."

The introductions were barely concluded when Zinnie screeched, "Lordy mercy!" She grabbed my hand and held it out to display the ring—the one I'd forgotten to take off. "That was my mother-in-law's ring. I gave it to Jed, hoping he'd find a good woman. I think I'm about to swoon."

She fanned her face and then looked puzzled. "What's it doing on your right hand?"

Jed took my hand.

"What *is* it doing on your right hand?" he asked. I knew I'd made a terrible mistake, but it was too late to do anything about it.

"When's the wedding?" Zinnie asked, while Amelia simply shook her head. Daisy was about to join the fray when Jed's whistle put a halt to the barrage of questions.

"I'll open a bottle of wine and we can have a nice, *quiet* discussion," Jed said as he led his grandmother to one of the easy chairs in the seating area.

I followed him to the kitchen while the members of his family watched us. "Would you like some help?"

"I'm good. But I would like to do this." Jed moved the ring from my right hand to my left. "If you're going to wear it, wear it properly." He handed me the bottle of wine he'd retrieved from the refrigerator. "Let me do the talking." He picked my hand up and kissed the base of each finger. That man had a way of handling an argument.

The women of the Collinsworth family were huddled on the couch. They probably had the wedding planned and the invitations ordered.

"First of all," Jed said as he placed the wine glasses on the coffee table. "Spring and I plan on a long engagement, and when we decide on a date, you'll be the first to know. In case you're wondering, which I'm sure you are, I gave her the ring the day before yesterday. We were going to tell you tonight."

Actually, that had never crossed my mind.

"Don't wait too long to have those babies." Daisy obviously felt like she had to throw in her two-cents worth. "Your eggs will get all dry and dusty. That's what happened to our cousin Charlotte, didn't it Zinnie?"

Amelia leaned forward, placing her elbows on her knees. "A discussion of babies is *way* too early. Let the young people tell us what they have planned."

Jed sent his mom an appreciative smile. "At this point, the ring symbolizes a commitment, rather than the announcement of a specific date. And if, or when, we discuss a family, it will be a private conversation. Right, Spring?"

"That's right." I glanced at my hand and noticed how the facets glittered in the sunlight. Then I hit on a brilliant way to divert this conversation.

"Ms. Zinnie, you said that this ring belonged to your mother-in-law. Why don't you tell us some of its history?"

Jed's cough sounded suspiciously like a disguised laugh. He shot me a wink as Zinnie launched into a family history lesson that proved to be both amusing and edifying.

"Hamburgers and hot dogs are ready," Cal Collinsworth announced. The spatula he was holding dripped unknown substances on a rug that probably cost as much as my car—or maybe even my house.

"Get that greasy thing out of here," Amelia instructed. "You're making a mess."

"Yes, ma'am." He grinned before giving his wife a mock salute. "I just wanted to let you know that the main course is ready."

I'd expected chateaubriand or roasted quail with caviar. Instead I was about to have a hamburger and potato salad. No butler. No maid. Not even a housekeeper. I had to admit that I was wrong about old money and people who live in mansions.

"Jed, would you take Grams and Aunt Daisy out to the pool and get them some sangria or a Margarita? And Spring, would you help me haul the rest of the food outside?"

"I'll be glad to," I said as I followed Amelia into the kitchen. She'd always been charming and lovely, but something told me there was more to her request than KP. We'd barely made it in the door before she turned and took my hands.

"There's something I think you need to know. Cal and I discussed this, and he told me to mind my own business, but with the ring..." She dropped my hand and leaned against the massive granite island, looking as if she was having an internal argument.

Obviously I couldn't help her make a decision.

"Let's sit down at the breakfast table." She pointed toward a large trestle table in the solarium adjacent to the kitchen. Under other circumstances, I would have thought it lovely.

She opened the refrigerator and grabbed an open bottle of white wine. Then she snagged two crystal flutes from a hutch.

After we sat down, she poured two glasses and then held hers up for a toast. "Here's to not making a mistake. I don't know if Jed has told you this, or not, but it's something I think you need to know."

"Jed hasn't told me much about his childhood, or even college, so I suspect I'm in the dark." My vivid imagination was conjuring up all sorts of terrible possibilities. Child molestation. Abduction. And the list went on and on.

"When Jed was at the University of Georgia, he fell in love with a girl named Heather. She was the most beautiful woman I've ever seen. Long dark hair, stunning figure, she was a Miss Georgia." Amelia smiled and shook her head. "And as you've probably noticed, we have a lot of gorgeous women in Atlanta."

That was true. And they always dressed to the nines.

"Heather was the only woman he's ever brought home to meet us, until now. That was shortly before spring break of his senior year. He confided to his dad that he'd bought a ring." Amelia poured more wine in her glass and held the bottle up in a silent question.

"No thanks." I was tempted to make the 'let's get moving' hand motion. I had a sinking feeling this story didn't have a happy ending.

"That spring, Jed had made arrangements with one of Cal's friends to spend his break at the law office. We all thought that would help him make up his mind about going to law school. And Heather went to Pensacola with her sorority sisters, or at least that's what Jed thought."

"But she didn't."

"No." Amelia shrugged. "She went to the beach, but it was with an old boyfriend."

Not good.

"And Jed found out." Amelia grimaced before continuing. "In the worst possible way. The police found his name and number in her purse and called him. They were trying to find her next of kin."

"Her next of kin!" I exclaimed.

"She and her boyfriend were shot and killed while they were in a part of town known for drug dealing."

"Oh, God!" That was too much like Tommy. "I didn't know."

"That's why I told you. I know that you mean a great deal to him. And more than anything, I want my son to be happy," she said, adding a sweet smile. "I'm not pressuring either of you to have kids. Lord knows, I have a passel of grandkids courtesy of Jed's sister. I understand your desire to be sure about such an important commitment, but I also wanted you to know how important trust and truth are to a man like my son. The situation with Heather was the reason Jed went into criminal law." Amelia stood. "But enough of that, we'd better get the food out to the patio or we'll have some guys tracking us down."

Jed pulled into my driveway and killed the engine. He turned in his seat. "Should we go inside and discuss what happened with the ring?"

"Yes, you're right." Actually I had better plans for him, but we did need to clear the air.

Jed followed me inside and immediately went to the refrigerator for a bottle of water. A couple of months back I'd given him a key to my house, and it delighted me that he felt at home.

He sat down on my couch and patted the cushion. "Let's start off with why you were wearing my ring on your right hand. Was that some kind of statement?"

Leave it to a veteran prosecutor to go to the heart of the matter. I sat down and snuggled up next to him. It was easier to discuss difficult topic when he was holding me. "I honestly don't know," I said when he put his arm around me.

"Do you think that subconsciously you don't want to be engaged?"

I was wondering how to craft an answer when I decided to go for the truth—or at least an abbreviated version of the truth.

"I love you and I know how lucky I am to have you in my life. Don't ever doubt that." I put my hand on his heart, feeling the steady beat. "And I want to marry you and have your kids more than anything in the world." I sighed wondering how to proceed. "But, as you know, I have some baggage left over from my childhood."

Jed turned slightly so he could look at my face. "And that's something I've wanted to ask, but I was hesitant to bring it up. Were you abused or molested as a child? I met your parents, and they seem like lovely people, but appearances can be deceiving."

I jerked back as if someone had zapped me with a Taser. "Good Lord, no! My parents are wonderful, and as annoying as my sisters could be when we were kids, they're the best."

"So what's the problem?" he asked. "For this

relationship to work, we can't have significant secrets."

"Your mom and I had a talk."

Jed fell back against the cushion. "She told you,
didn't she?"

I nodded. "So now that I know your secret, my
job is to figure out how to tell you mine. Kind of
like an 'I'll show you mine if you show me yours.'"
I couldn't resist a grin. "I'm seeing a therapist."

"Why didn't you tell me? There's nothing
wrong with talking about your issues with a professional."

"I realize that now, and I should have done it
years ago. But I am making progress. And as soon
as I get my head on straight, we can talk about the
rest of our lives."

"As long as I know that you love me, I can live
with that," he said. "When's your next appointment?"

"Tomorrow afternoon."

Jed pulled me into his arms. His kiss was like a
homecoming, warm and welcoming. I ran my fingers through his hair, thinking about how he was the
completion of my soul. If I lost him, my heart
would shatter into a million pieces and I'd never be
able to put it back together.

"You're thinking too much. Just relax and feel,"
he said as he turned me so I was leaning back on the
couch. "Clear your mind and think about us, and
this," he said as he slowly unbuttoned each tiny
pearl button on the bodice of my sundress, kissing
every inch of my skin as it made an appearance,

leading to my lacy bra. Then I felt his hand under my sundress, its objective the warm, moist place that couldn't wait to welcome him.

Our instant attraction and chemistry had somehow become an abiding love. There were times I wanted to crawl into his skin to be closer. And sometimes it was enough just to be with him, to talk, to chat, to cuddle.

No matter how I tried to rationalize what I was feeling, I realized that I was a goner.

Chapter 5

"I met Jed's grandmother and great-aunt yesterday," I said as I munched on one of Dr. Jill's brownies.

She poured herself another cup of tea. "How did that go?"

I couldn't resist a grin. "There was some discussion of dry and dusty eggs, and we're not talking about chickens."

"They want to see some little ones running around," she said, adding a smile. "We can't blame them for that."

"I'm sure my mother would agree. She has three daughters and not a single grandbaby."

"Women of a certain age want babies to hug and spoil. It's only natural."

"I know," I said. "But it takes a lot of thought and planning to pop out a baby with toes and fingers and little button noses."

"I wish more people had a plan, but that's neither here, nor there. Are you ready to get down to business?"

"Sure. The sooner, the better is my new motto. "More tea? Or another brownie?" Dr. Jill asked.

"No, I'm fine."

"When we left off last time there'd been a death at one of your dad's revival meetings. What happened after that?"

"For a couple of years, everything was fine. Daddy suspended the revival trips and I enjoyed being a kid. It wasn't until I was nine that Daddy decided we should go back to the mountains. That's when everything went totally upside-down." I shook my head, remembering that disturbing period of my life. "It won't be easy to relive, but it's something I have to do."

Late Spring 1988

Tommy was going to church with us, and afterward he was staying to play. It had been weeks since I'd seen my best friend.

Fiona plopped down on the porch steps. "Mama said not to get dirty."

I fluffed out the skirt of my best church dress. "She told me to wait patiently. It's hard, but I'm trying."

"What time is Tommy supposed to get here?" Fiona enjoyed having him around almost as much as I did.

"Mama said soon."

"So how soon is soon?"

I sat down on the porch steps with Fi. "I don't know, but she did tell Pearlie Jean that I was driving her cuckoo. Hey," I pointed at a cloud of dust on our lane. "There's his mama's car."

Seconds after Mrs. Herndon came to a stop Tommy jumped out and ran to the porch. He had on his Sunday duds, and even the sticky-up part of his hair was slicked down.

I ran out and grabbed his hand. "We're going to have so much fun. This is the Sunday that the church folks pound the preacher. It's not like they're going to hit him or anything."

"What's a pounding?" Tommy asked.

Mama had come out on the porch to wave to Tommy's mom. "I'm glad you could join us," she said after Mrs. Herndon drove off. "And to answer your question, a pounding is where folks give gifts to the preacher to show their appreciation. Usually it's stuff like food."

"Mama says they do it 'cause they don't pay Daddy much money," Fiona said, ignoring Mama's frown. "Last year we got a ham and two turkeys. And I'll betcha Miss Eula will give us another pound cake. She makes the best cake ever. I just hope Miss Thigpen doesn't show up with that stuff in a jar. Mama, what's it called?"

"Chow chow," Mama said.

Fiona wrinkled her nose. "It's got all kinds of weird stuff in it."

"It's not as bad as her pickled beets." I hated pickled beets. They made my mouth red.

Mama smiled. "You don't have to eat anything you don't like." She turned to Tommy and pointed at the paper sack he was holding. "Are those your play clothes?"

"Yes, ma'am, they sure are."

"Good, I'll put them in the house for you," Mama said. "Y'all go inside and play quietly until everyone is ready to go."

"Yes, ma'am," we said.

I took Tommy's hand. "Come with me to the

parlor. I learned a new card game called Five Card Stud. When Maeve was teaching us I heard Daddy whisper to Mama something about strip poker. I don't what he was talking about, but he had a funny grin on his face."

"Sometimes my folks say things that I don't get."

Even though Fiona had butted into our game, we were having fun when Mama told us it was time to go.

"Daddy's church is a really old building. Mama said that during the Civil War the soldiers tore out the pews and used the church as a hospital." I didn't know much about the Civil War, but the way some folks said it, I knew it hadn't been good. "We have pews now. Mr. Horton's grandpa carved angels on them, way back when."

"I read about the Civil War," Tommy exclaimed. "It was when the North and South started shooting at each other and things got really bad."

Maeve snorted, but Mama ignored her. "That's right. It was a terrible time, especially for the Shenandoah Valley." She pulled the van under an old oak and turned off the engine. "Here we are. Go play, but don't get dirty."

Everyone, including the twins, hopped out and ran to join some kids who were playing Hide and Seek. It was one of my favorite games and I knew places to hide where no one would be able to find me.

Later when the church bells rang, I left my hidey-hole and ran to find Tommy. "The services are about to start. My sisters and I lead the singing. Sit on the front row so when we finish I can come sit with you."

The church made me feel warm and comfy. I liked the wooden ceiling and the way the floors were polished and the sun would shine through the stained glass windows that told the story of Jesus.

"You'll feel right at home," I told Tommy as I led him to a seat at the front of the church. "Sometimes folks yell amen, but they probably do that in your Baptist church."

"Yeah, they do."

"So it's all the same."

"Right." His smile was as bright as a new penny.

Daddy preached the service on Mary Magdalene. It was one of my favorite stories. The congregation sang "Amazing Grace" and then went into "Joshua Fit the Battle of Jericho." My heart was so full of joy I was about to bust my buttons. It didn't get much better than good gospel music and best friends.

After the final amen the congregation went out on the lawn where the Ladies' Guild had laid out a picnic. There were freezers of homemade ice cream and plates of fried chicken. My tummy rumbled just thinking about the good food. Mama said that when country folks worshipped, they worshipped with abandon, and when they celebrated they did it with equal enthusiasm.

"Brother Micah, we've gathered here to do some poundin'." The man talking was Jonas Crabtree, the chairman of the Board of Deacons, and the acting pastor when we went on a mission.

"As you all know, the tradition of a pounding is where folks in the congregation bring a pound of their favorite food to fill the preacher's larder. But here we go a little more." He turned to one of the other deacons. "Brother Jim, would you please bring in Petunia."

"That's a pig," Tommy whispered. "Please tell me you're not gonna eat it."

"No." Just the thought made me gag. "We've gotten all kinds of things like chickens and pigs. One time we even got a guinea pig. Daddy just makes room for them at the farm. We eat the eggs, but everything that has a face turns into a pet."

"That's good."

"And look at all the goodies." The table was covered in gifts including baked goods and sacks of vegetables. There was even a patchwork quilt.

"It's cool that these folks like your dad so much," Tommy said. "Your family is fun, even the twins."

"Thanks. I think so, too."

Tommy pulled something brightly colored out of his pocket. "I brought you a present because we're best friends. It's a friendship bracelet. I made it." It was a bracelet made of twine and beads.

"That's the nicest gift I've ever had." I was trying to stop the tears that were oozing out of my eyes. "Pinky swear again that we'll be friends always." I held out my hand.

"I pinky swear that we'll always be best friends. Always and always."

Present Day

"You really loved Tommy, didn't you?"

"Yes, I did." The innocence of our relationship had always been very special.

"And I suspect the rest of the story will be a lot

more difficult to tell," Dr. Jill said. "Are you ready to quit for the day, or do you want to continue? "

"I want to get through this as fast as possible. I have a life to build, and a man to share it with. So, here goes..."

Windy Hill Farm-early summer

"Why do you think Daddy wants to talk to us?"

"I don't know, but it makes me nervous," Maeve replied. "I hope it's not like last year when he wanted us to dress up like elves and sing at that shopping center. That was *beyond* humiliating."

I thought being an elf was cool, but Maeve was almost a teenager so just about everything embarrassed her. She wouldn't even go to the Dairy Queen if the twins were invited, and in my opinion, passing up a Blizzard was silly.

"Your mama and I have decided to do a revival tour this summer," Daddy announced after we'd taken our seats around the pine table. "And Spring, you'll have your ninth birthday while we're on the road."

"But...but I wanted to have a party here and invite all my school friends. Tommy said he has a special gift for me." I was tempted to stomp my foot, but I knew that would get me in a mess of trouble

"Don't worry, sweetie. You can have a party when we get back." Mama was trying to make me feel better, but it wasn't working. I wanted to stay home, darn it!

"Can we take baths in the river?" Bubba asked, and then Beau butted in. "And not eat vegetables and have weenie roasts?"

Mama grinned. "Yes, to bathing in the river and the weenie roasts, and no to the veggie ban."

A week later we chugged into a place called Left Hand Hollow. It was so far up in the mountains that the paved road had given out several miles back.

"Micah, I think we're lost." Mama held up the map she'd been studying. "I can't find this place."

"If we're lost, which I don't think is the case, all we have to do is turn around and go back the same way we came in. I suspect these folks can use a good dose of God's word."

Mama glanced out the window and shook her head. "I suppose you're right. But I want our next stop to be...how should I say this...in a place that's a little more civilized," she said, adding a frown. "Now let's find a place to camp."

I saw the teenager when Daddy was looking for help in setting up the tent. The kid had a ponytail and a black leather motorcycle jacket with skulls on the back.

"He looks scary," Fiona whispered.

"His aura is okay, but it is kind of gloomy. I think he's just trying to look bad."

"I'll bet he doesn't show up at the service tonight. What do you think?"

"I suspect you're right."

Later, as I was helping Maeve put out the hymnals I spied a woman wearing a dress as big as a circus tent. There was gray fog rolling around her legs. I'd never seen colors like that. It scared me so bad I almost missed the fact she was pushing the teenager in the leather jacket into a seat on the front row.

"You need some learnin' about God," she hissed.

When I was passing the offering plate, I accidently touched the teenager's arm. A knife! Blood! Something awful was about to happen to him and I couldn't do a darned thing about it. Why would God let me see bad things and not give me a way to stop it?

If I told Daddy, he'd get upset, and I didn't want that to happen. And the awful woman wouldn't believe me.

When we went to bed it was hot and the mosquitoes were buzzing around my head. Plus, Fiona was hogging the space. I looked out the window and saw Mama and Daddy sitting down by the river. I really wanted to be held, so I carefully got out of bed and tiptoed down the steps of the bus.

"Come here, baby," Mama said and then pulled me into her lap where I felt safe. Maybe everything would be okay.

Mama kissed the top of my head. "Are you having a hard time sleeping?"

"Uh-huh."

"You know you can tell us anything, don't you?"

When the words started it was like water rushing down the drain.

"Hey, kiddo." Daddy ruffled my hair. "If something like that happens again, you let us know right away. We're here for you. For right now, why don't you close your eyes and get some sleep. Don't worry about a thing, okay?"

"Okay," I said, and then felt my head nodding. Later, Mama told me that I slept the sleep of angels. That sounded good.

Most of the next week was like a vacation. We spent our days fishing, swimming, eating junk food and singing gospel songs around a campfire. Daddy claimed that it was the perfect way to commune with God.

Mama said that all that nature was getting to her.

On Thursday she made an announcement that had us all clapping. "We're going to town to have dinner," she said. "We all need some vegetables and milk."

"Vegetables and milk," Fiona moaned. "I thought you meant hamburgers and French Fries."

"Me, too." I had to back up my sister.

"I could do with a nice greasy burger," Daddy said. He didn't seem to notice the bad look Mama was giving him.

"And fries?" Maeve asked.

"And fries."

"Micah!"

"Oh, yeah, and some veggies," Daddy said. "So everyone get dressed. Remember you shoes and let's get rolling."

At first, the trip down the mountain was exciting. But as we drove on and on, we got antsy.

"How much longer?" Fiona asked.

Instead of answering, Mama turned to Daddy. "I didn't realize we were so far from the nearest town."

"We wanted to be away from everyone, remember," he said and then glanced at me.

"You're right."

"We look like hicks driving around in this...this abomination." Maeve was using big words again.

"People will think the Clampetts have come to town."

Mama whipped around in her captain's seat. "Maeve Marie, I've heard enough. Get a better attitude or stuff a sock in it."

She didn't get mad very often, but when she did, we knew it was time to zip it.

"Look at this." Bubba presented his orange fingers. The twins had pigged out on an entire bag of Cheetos. "Do you think they're going to stay this color?" He stuck two fingers in his mouth and sucked.

The boys could be really disgusting. If they weren't trying to put boogers on you, or chasing you with a snake, they were wrestling. And worst of all, they were stinky.

"Hot diggity!" Daddy sounded excited as he pulled up in front of a building with a neon sign blinking on and off. The gravel parking lot was full of motorcycles, pickup trucks and rusted vans.

"You've got to be kidding! This place is a dump." Mama didn't look happy. "If you recall, I said I wanted to take the children to a café."

"I'll bet they don't have any cauliflower in there," Fiona whispered.

"And look." Maeve pointed at a hand-painted billboard advertising an Elvis contest. If there was one thing Daddy couldn't resist, it was singing Elvis songs.

"For heaven's sake!" Mama exclaimed and then slumped back in her seat.

"Tell me we're not stopping here. Mom!" Maeve turned that word into two and ended with a screech.

Mama didn't turn around. "Talk to your dad. He's driving."

"What are those people doing?" Fiona pointed at a group of men dressed in white leather jumpsuits decorated with fringe and sequins. "I'll bet they're sweaty and smelly."

"Big time," Maeve said. "And that poufy hair is just…just freaky."

I was too busy looking at all the different colors to say anything.

"Most of them do this as a hobby," Daddy said. "But it looks like there's a hefty prize. I'm sure that's why there's such a big crowd. I think I'll go check it out. I'll be back shortly." He was out of the bus before Mama could protest.

"We might as well get out, too," Mama said we rushed to the door. "Go down the stairs one at a time," she cautioned the twins.

"We need to find a proper restaurant," Mama said when she caught up with Daddy. "One where my children won't be subjected to…this." She waved her hands at the whole scene.

"I'll run in and see what's going on," Daddy said before disappearing in the door.

"Please tell me we're not going to participate in this circus. That would be humiliating," Maeve said. "I think I'm going to be sick."

Fiona called Maeve a drama queen, and that was like the pot calling the kettle black.

"Maeve Marie, I don't want to hear another word from you."

Oops. Mama was getting cranky.

"And twins, cool it! I've about had it." One thing about the O'Flaherty kids—we all knew when it was time to shut up.

We were quiet for almost ten minutes, but then Fiona whispered, "There's Daddy." She pointed toward the front porch where he was making his way through the crowd.

"Mom, are we going in there?" I asked. I couldn't take my eyes off a girl who had an aura that looked like spray-painted glitter.

"I'm afraid so. It appears that your dad has registered for the contest."

"Does that mean we have to sing, too?" Maeve asked.

"I don't know. You'll have to ask him. All I want is to get some good food into you guys," Mama said as Daddy strolled up carrying a piece of paper.

He was wearing a big smile as he announced, "We're good to go. There were so many people in line that they cut off the number of entries right after me."

"Lucky us," Mama muttered. "We have to feed these kids. Does the café look decent?"

"Yep, I checked it out. I even talked to one of the waitresses, and she assured me they have vegetables." He shot Mama a wink that she ignored. But then she grinned. Mama was getting happy, and that meant everything would be fine.

The sign said this was *The Place.* It looked like the country dance halls from back home. Everything was made out of wood—the ceiling, the floors, the stage and even the moveable walls that were propped out to let in a breeze.

Folks were already seated at the picnic tables surrounding the stage. Little kids were running around playing chase while their parents munched on peanuts and talked. A group of teens had staked out a couple of tables as far away from their parents as possible. The colors were all good, except for a couple of smudged gray ones, but all in all, it was okay.

"Do we have time for dinner, and where's the cafe?" Mama asked as she grabbed one of the twins who was about to make an escape.

"Follow me. My new friend Annabelle is saving us a table." Daddy picked up Beau and headed toward the back of the dance floor.

Mama took me by one hand and Bubba by the other. "Spring baby, don't touch anything or anyone. Okay?"

"Yes, ma'am." I'd learned the hard way that touching people I didn't know could be terrifying.

We had a down-home country meal of fried chicken, mashed potatoes, collard greens, cornbread and peach cobbler. I was so stuffed I could barely move.

"Girls, you're going to sing with me while your mama watches your brothers," Daddy announced.

Maeve groaned and rolled her eyes.

"We need to get warmed up. I promise this will be fun." Daddy had a way of saying things that made you believe him. That's probably why he was such a good preacher.

"They're scheduling the Elvis songs from his early records to his later ones, and since we're doing sacred music, we're on at the beginning."

When we trooped back through the main dance hall, I noticed that the huge room had the filled with people.

"Are you guys scared?" Fiona asked.

"There are more people here than at our services, but it's okay," I said. "A big crowd might be fun."

"I don't think so." Maeve could be really irritating. "I'm just glad Daddy isn't dressed like that." She pointed at a man in a bright blue jumpsuit covered in rhinestones. He even had rhinestones on his sunglasses.

"Girls, let's find a corner and do some vocalizing," Daddy said as he herded us toward the back of the stage while Mama and the twins claimed a table down front.

"What song are we doing?" Fiona asked.

"'How Great Thou Art' and if we get a call for an encore we'll do 'Amazing Grace.' I'll do the stanzas and you come in on the chorus."

While we warmed up, I could hear singing in the background, so I knew the show had started. But it wasn't until the announcer said, "And now we have the O'Flaherty family from Spirit Hollow, Virginia. That's a ways back east. And they're going to do one of Elvis's favorites,' How Great Thou Art.' Let's give these folks a big hand."

Daddy stepped up to the microphone. "You might have noticed our bus out front. That picture is Jesus, not Elvis," he said with a grin. "We'll be in Boone's Creek next week doing revival services. We invite you to join us. There'll be lots of singing and fellowship. It's a great way to affirm your love of Jesus."

The crowd clapped in appreciation, but when he started to sing everything changed. An electric zing rippled through the audience that made the hair on my arms stand up.

"*Oh Lord, my God, when I in awesome wonder consider all the worlds thy hands have made*," he sang and then we joined him in the chorus. It felt like God was in the audience.

By the time we sang the final notes, almost everyone was in tears. There was complete silence before the folks erupted in applause and whistles.

"Encore, encore, encore," the crowd chanted.

Daddy grinned and winked at us. "My youngest daughter and I will be doing *Amazing Grace*." Daddy and I sang a duet we did at church, and after we finished we could barely hear our thinking for all the clapping.

Daddy herded us off the stage and then whispered, "That went great. Let's go watch our competitors. Most of them can't carry a tune in a bucket."

I knew that meant they couldn't sing, but just the thought of someone carrying around a bucket with musical notes in it made me giggle.

After we sat down, Fiona poked me. "What's he doing?" she asked, pointing out a man who was making weird motions with his bottom. It looked a lot like clothes bouncing around in a front loading washing machine. .

"I don't know, but it looks strange."

Mama must have heard us. "He's doing the hip swivel."

"Oh." That didn't tell me a thing, but a lot of things didn't make much sense.

The singers were really bad, and the costumes were even worse, but the folks in the audience seemed to be having a good time. The guy singing was in the middle of a long "you-ouou-ouou" when I spied the sparkly girl standing on the edge of the stage.

"Look at that pretty girl. I wish I had a shiny dress just like that one."

"What girl?" Fi asked.

"The one on the stage."

Fiona's head moved back and forth. "I don't see anyone but that skinny guy in the dumb clothes. Good grief, he's terrible."

"You really don't see her?"

Fi answered with one of those silly eye-rolls she loved so much.

I was trying to come up with something snotty to say when the girl gave me a wink and a wave, and then disappeared. Poof. She was gone. I'd seen an angel! An angel! The Glory Place had to be special if that's how the little girls dressed

And even better, we won the five-hundred-dollar jackpot. Mama said that would go a long way toward keeping the tax man from the door–whatever that meant. Daddy claimed a heavenly chorus was clapping in appreciation.

Personally, I thought it was God's pat on the back for doing a good job.

The next afternoon we pulled into the camp ground in Boone's Creek. Mama and Daddy were checking out the camp site when a woman walked up. She was so skinny she could hide behind a telephone pole.

"Hey, preacher man. I heard you was a'coming, so I thought you and your family might like some home cooking." She set her basket on the ground and stuck out her hand. "Mavis Sue Callahan here. My nephew was at *The Place*. He told me you were plannin' on headin' this direction, so I kept an eye out for 'ya. We don't git enough God talk around here. Swear to goodness, if Jesus showed up he'd smack some these folks silly," she said with a chuckle.

Daddy shook her hand before pulling her into a hug. That was his version of a friendly greeting. "Glad to make your acquaintance, Mavis Sue. I'm Micah O'Flaherty and this is my wife Paloma," he said and then sniffed. "I think I smell fried chicken."

"Yes, sir, I make the best in the county. There's also some potato salad and brownies for your young'uns."

Mavis Sue was one of those people who could make you smile by just looking at you, and she had the prettiest aura.

Daddy picked up the basket and peeked inside. "I think I've died and gone to heaven."

Mavis Sue patted his hand. "You enjoy those eats and I'll see ya' tonight. All my neighbors are plannin' to come and get the Word. We're all lookin' forward to it."

It was a busy day getting ready for the service. We all had assigned chores. Fiona and I were responsible for setting up the chairs and putting out the hymnals. Plus, we had to take care of the twins.

Daddy's sermon was on John the Baptist. Toward the end when Mama played "Just As I Am" on the guitar and Daddy issued the invitation, Mavis Sue hopped out of her seat and headed down the aisle. She was surrounded by a white light that was so beautiful it brought tears to my eyes.

"Daddy." I tugged on his sleeve, but he wasn't paying attention.

"Dad-dy!"

He placed his hand on my shoulder. "Not now, sweetie. Miss Mavis Sue has something to say."

"But Daddy, I want to tell her that she's going to the Glory Place."

Daddy turned to me, his eyes were wide.

"What did you say?"

"She said I'm a'going to the Glory Place, and I sho' hope that little gal's right," Mavis Sue said and put her arm around my shoulders. I knew she'd be very happy in the Glory Place.

"Brother Micah," Mavis Sue said. "I've been sick for quite a spell, and I'm pretty sure it's my time to go. I'd like to be baptized. You think we can arrange that?"

"We certainly can, Mavis Sue." He turned to the congregation. "Please join us down at the river for an old fashioned dunkin'." A chorus of amens greeted his announcement.

"It looks like there's been a drought in these parts," Daddy said as he checked out the water rippling through the rocks.

A man in a John Deere ball cap nodded. "Yes, sir. That'd be right."

"Not a problem," Daddy said with a grin. "It looks like this will be more of a Methodist sprinkling than a real baptism, but just like John the Baptist did in the Bible, we'll make do." He rolled up his pant legs and held out his hand for Mavis Sue to join him in the creek.

"Paloma, would you and the girls please lead us in a singing of 'Down By the River?' I'm sure the angels will be singing right along with you."

Chapter 6

Three weeks later

"You know what I'd like?"

Fiona was reading her new Nancy Drew mystery so I knew she wasn't listening. "What?" she asked, without looking up.

"Spinach, I want a great big plate of creamed spinach."

"Un-huh."

Nope, she hadn't heard a word I'd said. I tossed my comic book on the floor of the bus. "I said I want spinach."

"That's nuts!"

The look on her face gave me a case of the giggles. "I said I want to go home."

"Me, too." She put down her book.

"I want to sleep in my own bed."

"Right on."

"How much longer are we going to be on this trip?" I'd been wondering about for a while.

"I heard Daddy say this is our last town before we head home."

"Yay!" Then I noticed that Daddy had pulled into a motel parking lot, and best of all, there was a swimming pool. A pool with blue water and a diving board! "Look at that! There's a pool. We can swim in clean water."

"And I see a cafe." Maeve had jumped on my bunk and joined us in looking out the window.

Daddy hopped off the bus and strolled into the office. Fiona and I held hands and crossed our fingers. "Please, please, please come out with a key," she muttered. "If we stay here we can have a hot breakfast, and cold milk and French Fries," Maeve said.

Our noses were pressed to the window when we saw Daddy carrying two keys with attached plastic tags.

I was bouncing on my bunk. And when I found out that Daddy would be preaching in a real church with hymnals, pews, choir robes and an air conditioner, I was so happy I could have danced a jig. A restaurant, a toilet that flushed, clean sheets, *and* a television was pretty hard to beat.

The church-goers in Parker's Corner called a revival a booster. Daddy's sermon that night was about Job–that poor man. No matter how many verses of the hymn we sang no one walked down the aisle to accept the invitation. Daddy was about to call it quits when a man strolled down the aisle, stopping to speak to people along the way.

"Finally," Fiona whispered. "I'm tired of singing, but he doesn't count. He's the preacher at this church, so I think he's already on a first name basis with God."

"Darn," Maeve muttered.

Something about him gave me the willies. "So that's Brother Fred?" His aura was weird.

Brother Fred sashayed and schmoozed before finally making it to the pulpit. He snatched the microphone out of Daddy's hands. If one of us pulled a stunt like that, Mama would have taken a switch to our backside.

"Brother Micah, thank you so much for that wonderful sermon." It sounded like he was talking in capital letters. No wonder his flock needed a booster.

"I'm sure my children appreciated your wisdom, I know I did." His children? "And your girls are beautiful creatures of God."

I took another look at his aura. He didn't look like a man of God. I was wondering what that was all about when he patted my head and his colors turned into a swirl of black, dark grey and muddy green. Little bits of electricity bounced around his head, almost like an evil halo, and something started squirming and wiggling around him like it was trying to scratch its way out of a sack.

I wanted to scream, but I couldn't utter a sound. It felt as if I had a balloon stuck in my throat. And then I fell into a place so dark and scary that I couldn't breathe, or say, or do anything, and even worse, no one else could see what was happening. I turned to run, but my sisters were in my way.

Maeve put her arm around my shoulder. "What's wrong?"

I was trapped, and the boogeyman was about to take me to hell.

"No! No!" My scream came out as a squeak. Don't let him touch me, I prayed, but God didn't seem to be listening.

Brother Fred touched my cheek and everything went dark.

That's when I saw the teenager. The girl was wearing bright orange lipstick and she had black goop around her eyes. Her neck was twisted like she was trying to look behind her.

Oh God! Oh God! Oh God! She was dead!

The minute that horrible thought crossed my mind, I started screaming and couldn't stop. I could hear Daddy and Mama, but it sounded like they were a long way away. More than anything, I wanted to crawl into Mama's lap where it was safe, but I couldn't stop screaming.

Evil had become a living, breathing monster. The story of the boogeyman wasn't something made up to scare little kids. He was real and his name was Brother Fred.

"Sh, sh, Spring honey. Take a deep breath." That was Daddy's voice. The next thing I knew, I was in his lap and he was rubbing my back.

But what were we doing on the floor? And where were all the people?

"I'm scared." I burrowed my face into Daddy's shoulder. Terrifying things were lurking out there, things that little girls shouldn't see.

"I know, baby, I know."

"Is Spring okay?" Fiona asked. Her freckles looked like dirt sprinkled across her nose and Maeve was wringing her hands.

"She'll be fine," Daddy said and then spoke to Mama, "Why don't you take the rest of the kids back to the motel café and get them burgers and milk shakes. Spring and I are going out for a treat."

"Are you sure?" Paloma asked.

"Yeah, we'll talk later. Kids, grab your stuff and go with your mom. And twins, you guys behave." Beau and Bubba responded with a 'Yes, sir.'

Scoops was an old-fashioned ice cream parlor

with white wrought iron tables and candy-striped wallpaper.

"Would you like to share a banana split?"

Most of the time I would have jumped at the chance to have chocolate, caramel and strawberries. But I kept seeing that girl's face.

"Banana split it is." Daddy's smile was sad, probably because I'd gone nutty in the middle of his service.

I tried so hard not to make a big deal about being different, not to draw attention to the fact I could see things other people couldn't, but tonight had been way too much. The colors, the smell, the girl– it was all too, too...too!

I wanted to stuff all the bad things into a place that I didn't have to think about.

"Give us the works, lots of chocolate and two spoons," Daddy told the teenager behind the counter.

"Right up, sir."

With the ice cream in his hand, Daddy took me to a table in an out of the way corner, away from the giggling teens and noisy families.

"I need a cuddle," he said, patting his lap. That was the best invitation I'd had in a very long time. Daddy wouldn't let the bad man get me. Just the thought of Brother Fred gave me chill bumps. Little girls should be thinking about dolls and pretty dresses, not seeing dead people.

"Do you want to tell me about it?"

"Uh huh."

"Let's talk, and remember, I won't let anyone hurt you. You know that, don't you."

I really wanted to stick my thumb in my mouth,

but instead I just snuggled closer to Daddy and nodded my head. I closed my eyes and thought about what I'd seen.

"She had dark hair with a bow."

"That's good." Daddy had taken a napkin out of the holder and was writing on it. "What else?"

"The lipstick and stuff looked like a clown. She had on a pink shirt and blue jeans."

"Could you tell where she was?"

I thought that would be harder, but then I had the answer. "She was in the woods near a road. I saw a sign that said Bubba's Beer and Bait. Will that help?"

Daddy kissed the top of my head. "I'm sure it will, little one."

Once I started talking, it seemed I couldn't stop. It was like the time I'd puked up some bad chicken salad; once it was all gone I felt better.

But I was still really, really scared.

Present Day

"Spring, come back to me."

I was so immersed in my past that Dr. Jill's voice came as a shock. "Oh, right. Sure." I shook my head like a dog that had just come in from the rain. "I'm sorry, I..."

Dr. Jill took my hand. "You just relived a very traumatic incident in your life. That'll take a toll." The way she was looking at me I knew she was assessing my condition. I wondered what she'd do if she thought I was about to flip out.

"I'm okay, really I am. That was a hideous time in my life."

"Do you feel better for talking about it?"

"I think I do, but I'll let you know tomorrow." And please God, the nightmares would be held at bay.

Dr. Jill leaned back in her chair. She obviously didn't think I was about to freak.

"I'm curious, what did your parents do?"

"I didn't find this out until much later, but Daddy and Mama decided to call the sheriff, even though they were taking a chance by accusing a pillar of the church of murder, especially in a small mountain community. But fortunately, the sheriff believed in second sight, and he'd also been at the service. He told Daddy that four teenage girls had been murdered in the county, and the last victim's neck was broken. In fact, he said that God had sent me to stop the murders."

"That's a lot for a child to handle."

Despite my best intentions, I let out a snort. "You don't know the half of it. Daddy called his brother, Hiram, who showed up with his son to follow our bus back home. Knowing Uncle Hiram and my cousin Jerome, they were armed to the teeth."

"Sometimes, that's what it takes," Dr. Jill said, adding a nod. "Where do you want to go from here?"

"Truthfully, I'd like to go home and pull the covers over my head, but I have to get this off my chest. I told you that I don't have visions about the people I love, but I have a feeling that something really life-changing is about to happen. And I have a sneaking suspicion that I don't have a lot of time, so let's do this again tomorrow."

A day rarely went by that I didn't hear from Jed, but today he must have been busy. I didn't have any messages or missed calls on my phone. So I was so pleased when I pulled into my driveway and found him sitting on my porch swing. He was my touchstone, my lifeline to reality. Truth could be ephemeral, but in this case there were things he deserved to know.

"You look comfortable." I dropped my briefcase on the floor and sat down next to him on the swing. "It's been quite a day."

"Come here." Jed put his arm around me and pulled my head down to his chest. I could spend hours listening to his heartbeat. "Did something unusual happen?" he asked.

All of a sudden, I was so tired I could barely speak and my bones felt like melted butter. "I had an appointment with my therapist, and right now I'm wiped."

"I'll get you a glass of iced tea."

"That would be great." I leaned back and closed my eyes, comfortable in letting Jed take care of me. He deserved the truth, and I knew that once I was able to verbalize it all to Dr. Jill, I wouldn't be afraid to tell him everything.

Chapter 7

Dr. Jill always looked gorgeous in her designer clothes, but today she seemed even more professional in her dark navy suit and fuchsia silk blouse.

"Do you have an important appointment after our session?"

She sighed. "I'm testifying in court later this afternoon."

"I thought everything that's said here is privileged."

"Don't worry, it is. This is a third person analysis requested by the defense team."

"Good."

"So let's get started. I think we're making progress."

"I do, too. I remember..."

Windy Hill Farm

"Three days after we got back to the farm, my Auntie Aurora came to see us. She was funny and funky, and wore tie-dyed clothes and Birkenstocks. And even better, she had second sight, or at least that's what Mama said. he was also a healer for folks up in the mountains who couldn't go to the doctor. The minute we spied her car, we ran out to greet her.

"Auntie Aurora," Fiona squealed, as the other kids sprinted across the lawn. I was feeling shy, so I held onto Mama's skirt.

"Hey, kiddos." Aurora gathered everyone into a hug. "Welcome home."

"Look, my front tooth fell out." Bubba stuck his tongue between the gap. "I got some money from the Tooth Fairy. I'm thinking about pulling the other one out."

"Don't even consider it, young man," Mama yelled from where she was standing on the porch. "Pearlie Jean has some fresh cookies, so you kids run in and see if she'll give you one."

Cookie was the magic word for the twins. They were in the house so fast the screen door didn't hit them on the butt, and Fiona and Maeve weren't far behind.

Mama ruffled my hair. "You too, sweetie. Your daddy and I need to talk to Aurora."

Mama, Daddy and Auntie Aurora were in Daddy's office drinking the sweet tea Pearlie Mae had made. I knew it was wrong, but I couldn't resist tiptoeing up and lying down to watch through the crack in the door. From there I could hear most of the conversation. Mama would snatch me bald-headed if she knew what I was doing, so I was very quiet.

"Spring's not eating and all she wants to do is hang on me." Mama said. "I was hoping that being home would solve the problem, but now I'm not sure. I invited Tommy out to play yesterday, and even he couldn't cheer her up."

"She won't sleep in her own bed," Daddy added. "All things considered, I'm sure that's normal, but I'm worried." He paused as if dreading what he had to say next. "The sheriff from Parker's Corner called about an hour ago. They used Spring's information and found the girl's body. From there they were able to get a search warrant for Brother Fred's home and discovered the souvenirs he'd kept. The cheerleader wasn't his only victim."

"Oh, dear God!" Auntie Aurora exclaimed. "What is this world coming to?"

"The good news is that the sheriff thinks this will be a slam dunk for sending him to death row. We won't have to worry about him showing up here, and that's a huge blessing."

"Amen," Mama agreed. "We'll share that with Spring, with some modifications, of course. But I'm afraid it might make the problem worse."

Daddy leaned back and rubbed his temple like he had a bad headache. "We've talked about taking her to a therapist, but I'm not sure conventional methods will solve her problem. I believe this is more spiritual."

Mama nodded in agreement. "I'm hoping you might know someone who can assist us."

Auntie Aurora was a hippie right down to the tips of her sandals. "I've done some research and I think I may have found someone," she said, playing with the end of her blonde braid. "I don't know her personally, but the people I talked to are quite impressed. Word has it, she has a special touch with animals, sort of like a horse whisperer," she said. "If you want, I'll send her a message through a mutual acquaintance. She doesn't have a phone."

"Do *you* think it's a good idea?" Mama asked.

"I don't see that you have a choice, unless you

want to take her to a doctor. And like Micah, I don't believe that's the answer," my aunt said. "I'll stay with her the entire time, and you know I wouldn't let anything bad happen to Spring. If nothing else she'll have a vacation in the woods away from her normal life."

Daddy and Mama looked at each other, and then Daddy said, "We'll do it. You make the arrangements."

It was time to get lost, so I slithered back and then quietly made my way outside. Where were they sending me, and would it be scary? I was glad Auntie Aurora was going with me.

A couple of days later, I was in my room reading when Auntie Aurora tapped on the doorsill. "May I come in?"

"Okay."

Mama and Daddy were right behind her.

Aurora plopped on the bed. "Whatcha' doing, sweetheart?"

"Reading."

"Would you like to go on a trip with me?"

"Where to?"

"I thought we'd head up to the mountains and visit an acquaintance of mine. She has horses and dogs and cats."

That sounded a lot better than sitting around here worrying.

I glanced at Mama, "May I go?"

"Sure," she said even though she didn't look happy.

"I thought we'd leave this afternoon, if that's okay with your mom and dad. Are you game for an adventure?"

I jumped up and reached under the bed for my backpack. "Are we spending the night?"

"Maybe even a couple of days. How do you feel about that?"

Having two whole days away from the bad thoughts sounded like heaven.

"Pack some shorts, a couple of nighties and a toothbrush. While you do that your mom and I will go down and put a lunch together. We'll stop somewhere and have a picnic."

The trip to the mountain took longer than I'd expected. The winding road went up and up, and then we turned on a gravel trail that went into the forest. Splotches of sun barely made it through the thick arches of trees.

"Are you sure we're going the right way?" What if we got lost on the mountain and no one found us for days? There were wild animals in the forests—bears and big cats and even poisonous snakes. Even so, I'd learned there were things much worse than a stray bear, or even a copperhead.

"Here we are." Aurora pulled into a clearing and turned off the engine. "At least I hope this is the place," she muttered.

Spirals of white smoke drifted from the chimney of a small log cabin that had a wide front porch. A palomino pony and a chestnut gelding were grazing inside a stockade fence. A calico cat was sunning on the stoop. An old hound came out to greet us while a couple of his buddies watched from the shade of an ancient tree. The smell of wood smoke, pine sap and fresh air was almost as comforting as Pearlie Jean's cinnamon rolls on a cold winter morning.

Birds were singing and wildflowers covered the meadow. It was really pretty, but it didn't look like any vacation place I'd ever seen—no swimming pool, no restaurant and apparently no indoor plumbing, not if the outhouse was any indication.

What if we had squirrel, or possum or even worse, rattlesnake for dinner? That would be gross.

"Come on." Auntie Aurora opened the passenger door and held out her hand. "Let's go meet Sister Sarah."

"Sister Sarah?" That was a strange name, but everything about this trip was turning out to be weird.

I squatted down to pet the cat while Auntie Aurora knocked on the screen door.

The woman who answered was tall with coal-black hair and eyes that twinkled like the stars. Most of Auntie Aurora's friends were partial to tie dye T-shirts and peasant skirts, but this lady was wearing jeans and a man's white dress-shirt.

"My, my, my," Sister Sarah exclaimed. "Aurora, it's so nice to finally meet you." She extended her hand in greeting. "And little one, come here and let me see you."

Her aura was shimmery, almost like the girl at the roadhouse. I held out my hand and when Sister Sarah took it, a calm flowed over me.

"Let's go in and have a cup of tea and a chat."

The cabin was decorated with chintz curtains and an overstuffed sofa covered in a rose-patterned fabric. Everything smelled like fresh laundry and honeysuckle.

Much to my relief, I didn't see any boiling cauldrons or skinned animals hanging from the rafters. Instead, a white Persian was grooming itself in front of a stone fireplace. And the coffee table was stacked with books and magazines.

"Have a seat, ladies. I'll brew some tea. Is peppermint okay with everyone?" Sister Sarah asked. "Spring, I'll make yours iced." She reached into a small refrigerator and brought out a bowl of ice.

Mountain people generally made do without lights and refrigerators, and lots of stuff that I couldn't imagine living without, so how did this lady have all the goodies?

"After we finish our drinks, Spring can help me in the barn. Aurora, there's a wonderful swing on the porch. It's a great place to take a nap."

"I think I'll take you up on that suggestion. In fact, I'll go out there and sip my tea." Auntie Aurora grabbed a sugar cookie as she left.

Sister Sarah walked with me to a small wooden barn. "Have you ever mucked stalls?"

"No, ma'am. We have lots of animals, but no horses. Folks at church have given us chickens and pigs and even a guinea pig. They think we're going to eat them, but we don't."

Sister Sarah's laugh was the prettiest sound I'd ever heard.

"Is that right?" she asked as she grabbed a pitch fork. "Doing barn chores gives me time to meditate about life and God and all kinds of things. Do you ever meditate?"

"Not really." Did little kids really sit around and med…medi…what?

She handed me a smaller pitchfork and opened a stall door.

"Our job today is to pick out the horse apples. That's what we call the poop because it's round."

She stuck her pitchfork in and sifted through the bedding. "See. It's easy."

"Okay." I wasn't very good at it, but before long, I was halfway through my first stall.

"That's really good." Praise from Sister Sarah felt like manna from heaven. Daddy used that in sermons.

As we mucked the stalls, cleaned the buckets and put out flakes of hay, Sister Sarah asked questions and told me funny stories. In return, I told Sister Sarah about the colors, and the dead people, and even Brother Fred. When I finished she pulled me into her arms and held me.

After a few minutes Sister Sarah said, "Let's go see Emmaline."

I discovered that Emmaline was a soon-to-be a mama mare. Her coat was a velvety chocolate brown, and she had a great big tummy. Her wet nose made me giggle when she nuzzled my hair. "She's so cute!"

"Yes, she is, and she's a love. Foals are so much fun." I could tell that Sister Sarah loved her animals.

"Are you ready to go in and have a snack?"

My tummy rumbled. "Oh, yes."

Auntie Aurora was sitting on the porch rocking when we got back to the cabin. "How are the ponies?" she asked.

I plopped down next to her. "Emmaline's gonna have a baby. And the other horses came right up to us when we went to the pasture with a feed bucket. Do you think I can get a horse?"

Auntie Aurora chuckled. "I don't know. That would be up to your mama and daddy."

"I heard that you rescue animals," Auntie Aurora said.

Sister Sarah was leaning against the porch rail. "I give homes to my animal friends." Her smile was so pretty. "Let's go in and wash up. I'll bet I can find some cookies. And Spring, you can help me cook our evening meal."

Supper was a feast of stew, fresh vegetables and hot bread. Auntie Aurora leaned back in her chair and rubbed her tummy. "I'm so stuffed, I'm about to pop."

"Technically speaking, I doubt that'll happen," Sister Sarah said, adding a smile. "Let's get the dishes done. Then we can sit around the fire and chat." It was summer, and even though the fire was burning brightly, the room wasn't too warm.

After the dishes were washed and the sun had set, Sister Sarah turned to me. "Let's talk more about the colors."

Auntie Aurora looked surprised, but she didn't say a word.

"Okay." No one had ever explained why I could see the colors.

"Do you know what they are?" Sister Sarah asked.

"No."

She waved a hand to indicate the whole world. "All living creatures are surrounded by electrical impulses that create a color. And the colors are indicative of the person's soul. Aurora's is turquoise. That means she's good at influencing others. Yours, my little one, tells me that you're one of God's special children."

"Really?"

Sarah smiled. "Yes, really."

"Why can't everyone see them? Most of the time they're pretty. Except. . . uh, Brother Fred. His made me scared."

"I know." Sister Sarah put her arms around me. "He's a really bad person, but he can't hurt you, not anymore."

"Are you sure?" My biggest worry was that he'd find me and do awful things.

"I promise, and I don't break promises. Now let's talk about the good stuff. Most people aren't as sensitive as you are. Kids, and sometimes teenagers, have bright colors because they are a new energy. As people get older their colors get fuzzy around the edges and look sort of pastel."

"Like the Creamsicle® people."

"Yes, just like the Creamsicle® people," Sarah agreed. "Have you ever wondered about halos?"

Aurora leaned forward. She seemed to be as curious as I was. "I've seen them in the paintings about Jesus, but what are they?"

"They're similar to an aura. The Renaissance painters had the ability to see auras."

"Wow!" That made my day. "You're talking about the famous guys in the art museums, right?"

"Absolutely."

"Cool!"

Later, Sarah tucked me into a cozy feather bed in the loft and kissed me goodnight. The evil was gone and my dreams were happy.

Windy Hill Farm

"Mama," I squealed as I hopped from Auntie Aurora's VW bug and ran into my mom's arms. "I had the best time! We mucked stalls and took care of the horses. Then we played with the dogs and cats. And I told Sister Sarah all about the colors, and how I was afraid of Brother Fred."

"You did?"

"Yeah, and it made me feel better. She explained all about the auras, that's the colors. Did you know that famous painters from long ago saw the colors?"

"I didn't know that."

"She said she thinks I have something that's called," I looked to Auntie Aurora for help.

"Precognition and retrocognition. The precognition is seeing things before they happen."

"Like that old man dying at the feed store. That must have been precognition."

"Yes," Aurora said. "And retrocognition is seeing things that have happened in the past."

"She told me it's a gift from God. I was afraid it was something bad, but she told me that I'm special."

Mama and Auntie Aurora glanced at each other. It was like when Fiona and I could talk without really saying anything.

"So you're glad you went?" Mama asked.

"Yeah. She told me that I'd still be seeing the colors, but the yucky stuff would go away until I was ready to make a decision whether to use it or not. I'm not sure what that meant, but I think it's good." And I wouldn't be scared that the boogeyman would get me.

Present Day

"What do you think happened on that mountain?" Dr. Jill asked.

99

"To be perfectly honest, I believe she was an angel."

Dr. Jill looked pensive and then nodded. "You might be right. In my business, I hear a lot of things that are seemingly impossible. But who am I to determine what is, and what isn't possible. I'm a mere mortal. For you to admit, even to yourself, that you spent a week with an angel, means we're making progress." She stood and straightened her skirt. "Now, I'm afraid I have to scurry to the courthouse," she said as she grabbed her tablet. "How about day after tomorrow? I have all afternoon open. Let's say one o'clock?"

"I'll be here. That'll give me time to get some work done. I don't want my clients to feel as if I've slighted them. They want answers based on law. I'm afraid they wouldn't understand my unique, and bizarre, situation," I said with a laugh. "Frankly, I don't understand it."

Chapter 8

The next two days proved to be busy. I hadn't confided in Sam, my boss and friend, about my intensive therapy sessions, but I didn't want him to think I wasn't pulling my load, so I worked through lunch and dinner.

At any rate, my desk wasn't piled high with work when I showed up at Dr. Jill's office. And after our perfunctory tea and cookies, I was ready to get to work.

"Everything was calm for the next couple of years, except for one disturbing incident when I was eleven."

Windy Hill Farm—1990

My world was still full of Popsicle and Creamsicle® people, and occasionally I'd run into someone with a dirty gray aura. Fortunately, there hadn't been a repeat of anything like the Brother Fred mess. But then something happened the summer before my fifth grade. Auntie Aurora was on a retreat in the Himalayas, and she'd promised to send us a special treat.

"Let's ride our bikes to the mailbox to see if we have a package," Fiona said. "It's neat that

Auntie Aurora gets to go up on those huge mountains with Sherpa's and all that stuff. Don't you wish we could go someplace special?"

"Yeah, but Mama said money's tight this year," I didn't want to complain, but I really wanted to do something exciting.

"Let's race," I yelled as I jumped on my bike. We went pedaling off like crazy. When we got to the end of the lane we threw our bikes down and collapsed on the grass.

"I won," Fiona crowed.

"No, you didn't"

"Yes, I did!"

"Only by an inch."

"That's as good as a mile."

I was so busy trying to come up with a response that I didn't hear the rusty pickup come to a stop in the middle of the highway.

A grizzled old man leaned across the seat and motioned at us with a tobacco-stained finger. "Hey, little ladies, can you point me in the direction of Helen's Holler?" When we didn't move, he motioned again. "Come closer. I'm a mite hard of hearing."

That's when I heard the voice. *"Run! Forget the bicycle and run as fast as you can through the field toward home. Now!"*

"Run!" I grabbed Fiona's arm and pulled her toward the fence.

Fiona didn't miss a beat. She was right behind me as we sprinted across the field. It wasn't until we reached the trees close to the house that we stopped, out of breath and terrified.

Fiona was leaning over wheezing. "What just happened?"

I didn't know where that voice had come from, but I did know that if we'd waited a second longer, something horrible would have happened. "A voice told me to run. That man was bad."

Fiona didn't flinch, a testament to her confidence in my gift. "I didn't know you've been hearing voices. How long has that been going on?"

"That was the first time."

"Neat."

"Not really." Hearing voices wasn't my idea of fun.

Ever since Brother Fred, I'd been really mad at God. I went to church, and did all the things that people expected of a PK–that's what some folks call a preacher's kid–but I didn't want to talk to Him. But things changed when I was baptized...

Down by the River

Daddy and Brother Josiah, pastor of the Church of the Holy Apostle, were holding revivals in the nearby counties. One beautiful day in April, my sisters and I we went with Daddy to a baptism at Lake Thompson. The mist had just lifted when we arrived, and Brother Josiah was setting up a temporary pulpit by the water's edge.

"Brother Micah, good to see 'ya." Brother Josiah was a big Teddy-bear of a man with skin the color of coffee with cream. "This is a day of the Lord."

"Amen, brother, amen. Do you think folks will show up this fine morning to make friends with God?" Daddy asked.

"You bet. Just take a look." Brother Josiah pointed toward the gravel lane where a line of cars, pickups and minivans were slowly chugging toward

the lake. "Our brothers and sisters are on the way."
He glanced at Daddy's khaki's and asked, "Would
you like to borrow a robe. My flock's partial to getting dressed up, especially for church, and that
goes double for preachers."

"Okay." Daddy chuckled. "I get the hint."

The big preacher grinned before producing a
purple choir robe embellished with gold stitching.

Fiona looked enraptured. "Daddy looks like he
should have angels singing back-up."

"He certainly does," Maeve said in agreement.

"It's nice that you girls could join us." Brother
Josiah pinched Fiona's cheek.

"Mama was busy with the twins, so she sent us
to keep Daddy company," Fiona said. "And he
promised to take us to the mall on the way home.

Brother Josiah let out a belly laugh. "Why don't
you young ladies stake out a spot under a tree? It
gets mighty hot out here, and I 'spect this baptism
will take some time. Lots of our folks have been
hankerin' for a revival."

We took his advice and found a shady place to
get comfortable. As PKs we'd attended all kinds of
ceremonies—from funerals to weddings—but this
seemed different.

The crowd was getting bigger and bigger. Families with small children were setting up playpens,
old folks were unloading folding chairs, and teens
were milling around. But more impressive were the
baptismal candidates in their shiny white robes.

Daddy and Brother Josiah stood hip deep in the
water, waiting for the folks who wanted to be baptized to join them one by one. The people on the
banks of the river were singing spirituals. The
preachers took turns dunking the new congregants

and reaffirming the faith of older members of the flock.

The auras were an array of beautiful colors. These folks were in love with their God, and that was something I'd been missing. After the last person walked out of the water, Brother Josiah and Daddy shook hands, indicating the end of the service.

"God has a whole new flock," Brother Josiah said in a voice that could reach the heavens. His proclamation was greeted by a chorus of amens. "Is there anyone else who'd like to come forward?"

Much to my own surprise I jumped up. "I do."

"Sister Spring, come on down," Brother Josiah boomed. "Come on down."

Daddy didn't say a word, but the look on his face was something I'd remember the rest of my life.

Someone handed me a kid's size robe that barely came to my knees. God hadn't answered my prayers in a long time, and now I was hearing voices. Maybe a baptism would get my relationship with Him back on track.

I walked into the water and took Daddy's hand. He leaned forward and whispered, "I'm so proud of you." He led me into the lake. "As John the Baptist said, I will baptize you with water. He will baptize you with the Holy Spirit." Then he leaned me back into the cool water.

The baptism seemed to be exactly what I needed. My friendship with God started to improve, and for almost five years I led a normal life. Occasionally I'd hear the voice of what I'd started thinking of as my guardian angel, but that was only when I was about to do something incredibly stupid.

It was one of the few times I remember being really happy. High school proved to be challenging and I was doing well in sports. And best of all, I was madly in love with Tommy. He spent most of the summer before our junior year working on his grandma's farm. I missed him like crazy—and finally—he was on his way to see me.

I stationed myself on the front porch looking for the rooster tail of dust to billow up from the gravel lane, and when Tommy's rusted-out pickup came into view my heart almost jumped out of my chest.

"Didn't he call you just a couple of minutes ago?" Fiona asked as she plopped down on the steps.

"Fifteen to be exact. I hope he didn't get a ticket." I couldn't wipe the smile off my face. "I think he's anxious to see me."

"Ya think?" Fiona shot me a sly grin. "Do you want me to run out and greet him with a big fat smoochy kiss?"

I couldn't resist giving Fi a poke, just for being a wiseacre.

"Ouch." Fiona rubbed her bicep. "I think I hear someone summoning me."

"Good call." Seconds later the truck came to a sliding stop in the circular drive.

"Tommy." I made a mad dash across the lawn stuck my head in the driver's side window. "When did you get back?"

"About twenty minutes ago." He hopped from the truck and pulled me into a huge hug. "I missed you!"

He'd grown over the summer and towered over me. And even more amazing was how muscled he was. He must have been toting a lot of hay bales.

"Let's take a walk. I have a present for you," he said, taking my hand.

"For me?"

"Just for you. Let's go to the orchard."

On the way to our favorite swing we talked about anything and everything.

"I missed you." Tommy pulled me into his arms and *really* kissed me. It was just as I remembered—his lips were soft, but firm and it made all my lady parts get tingly. It was new, exciting and scary.

When Tommy finally pulled away, he rested his forehead against mine and took a big gulp of air. "That was...uh, great. Here's a gift for you." He pulled a small box out of his pocket. It was from a boutique in Charlottesville. "It's your birthday present, but it's also because I missed you."

The Hearts and Flowers Boutique was so girly that it was hard to imagine Tommy shopping there. Everything in that place was expensive, and when I opened the box, I almost fainted. Nestled in a nest of tissue paper was a silver Claddagh ring—a traditional Irish token of love.

I'd loved Tommy Herndon almost my entire life—first as a best friend, and now as my soul mate. I knew I'd love him forever.

"It's a...a friendship ring, but it's also a marker for something even better in the future." When he looked deep in my eyes, I knew this wasn't just a teenage crush.

Present Day

I slumped in the chair, feeling drained, but strangely exhilarated.

"Remembering was actually fun."

"It sounded like you had a good time as a teenager." Dr. Jill crossed her legs, a seemingly casual pose, but with her it was hard to tell.

"I had a good life. Tommy and I were inseparable. I thought I'd be with him my entire life, but that wasn't to be."

"That sounds like a story for another day," Dr. Jill said as she retrieved her tablet.

"How are you feeling about our sessions?"

My answer came immediately. "Good. Really good. Talking about it with someone impartial makes me feel more confident about telling Jed. And once I do that, I'll be able to continue with my life, instead of living in my self-imposed purgatory."

Dr. Jill smiled. "You're sounding more and more like a recovering patient. I'm pleased with how far you've come."

"Me, too."

We made arrangements for another appointment, and I was almost home when my cell beeped.

"Sweetheart, I'm afraid I won't be able to come over for supper. We have a meeting concerning the triple murder that occurred last week."

"Did they find the guy?"

"Yeah, but it wasn't a guy. Allegedly, it was a twenty-year-old woman who was mad at her boyfriend, so she killed him and his parents." Jed's sigh sounded like it came from the depths of his soul. "I don't know about people. Sometimes I wonder if we're even civilized."

"I know. So, you've assigned someone the case."

"My best prosecutor. I'm tired of people getting off on a technicality, or pleading this, that, and what have you, and never spending a day in jail."

"Would you like to come over for a drink when you get finished?"

"I can't think of anything better."

Chapter 9

Jed and I *talked* well into the night. Or at least we did when we weren't making love. It was better than anything I'd ever experienced. At first it was hot and passionate. But the next time it was slow and easy, soft but carnal. It was well past midnight before we fell asleep, spooning and dreaming.

No wonder I was exhausted. Regardless, I went to work, cleaned off my desk, and had a meeting with Sam. It was my way of not feeling guilty for taking the afternoon off. Tommy's story was the last part of my childhood that I needed to excise. I was so close to the finish line that I could almost feel victory."

Quick Stop, Harrisonburg, VA, July 1997

"Where are you guys going tonight?" Fiona asked as we were getting ready for our dates.

The ink was barely dry on our high school diplomas and Tommy and I were excited about going to college together. "I don't know, but Tommy told me to dress up." I had a feeling that something important was about to happen. I plopped on the bed clad only in my underwear and slip. "He's been secretive lately."

"Swear to goodness, the way that boy looks at you makes *my* heart go pitty-pat," Fiona said. "That's luv with a capital L."

"I know." I couldn't keep the sappy look off my face. "I wonder what he's got up his sleeve?"

Everything would be perfect if I didn't have that niggle of...something that I couldn't quite put my finger on. Normally, I knew what he was thinking, but this time he was blocked, even though he'd been hinting that he'd bought me a special graduation present.

Tommy had made reservations at a restaurant in Harrisonburg. We were almost to our destination when he wheeled into a convenience store parking lot. "I'm dying for a candy bar." When he got nervous he had a wicked sweet tooth.

Tommy hopped out of the car, but before he made it to the door he returned to the passenger side and stuck his head in the window.

"Are you sure you don't want anything? A Fudgesicle? A Coke? Me?" Without waiting for an answer he leaned in for a kiss.

Tommy was of those people who had grown into his body. Gone was the kid with the red hair and freckles, replaced by a handsome man with a mop of russet hair and a gorgeous body toned by hard work on the farm.

Tonight he was wearing one of those ear-to-ear grins that I loved so much.

"I'm good," I said after we finished our kiss.

"I'll be right back," he said and then disappeared into the store.

I was wondering how I got so lucky when an ancient Oldsmobile pulled and parked.

Throughout my teenage years, the auras had

receded to the background, until they were almost like white noise. I rarely took notice of them; that is, until the man got out of the car. His aura looked like the turbulent clouds that preceded a bad thunderstorm. If that wasn't bad enough, he was wearing a bulky parka and had on a ski mask even though it was ninety-degrees and humid.

The moment he entered the store my clairvoyance returned with a vengeance. Tommy was in terrible, terrible trouble. I had to get out of the car, but I was caught on the seat belt.

Tommy, please, please don't do anything heroic! Don't die! I was trying to send him a message, but I realized that he wasn't hearing me.

That mantra was looping through my brain as I ran to the door. I didn't hear the shot, but I felt the bullet as it ripped through Tommy's body.

Oh, God! No! The pain was excruciating. I couldn't breathe. I couldn't think. Blindly reaching for the handle, I froze as the door flew open and the man in the parka raced out. He knocked me down and the evil came boiling up, clutching at me, tearing at my hair, trying to reach my soul. It was the same seething blackness of my childhood. The portal I thought I'd closed all those years ago had been flung open.

I didn't see the man's face, but I knew exactly what he planned to do with the gun. But that was for later. Right now I had to get to Tommy.

He was lying in an ever widening pool of crimson. The store clerk was kneeling beside him holding a towel over the entrance wound. I dropped to my knees and pulled his head into my lap.

"I called 911 and they're coming," the clerk wailed. "What should I do? What should we do?"

There wasn't anything either of us could do. Damn it, damn it all! Tommy's beautiful green aura, the essence of his soul, was fading to white. His time was drawing near, and all I could do was hold him and love him.

"I'm here, Tommy. I'm here," I said as I stroked his silky hair. It was imperative that I touch him while he was still in this realm.

"Look in my pocket." His voice was weak, but his will was strong. When I found a small velvet box, I wanted to die right along with him. Oh my God! He was about to propose.

Tommy's voice was getting weaker by the second. "Put it on. I want to see it."

The tiny diamond glimmered through my tears. How could I survive without the person I cherished more than my own life?

"I'll always love you. And when you need me, I'll be with you. Remember that," he said, smiling as he closed his eyes. "They're waiting for me."

"I love you. Please don't go," I pleaded, although I knew it was useless.

"I have to. Don't worry about me. Everything will be fine." With those words on his lips, the light left his eyes.

The bright white of Tommy's soul was gone. The vivid crimson of his blood, and the red and blue lights from the police cars were a stark contrast to the bleakness of my soul.

It was as if I'd ceased to exist. Talking to the police and riding in the ambulance were all a blur. There was so much blood on my clothes that the EMT guys mistakenly thought I'd been injured.

My next recollection was the frenzied activity in the hospital emergency room. How could life be going on when I could barely put one foot in front of the other?

A nurse with a peaceful smile walked into my cubicle. "Miss O'Flaherty, your parents are here."

Mama rushed in and wrapped me in a hug that was as warm as an early summer day.

"Oh, baby, I am so sorry." She sat down on the bed and rocked me back and forth; reminding me of the times we'd sat on the swing.

Daddy was pacing. He was more distraught than I had ever seen him. Had I been shot and not realized it? My body was numb, so I figured that anything was possible.

Daddy finally stopped making circles around the room. "The doctor says we can take you home. Do you want to stay here, or would you rather go to the farm?"

Going home sounded as good as anything else. Actually, all I wanted to do was die. Unfortunately, that ennui lasted well into the next week.

Everyone tiptoed around like I was either a mental case or had a terminal illness. Truth be told, I wasn't nuts and I wasn't contagious. That would have been a blessing. Instead, I'd turned into a zombie. I was a fossil like those found flash frozen in the Arctic. Everything was cold, so very cold.

I spent most of my time in bed wrapped in one of Auntie Aurora's quilts. Shards of ice seemed to be floating in my blood. Would I ever be warm again?

I'd been studying the stitches on the quilt when I glanced up to see Daddy standing in the door. He looked as if he needed permission to enter.

"Sweetheart, may I come in?"

"Sure, Daddy. Come on in."

He sat down on the side of the bed and took my hands. "We're all worried about you."

"I know, but I can't seem to help myself." I hated that I was making everyone sad.

He sighed. "Let me tell you a story."

Daddy had a tale for almost every occasion, and usually they were perfect for the situation, but nothing he could say would help.

"Do you remember Mary Jeannine Williams? She was Bubba and Beau's classmate when they were in elementary school."

That name hadn't come up in years. Mary Jeannine was a cute little girl with braids who'd passed a long time ago. "I remember her."

Daddy ran his hand down his face. "Conducting the funeral of that child was enough to send me to my knees." Sorrow was etched on his face. "I've been in that position more than once, and every time it happens, I wonder if I'd be able to survive if something bad happened to one of my kids. I have to admit that I probably would have gone off the deep end," he said. "Parents want their children to be with them. But maybe God wants some of his babies back."

That was something I hadn't considered.

"I recall the day she died like it was yesterday," Daddy said, continuing his narrative. "She had leukemia. Her parents realized that she was in bad shape so they had a party with a clown and ponies and balloons. Just about everyone in town showed up, and when the festivities were over Mary Jeannine snuggled up in her mother's lap and held her dad's hand. Then she said that an angel told her God was going to have a party for her when she got to heaven. After that she gave each of them a kiss and said she wanted to go to sleep."

"When they told me that story I knew for sure there was a Glory Place. I also knew that I'd see Mary Jeannine there. I feel sure the same goes for Tommy. Death is devastating for those who are left behind. At times it feels like there's no rhyme or reason to it, and that's especially true when it involves violence or a youngster. We have to take it on faith, and accept that there are things we'll never understand."

"But why Tommy? Why someone so full of life? And why couldn't I warn him? It wasn't until the very last minute that I knew something horrible was about to happen. You keep telling me that I have a gift from God. Well, screw that!"

He took me in his arms. "Oh baby, I'm so sorry. One day in the future, you'll be able to speak to Tommy again."

What Daddy didn't realize was that I'd already been communicating with Tommy. The voices of my childhood were back, but this time I knew exactly who was doing the talking.

The day of Tommy's funeral dawned with a thick fog. It was one of those spring days where there was a chill in the air, and the sun never quite made its way over the mountain.

My entire family was worried because I hadn't been out of bed for any length of time, except to take care of the necessities.

"Eat this!" Fiona poked a piece of toast in my face.

"I don't want it."

"Too bad, you're gonna eat if I have to stuff it down your throat."

My sister didn't make idle threats so I sat up and grabbed the toast. It tasted like cardboard.

"There, are you satisfied?"

"Not quite. Keep going," she ordered.

Damn her hide! A couple of bites later I realized I was ravenous.

While I was eating, Fiona rummaged through the closet pulling out an array of skirts and dresses, tossing them on the bed. "Now get up. I'm not telling you twice."

No funeral, not now, not ever. Why couldn't everyone leave me alone? And that went double for Tommy.

Late at night, he'd come in my room and natter on about how I was the only who could catch his killer. He'd start off by using reason, and when that didn't work he'd switch to guilt. He said I had to stop the bad guy before he killed again. Tommy was determined to make me do things his way, and he wasn't about to let up until I capitulated. Damn it! I loved him with all my heart, but frankly, his nagging was getting annoying.

At times it felt as if I was merely observing my life. Could it be that my soul had gone and I was left with the shell of a body? Perhaps that was why I could hear Tommy.

I decided to worry about that tomorrow. Today, I had a funeral to attend. "Oh, all right. Pick out an outfit. I don't care what. I'll get a shower."

"Hallelujah!"

"Smart ass." The spray of hot water hit my face, rejuvenating me.

I rode with Mama and Daddy while everyone else piled into Auntie Aurora's car.

"Take a look at that," Mama said, indicating the

huge crowd outside the church. "It looks everyone in county is here." Cars lined the street, and people were streaming toward the church lawn.

Daddy pulled in behind the hearse and the Herndon family vehicles. "There are a lot of folks here to say goodbye," he said. "Tommy was loved."

"I know." The ring on my left hand twinkled.

"Pretty cool, huh?" Tommy had taken to visiting me in the daytime.

"Um-huh."

"Did you say something?" Mama asked.

"No, just talking to myself."

"Okay, well, let's go in and find our seats." Mama was obviously at a loss concerning her daughter.

I spaced out during the entire service, lost in a fugue that was my environment of choice. When the formal service was over a huge caravan slowly made its way to the cemetery. The family and close friends had reserved places under the tent, and we were seated next to Tommy's parents.

It wasn't until the graveside service started that the ice in my heart started to crack and slough off like a glacier in Prince Edward Sound. The cold had almost become comfortable, and when the ice splashed into my sea of tears, I almost freaked.

Mrs. Herndon grasped my hand and stared at the ring. "He saved all year to buy it." She patted my hand. "He loved you. We love you, too."

"I loved him." The rose I held was the color of blood, a vivid contrast to the gray of Mrs. Herndon's aura.

I glanced at the crowd and noticed that our classmates were dressed in the school colors. During one of our nightly conversations, Tommy had expressed a preference for having mums at his funeral. I had to giggle at his suggestion we decorate his casket in purple and gold crepe paper. That would have kept the gossips going for years.

"Will you help the police find my killer?" Tommy whispered in my ear.

"If I do it, will you leave me alone?" I muttered.

"What did you say?" Mama asked, squeezing my hand.

"Nothing."

"Absolutely." Tommy had a grin in his voice.

That's when I knew that I'd be making a return trip to Sister Sarah's.

"All right, I'll do it," I whispered. "And then you should leave."

As comforting as his presence had been—and even though his nagging was getting on my nerves—I realized that his life force was not destined for this plane.

"You're right. And I'll be going as soon as we get through this," he said. "But I'll always be with you. And I want your promise that you'll go on with your life."

"I promise." By that time, people had to be doubting my sanity.

Present Day

"I've never told that story to anyone." I collapsed against the back of the sofa and rubbed my neck.

"I feel like a mashed up overripe banana."

Dr. Jill grinned. "I've heard that sentiment before, but not exactly in those words. It's amazing how cathartic talking about your worries and secrets can be." She stood and placed her tablet on the desk. "Would you like a glass of iced tea?"

"I'd love something cold to drink. I'm parched." While Dr. Jill was puttering around in the kitchen, I thought about how far I'd come in this journey. I could see the light at the end of the tunnel. Once the entire story was told, I'd be ready to go on with the rest of my life—with the man I loved. I couldn't wait to be free of the secrets, to trust again, to live!

Chapter 10

The iced tea was exactly what the doctor ordered, literally. "Thanks, this is so good. And the peanut butter cookies aren't half bad either." Dr. Jill had spoiled me with all the goodies. With everything going on in my life, it was a rare day that I took time to bake.

"It's a new recipe. So, you really like them?" she asked as she settled into her favorite chair.

"I do." Should I, or shouldn't I take another one? Why not? I thought as I grabbed two more cookies.

"Are you up for continuing?"

I nodded. "I am. I'm almost to the end of this story. And I know that when I get it off my chest, I'll feel so much better."

"Good. I'm glad that I can help. You're a very special patient."

I wasn't sure if that was good or bad.

Windy Hill Farm

I knew that I had to talk to Sister Sarah before I contacted the police. Daddy, Mama and Auntie Aurora were less than enthusiastic, but after a lengthy discussion, they finally acquiesced. So by noon the next day, Auntie Aurora and I were on the road.

"I'm not sure we should be doing this." Auntie Aurora's fingers were white from gripping the steering wheel.

"I know. But I have to make this trip." I didn't intend to tell her about Tommy.

The paved road turned to gravel, and then the vegetation completely took over. Aurora stopped the vehicle. "Remember, we have to walk from here."

"Okay." I grabbed my backpack and got out of the car.

The canopy of overgrowth and the small dapples of sunlight reminded me of my first visit to the mountain. We entered the meadow where the wildflowers spread out in a vivid array of color. It was as if time had stood still—the cabin, the horses in the meadow, the old wooden barn, the cat curled up on the step and the beautiful woman standing on the porch. She could have been as old as time, or as new as the dawn.

"Aurora, so good to see you, again," Sister Sarah said. "And Springen, you're all grown up. I was wondering when you'd come back." Her comment was almost as interesting as the fact that Tommy was standing on the porch. He was listening, but he remained silent.

"You were expecting me?"

"I knew you'd be back when you were old enough to learn how to deal with the devil. The last time you were here, I gave you some tools to help you cope with your situation. This time it's my job to teach you how to slam the door in old Beelzebub's face."

"May I stay with you a couple of days?"

Sister Sarah walked down the steps and took my hand. "Of course. It's your destiny."

That was exactly what I needed to hear. "Auntie Aurora, would you pick me up in a couple of days."

"Are you sure you want to do this?"

"Yes. I'll walk you back to the car."

We strolled down the lane to where we'd parked. I gave my aunt a hug. "Don't worry about me. I'll be fine."

"That's easier said than done." Aurora paused as if deciding what to say next. "There isn't any phone service up here, but I heard a rumor that an old man lives up the path a mile or two. If you need help with anything, run in that direction. I'm sure you can find his house."

"I won't need anything. Just come back to get me."

Aurora opened the car door. "You know I'm not wild about this, but you're almost an adult, so I can't stop you."

"I am an adult." I tempered my words with another hug. "I love you."

"I love you, too." Aurora got in and started the engine.

"There are potholes out there, so watch out," I yelled as Auntie Aurora carefully made her way down the lane. I had a fleeting moment of trepidation, but that was quickly overtaken by optimism.

The next two days were déjà vu of my first visit to the mountain, but on an adult level. Sister Sarah was amazingly informed about current events. She could talk for hours about politics, religion and even pop culture. The herbal tea flowed freely. I suspected that she doctored it with something other than tea leaves.

It wasn't until we'd finished a supper of pot roast and fresh tomatoes that Sister Sarah broached the subject I'd been anticipating. "We need to talk about why you came to see me."

It was a conversation that I looked forward to—and dreaded—but I couldn't remember a single word of my carefully rehearsed explanation, so I went straight to the truth.

"My boyfriend, Tommy was killed in a convenience store robbery, and now he wants me to help the police find his killer." Then I told her everything—from seeing the killer in my mind to Tommy trying to convince me to help the police.

"I was just a child when I had that episode with Brother Fred. Since then life's been good. I'm terrified that if I open that psychic box, I'll never be able to replace the lid." I prayed that she would understand. "I don't think I can live that way. And I'm having doubts about God again. I can't understand why He'd take someone as good as Tommy."

"Springen, sweetheart." Sister Sarah's smile was as comforting as it was calming. "Let's have a little discussion about God. Then we'll figure out how to deal with Tommy's request." She took my hand and a warmth spread throughout my body. "When Tommy's job on earth is done he'll go home to his Father. You'll know when that time has come."

The entire experience was an esoteric combination of the mundane, the metaphysical and the spiritual. And it was also the beginning of our discussion about good and evil, and God's plan.

Sister Sarah assured me that my ability was a gift, and like the parable of the talents in the New Testament, talents should never be ignored, and wasting them could be construed as a sin.

Several days later Aurora tapped on the screen door. "Yoo hoo," she called. "Anyone home?"

"We're in the kitchen," Sister Sarah said. "Come on in. We went blackberry picking yesterday and Spring thought you'd enjoy a pie."

"I have wounds to prove my berry picking prowess." I held my hands out to display my scrapes and scratches. "I've discovered that baking is a great way to meditate." I handed Auntie Aurora a piece of pie.

"This is delicious," she said as she forked up a bite. "Sarah, I'd like to get a couple of recipes from you."

"Certainly. I'll give you several of my favorites before you leave. I take baked goods to the man up the hill. He needs some tender loving care." Sister Sarah laughed as if she knew a secret. "I'm trying to introduce him to God, but he's a tough nut to crack."

As we were leaving, Sister Sarah pulled me into a hug. "Remember the things we discussed. Just follow your heart and everything else will fall into place."

What she said next wasn't quite a whisper, but it was for my ears only. "God loves you and he won't give you a task that's too big to handle."

"I hope you're right."

"I am. I have it on good authority. Just listen to your heart."

"Are you ready to go?" Aurora had returned from her visit to the bathroom. "I'd like to get off the mountain before it gets dark."

I kissed Sister Sarah's cheek. "Thank you so much. The last couple of days have been extraordinary. I know what I have to do."

Sarah opened the screen door and ushered us out. "You ladies better get on your way. There are potholes out there."

That was almost word for word what I'd told Auntie Aurora when she'd left me several days ago. Before we reached the curve that would obscure my view of the cabin I turned to wave, but everything was gone. There wasn't a cabin. There wasn't a woman standing on the porch. There wasn't even a calico cat sunning on the grass. Nothing remained but the meadow of wildflowers.

"What..."

"Don't ask. Just believe."

The drive home was silent except for the perfunctory niceties. Thinking back on my mountain experience, I realized that between mucking stalls and walking in the woods, there were times when I was transferred to a place beyond this realm. My relationship with my Maker was still iffy, but for now, I had to concentrate on solving the crime— and getting Tommy off my back.

The turnoff for Windy Hill Farm was in sight before I finally took on the eight-hundred-pound gorilla in the car. "I'm sure Mama has told you about my powers."

Aunt Aurora glanced at me and smiled. "I've known about them since you were a toddler. You're a very special person."

I couldn't keep from returning her smile. "That's debatable. At any rate, when the guy who shot Tommy flew out the door he bumped into me."

"Did you see something?"

"I didn't glimpse his face, but I know what he did with the gun. But before I became even more involved, I wanted to get Sister Sarah's advice. Now I know that I have to contact the police."

Aurora patted my knee. "I'm so sorry. I know how hard this is going to be."

"It'll be hideous. But it's something I have to do."

The next two weeks passed in a blur. The only thing that really stood out was my interview with the police detective. He was skeptical until they found the gun where I said it would be. Then he did an about-face.

Fortunately, the killer forgot to wipe his fingerprints off the gun before he threw it away. And now the police had the evidence they needed.

My job was done. At least that's what I thought before the sheriff came to the house, and my life took a down-hill turn.

"I'd planned to keep your involvement on a need-to-know basis." The words sounded good, but the way he was twisting his hat sent my stomach plunging.

"We apparently have a leak in my department." He slapped his hat on his leg. "Believe me, when I find that person, they're toast. But that's not what I'm here to tell you. The bottom line is that the press knows we used a psychic." He paused and then said, "They have your name and address."

"What!" Daddy looked like he was about to put a hurting' on the lawman.

"Micah! Sit down." It was Mama's turn to be the voice of reason.

"Humph." Daddy snorted.

"So what does that mean?" Mama asked.

"Rumor has it there's going to be an article in the Harrisonburg paper."

"Dear God!" I dropped my head in my hands. That story would spread like wildfire.

The sharks—aka the press—set up their satellite trucks on the lane leading to our farm. In an effort to stop the madness, Daddy took out a Temporary Restraining Order. Regrettably, it couldn't be enforced unless the paparazzi stepped foot on our land.

We were prisoners in our own home. We couldn't go anywhere without being hounded, so after a couple of days of craziness, Daddy called a family conference.

"I suggest we ignore them," Mama said.

"That's easier said than done," Beau groused. "Yesterday one of those yahoo's jumped in the bed of my pickup." He had on one of his *I did something bad* grins. "I took him up on Bald Mountain and tossed him out on his keister."

Mama gave him the *eye*.

"Beauregard O'Flaherty, that's at least ten miles from here."

"Yep, it is. I'm sure it took hours to walk back."

"Don't do anything like that again." Although Daddy's words sounded like a chastisement, his smirk gave him away. "I talked to Maude this morning. She wants Spring to work for her at the diner."

Maude's Diner was the only place in the county to get a home-cooked country breakfast or a good greasy burger. Working men and retirees came from far and wide to fuel up on ham and red-eye gravy, eggs and butter grits.

"Do you think that's a good idea? Doesn't that give the press a better chance to ambush me?"

"Here's the good part," Daddy said. "The town's people have decided to rally around us. They're not providing services to reporters, or gawkers or anyone else who looks suspicious. Maude thinks you'll be fine. And working will keep your mind occupied. I think it's a good idea, but it's up to you."

"Do you honestly believe it will be all right?"

"I do," Daddy said. "And if it makes you feel better, I'll give the twins time off from their farm jobs to act as your bodyguards."

"Bodyguards, the twins, are you kidding?" I couldn't resist a chuckle.

Bubba was the first to comment. "Stuff it."

"Yeah," Beau agreed. "We'll be good bodyguards."

That was debatable, but desperation and all that rot. "Okay. When do I start?"

"Maude's expecting you tomorrow morning at 5 AM for the breakfast shift. And guys, Maude offered to feed you, but don't make hogs of yourselves."

"Yes, sir." Bubba glanced at his brother. When it came to food, the twins were like pigs at a trough.

Surprisingly, my brothers proved to be effective watchdogs. Only the bravest of the brave tried to make an end run around the hulking teens.

Unfortunately, they couldn't keep everyone away. One Saturday toward the end of summer, I was working the lunch rush while Beau was trying to eat his way through Maude's inventory.

"Burgers are up," Maude yelled. The order was for a booth of hungry truckers.

I'd just retrieved the food when a well-dressed middle-aged couple walked in and took a table by the front window. Sadness clung to them like a shroud. My gut reaction was to run, but considering

I was carrying three plates of double cheeseburgers with extra fries, that wasn't an option. I was so busy keeping an eye on the newcomers that I almost dumped a burger in the lap of one of my favorite customers.

Bud Tucker, a local tow truck driver, grabbed the wayward plate. "You look a bit frazzled. Is there something I can do to help?"

"I'm good, thanks." But was I really?

The woman tugged on her husband's arm and pointed in my direction.

Maude had obviously sized up the situation and wasn't comfortable with what she observed. "Do you want me to take that table?"

"No. I'll do it." I took a deep breath, plastered on a smile and pulled out my order pad. "May I help you?"

There was a strange mixture of sadness and hope in the woman's eyes.

"Are you Springen O'Flaherty?"

"If you're with the press, I have nothing to say." Please God, my voice wasn't as quivery as I thought.

"Please leave me alone."

"We're not reporters, I promise. I'm Jack Kirkpatrick and this is my wife, Patricia." He had the mesmerizing voice of a trial attorney. "We just want to talk to you. If you'll give us a few minutes we can explain. Then if you still want us to leave, we'll go quietly."

It felt as if my feet were glued to the linoleum. "Okay, one minute, no longer." Why was I agreeing to anything?

"Would you like to sit down?" The woman scooted across the bench seat to make room.

"No. I'll stand." That is if my knees didn't give out.

The man was obviously the spokesman. "Our beautiful daughter disappeared from her dorm last year. We've searched everywhere and offered a substantial reward, but so far, we haven't found anything. We're desperate. You can't imagine what it's been like. After Patty read that article, we thought…we hoped you could help us find her."

"I…I…can't do stuff like that. It's simply not possible."

"Please, please help us." Tears streamed down the woman's face. "All we want is our baby back. I beg you."

My heart was beating so hard I was afraid it might pop out of my chest. There was no such thing as fight or flight in this situation—it was flight, all the way. Before I knew what was happening, I was out the front door and down the block.

The farm was three miles from town, but I knew all the shortcuts. I'd made it halfway across Mr. Thompson's field before Beau caught up with me.

"You going' somewhere?"

"Home."

"Maude's worried about you."

I didn't slow down. "So am I."

"Do you mind if I walk with you?"

"Nope. Just don't talk."

Miracle of miracles, my brother did exactly as instructed.

Mama and Daddy were waiting for us on the front porch.

"Oh, baby." Mama took me in her arms. "Everything's gonna be okay."

That was debatable, especially considering how

fast my life was unraveling. Going back to the diner wasn't an option. And college was probably out of the question unless I changed my name and had some quick plastic surgery

Tommy's spirit had disappeared after I went to the police. I'd wake up at night, and then cry myself back to sleep. As annoying as he'd been, I missed him so much that I physically ached.

The only way I could survive was to take it one minute, one hour and one day at a time.

Chapter 11

Summer was almost over and I was feeling adrift. Going to the University of Virginia was out of the question, at least until this ordeal was but a memory.

Tommy's murderer had plea bargained the charge down to second degree murder, and his sentencing was scheduled for today. Talk about a conundrum—I wanted to see him led away in handcuffs, but I was afraid to be in the same room with him.

"Are you going to the courthouse today?" Fiona asked.

I took a deep breath, trying to slow down my heart rate. Just the thought of making eye contact with the scumbag made me want to hurl. "I'm going to pass."

"Do you want to go to Richmond shopping?

"Are you buying lunch?"

"As long as it's cheap."

"Will you spot me some money for a new out-fit?"

"Don't press your luck," she said as she poked my arm.

An hour and a half later we were at the Nordstrom's coffee kiosk waiting for the store to open.

Fi pointed in two different directions. "Clothes or shoes?"

"You can't go wrong with shoes." That was my story and I was sticking to it. Our shoe orgy involved trying on everything from boots to stilettos.

"I'm starving," Fiona announced as she admired her new strappy sandals. "Spending money is hard work. Fast food or sit down?"

"Sit down."

"How does Italian sound?"

"I never turn down free food." It felt good to laugh. "And I love Italian."

It didn't get much better than fine cuisine, shoe shopping, and having fun with my best friend. And even better, I didn't have to worry about police, or bad guys or pesky reporters.

I was in the best mood I'd been in since that awful night with Tommy. We were almost home before my world fell off its axis.

Fiona slammed on the brakes, almost rearending a satellite truck parked in the middle of the road. Vehicles were lining the gravel lane.

"What are these idiots doing here? I thought we'd gotten rid of most of them." Fi beat on the steering wheel to emphasize her point.

"Tommy's killer was sentenced today. They're probably here to talk to me."

"Good grief!" Fiona laid on the horn as she pulled around the van. "What could *you* tell them? You don't even know what happened." She eased through the crowd, heading toward the front of the house.

"They're brave enough to come in the yard so they must think I know something. Pull around back." I slumped down in my seat. "We'll go in the kitchen door."

Fiona made a quick right turn that took us to the

barn at the back of the house. From there we made a dash for the back door.

We'd barely made it inside before Pearlie Jean pulled us into her skinny arms. "Thank goodness you're back. Your mama and daddy have been worried sick."

"Why are *they* out there?" Fiona was on the verge of hysteria.

Pearlie Jean made a tsking sound that meant something bad was going down. "I'm not rightly sure." She turned and yelled, "Paloma, get yourself in here! The girls are home." That's all it took to summon Mama.

"Those vultures have been camped out front all day and..." She wasn't able to finish her thought before the doorbell rang, followed by an incessant banging on the back door.

"Good heavens!" Mama threw her hands in the air. "Pearlie Jean, please check the locks on the doors and windows."

"I'm gonna get that old Colt .44 I have under my bed," the housekeeper muttered as she stalked toward the door.

"Your dad and uncle Hiram are taking turns running them off, but some of them must have made their way through."

Fiona dashed to the front parlor to peek out the window. "I want to see what's happening. Spring, get yourself in here."

I was curious, but first I had a question. "Do you know what's going on?"

Mama held up a copy of the National Tattler. "*This* is what's going on."

Pearlie Jean shook her head. "I don't know what this country is a-comin' to."

One look at the headline, and it didn't take special powers to realize that things were about to get much worse.

Teenage Psychic Provides Clues,
Murderer Gets Long Prison Term

That rag contained all my information, including my name, hometown and everything in between. Why hadn't they included my bra size?

"I'd like to wring this...this," I checked the byline, "this Jason Jarvis dude's neck."

"You'd have to get in line," Daddy said before giving us both a hug. Then he grabbed the phone. "I'm calling the sheriff again. The situation is totally out of control."

"Apparently some jerk in the court house alerted the national media, and it blew up from there," Mama said.

"Blew up! Blew up?" I plopped in the nearest chair. This flat-out sucked.

"I know it's bad, but we'll get through it." Daddy patted my arm. "I promise. But first I'm feeling the need to get rid of some pesky critters." He punched a series of numbers into the phone.

"Sheriff Irving, please. This is Micah O'Flaherty. Sure I can hold," he said and waited a few seconds.

"Sheriff, I thought I should tell you that my brother and I are going to do some skeet shooting. Do you have any problem with that?"

He paused before giving his girls a conspiratorial grin.

"Yep, Hiram is the national skeet shooting champ." There was another silence. "Nope, he never misses, not unless he means to." His laugh said it all. "Tell you what. I'll call you when we get through with our *practice*."

Mama shook her head. "Micah, please tell me you're not going to do something silly."

"Not silly, just effective," he said, adding a belly laugh. "You might want to come to the window and watch. I think we're about to have some fun," he said and then strolled out.

"Is he planning to do what I think?" Fiona asked.

"I suspect so." Mama smiled. "But I never second guess anything when it comes to those two. They're both nuts."

Pearlie Jean's grin was leaning toward the devilish side. "I don't know about you, but I wouldn't miss this for the world."

By the time we made it to the front window, Uncle Hiram was on the porch holding his favorite double-barrel twelve-gauge shotgun.

"I think you fellas might want to step back a 'ways," he yelled. "I need to do some practicin' for my next competition. Right now I'm pretty rusty, so I don't know where this buckshot might go." Although he had a college education, he could do hillbilly with the best of them.

Hiram racked his gun and—surprise, surprise—the news folks scattered. Then the old dog—that being Uncle Hiram—turned and gave us a sly wink.

Daddy pointed the skeet machine toward the lawn. "Hiram, I'll be right back. I'm going to the barn to get that box of clay pigeons."

"No hurry," Hiram said loud enough to be heard by any reporters who were lurking at the edge of the grass. "I've got some real pigeons that I can practice on." He fired a shot toward the orchard.

Bam! Bam!

Hiram knew that what he was doing was harmless, and the O'Flaherty women were in on the joke. It was *too* bad the press hadn't been briefed. They skittered to their trucks as fast as their legs would carry them, resulting in a traffic jam of reporters in cars and vans trying to make a get-away.

Daddy and Hiram were laughing so hard they had to sit down on the porch steps.

Hiram propped his gun against the railing. "That went well, don't you think?"

"I'd say so." Daddy put his arm around his brother. "It was a classic. I about busted a gut when I realized what you planned to do. Did you see that weasel from the National Tattler, the one with the salt and pepper beard? He was out of here so fast I thought you'd singed his tail feathers with that load of shot."

"Pretty cool, huh?"

"Pretty cool," Daddy said and then signaled to us. "You girls can come out now."

Pearlie Jean was the first out the door. "There's nothing like a little target practice to put hair on a man's chest, especially when he thinks he's the target. Yes, siree. That was pure genius."

Mama sat down next to Daddy. "I hope you guys don't get in trouble."

He rubbed her knee. "We won't, I promise."

"I hope you're right because here comes a cop car." She indicated the cruiser that had come to a halt by the front porch.

"I haven't seen him before," Fiona whispered. "He's cute."

"I'll reserve judgment until I see if he hauls Daddy and Uncle Hiram off in handcuffs." I said, although Fi had nailed the deputy's cute quotient right down to his beautiful brown eyes and Colgate white grin.

"Howdy folks," he said, touching the bill of his ball cap. "The way those guys were heading out of here it looked someone had called a blue light special down at the K-Mart." Fortunately, the young deputy whipped out a grin instead of a pair of handcuffs.

"The sheriff wanted to make sure everything was okay," he said, eyeing the .12 gauge and the skeet machine. "Are there any problems I should know about?"

"Nope. Can't say there are," Daddy answered with a straight face, but he was obviously fighting off a smile.

"Good. The sheriff said to tell you that he found the guy who talked to the press, and he's taking care of it. To tell you the truth, I wouldn't want him on my rear. If there's nothing else I can do for you folks, I'll be on my way. Call if you need me."

"I think I might do that," Fiona mumbled. She hadn't intended him to hear her, but he must have, because he turned and gave her a wink.

Daddy walked the policeman to his car and talked to him for a few minutes. When he returned to the porch, he put his arm around my shoulders.

"I'm afraid we haven't heard the last of this. I'm so sorry. But I might have an idea. I just need to make a couple of calls."

I desperately wanted my life back. Right now, I was surviving more than living.

A couple of days later I was in the orchard reading.

Daddy sat down on one end of the swing while Mama took the other. "We need to talk," he said.

"Please tell me this isn't something bad."

"Nope, it's not bad. Your mom and I realize you're at loose ends."

"You think?" I realized that I was sounding sarcastic.

"I called a couple of old friends, and I think maybe we've come up with something."

"What?" I asked, even though I wasn't particularly interested. What could I lose by listening?

"Gerald Alvarez is a buddy from my Nashville days. Now he's doing mission work in the mountains of Mexico."

I was sorely tempted to throw in a 'so what,' but I wisely kept my mouth shut.

"I called him yesterday and filled him in on what we're facing. We had a little prayer session and he came up with an idea. He'd love to have you come down and take over his music program. The guy he had left to play the guitar in a mariachi band."

"You want me to go to Mexico?"

"Yep."

"Do they have tabloid papers down there?"

"Nope."

My knee-jerk reaction was an instant 'I'm in,' but then I had second thoughts. "How long would I have to stay?"

"As long as you want—six months, a year, shorter, longer, it's up to you," Mama said.

"Okay, I'll do it."

As a result of that spur of the moment decision, I spent almost a year working in Brother Gerald's church. The music soothed my soul and I adored the people. And I'd forever be grateful to the Alvarez family for giving me a goal and a reason to get up in the morning.

That didn't negate the fact that I was seriously peeved at God.

Part Two

Going Home

Chapter 12

Atlanta-Present Day

My session with Dr. Jill had left me both exhilarated and exhausted—exhilarated because I'd finally be able to confide in Jed, exhausted because the truth had been torn from my soul.

I walked out of the office and discovered that the beautiful weather had suddenly morphed into the frizzy-hair humidity that occasionally defined Atlanta's weather. We were also under a tornado, flash flood and hail watch. And if that wasn't bad enough, something dark, but indistinct, was nagging me. Please, don't do this happen again.

That plea went unheeded. When my home phone rang, I realized that a different type of tempest was at my door. I grabbed the cordless and clicked the on button with a dread that I hadn't experienced in almost two decades. Cold chills were running up and down my spine.

I hadn't chatted with the Big Guy lately, but perhaps this would be a good time to dial Him up. But what would I say? Hey, I'm still mad at you but I need a favor. That probably wouldn't float, so I aborted the idea.

"What?

"Springen O'Flaherty, Mama would have a fit if she heard you answer a phone like that!" It was Fiona and she sounded distressed.

"I'm sorry."

"Oh, Spring, something horrible has happened." When she ended her sentence on a sob, I knew this day was about to get much, much worse.

"What's going on? You're scaring me!" I was a nanosecond away from sheer panic.

"Daddy..." she sputtered to a halt.

"Daddy what?" Deep down I knew the what. I suppose I should have asked how.

"Daddy passed this morning." She was crying so hard I could barely understand her, but the words 'Daddy passed' came through loud and clear.

No! That couldn't be right. It had to be a mistake. She'd always been a drama queen. She had to be wrong!

I was desperately striving for a sense of normalcy. "Tell me everything, very specifically and very calmly."

"Cut the ice princess crap!" Even through the tears and hiccups, she managed to take me down a peg, but then she obviously reconsidered. "Oh, sweetie, I'm sorry. Here's what I know. Maeve called during my break and said that Daddy had been at a bank when it was robbed and someone shot him. She wasn't making a whole lot of sense, so I'm fuzzy on the details."

She paused before continuing. "I talked to Bubba, but he wasn't much help, either. I do know that he and Beau are at the farm."

Fiona was on a roll, so I didn't interrupt her. "Maeve's on her way home and I'm catching a plane in a couple of hours. I'll get to Charlottesville in the middle of the night, so I don't know exactly what time I'll make it to the farm. You know how it is with flying and renting a car..."

Then it really hit me. Daddy was dead! The rest of her sentence trailed off when I dropped the phone and plopped to the floor. My blood pressure had taken a nosedive, and my brain had quickly followed suit. I was cold, so very, very cold—it was déjà vu of another time and place.

"Spring, Spring, honey, are you okay? Answer me!"

My sister's muffled voice was coming from ...well, actually from under my butt. On my trip to the floor I'd managed to sit on the receiver. I wanted to get up and say something, but there seemed to be a disconnect between my brain and the rest of my body.

"Spring, snap out of it!" That voice was my dad's beautiful baritone voice, and it was as clear as a bell. "Don't freak out, it's me and we have some things to discuss," he said.

"Oh my God, oh my God, oh my God." I'd always suspected that I was crazy, and this merely confirmed my fear.

"There's nothing wrong with you." He was using his church voice. "Fiona is about to lose it, and you need to be her rock."

My sister was a fiery redhead who could turn a hangnail into Armageddon. But I was talking to my dead father. I took a deep breath before I asked *the* question.

"What do you want from me?"

"Your sisters are both going through a rough patch, so I'd appreciate you being there for them."

"What about Mama?"

"Your mom is a strong woman. Plus, she knows that I'm going to the Glory Place." I could almost feel the smile in his voice. "It'll be hard for her at first, but in the long run she'll be fine. In fact, we'll both be as right as rain, but for now she needs her family. The boys are good, but there's nothing quite like support and practical advice from her girls."

That was easy. Law school had turned me into the ultimate pragmatist.

"And one last thing. You'll have some backup in dealing with this."

Backup? What did he mean by backup?

"Hi, Spring." I'd know Tommy's voice any- where.

"What are you doing here?" I thought—or as- sumed—that he'd passed into the next dimension. He'd been an integral part of my past. But that was then, and now I had a future that I wasn't about to jeopardize.

"Springen O'Flaherty! I can hear you talking to someone. Pick up the phone. Immediately! If you don't answer in the next second I'm calling nine- one-one. Do you hear me?" Fiona screeched.

I took a deep breath and retrieved the telephone. Was hearing voices my way of coping with a reality that was too devastating to process? There were so many things left unsaid, so many I love you's hanging in the air. So much left to do, but it was too late. Daddy was gone. Or was he?

"Fi!" I had to yell to be heard over my sister's hysterical babbling. "I'm okay. Really I am."

"Are you positive?" She punctuated her question with a sniffle.

"Yes, I am." That wasn't quite the truth, but I wasn't about to tell her the whole story.

Then I had another thought. "Why didn't someone call me earlier?"

"Don't get prissy with me. I'll have you know I've been trying to get you all day. I called your receptionist so many times that she probably thinks I'm a stalker. And I've punched in your cell number so often that I'm about to get carpel tunnel. So there!"

An apology was in order. "I had an appointment for most of the day and I forgot to tell anyone where I was going. My cell was dead so I left it home," I said by way of an explanation.

Enough distractions—it was time to ask the important question.

"How's Mama?" Daddy said she was fine, but I wanted to hear it from someone located on terra firma. Mama was the most optimistic person I'd ever known, however; this might test her rosy view of life.

"Bubba said she's okay, considering the circumstances. Pearlie Jean and Auntie Aurora are in mother hen mode."

Talk about the indomitable duo. Auntie Aurora

was somewhat eccentric—actually a whole lot off center—but she'd do anything for her sister. As for Pearlie Jean, she could have organized the D-Day invasion and had enough time left over for a leisurely tea party.

"The wake is tomorrow night and the funeral is set for the next day," Fiona said. There was a crash followed by a muffled 'Oh_sugar' before she came back on the line. "Hey, listen, I've got to run. I still have to pack."

I could picture Fiona throwing clothes wily-nilly into her suitcase.

"When do you think you'll get to the farm?" she asked.

"I don't know," I said. "I have to take care of a couple of things. Once everything's settled, I'll leave a message on your cell."

"Okay. I'll see you soon. I love you." I could tell she was about to cry.

"Same to you."

I managed to keep the tears at bay until we disconnected, then they came in a flood of biblical proportions. I was achy, my nose was stuffed from crying and my chest ached.

I staggered to the couch and collapsed on the cushions. It was usually my favorite place, but tonight the downy soft pillows didn't offer the solace I needed.

Daddy was dead. I couldn't believe it. How could someone with that much charisma pass with only a whimper? Not that I thought of it often, but I'd assumed when his time on earth came to an end, it would be written in the sky and heralded by the angels, not announced by a phone call.

I wanted to wail, and moan and gnash my teeth, but if I started, I wouldn't be able to stop. I loved Mama and Daddy with all my heart, but deep down, in a place I didn't want to acknowledge, I was embarrassed by my mountain heritage.

Why couldn't I just accept that I was a country girl? Daddy had never been embarrassed by who he was. What you saw was what you got. But that type of introspection was a project for another day.

Daddy had told me to focus on the common sense stuff. That was easy. Practicality was my natural default. It was certainly less painful to concentrate on mundane tasks than to contemplate the big picture.

First, I had to call Jed. All the other stuff–like packing a bag, contacting the office, or even hopping in bed and pulling up the covers could wait.

I punched in his cell number. One ring, two, three–on four it would pop over to voicemail. Please, please, please answer.

"What's up?" He sounded breathless.

"Uh." Why couldn't I get my brain to communicate with my mouth?

"Spring, honey, what's wrong?"

"Uh…uh," I stuttered and then came unraveled like an old afghan, stitch by stitch as I told him about Daddy.

"Hang on. I'll be there in ten minutes. Fifteen tops."

I could tell by his heavy breathing that I'd interrupted a jog. His favorite place to run was a park only a couple of miles from my house. I settled down on the couch trying to put my brain on hold.

I don't know how long I'd been sitting there in a stupor, or in shock, or whatever when I heard the front door open. And there he was, just as gorgeous as ever, even though he was sweaty and wearing a pair of running shorts and a T-shirt. That didn't matter when he pulled me into his arms and tucked my head under his chin.

"I'm so sorry." Jed ran his hands up and down my back. "What do you want me to do? You name it and I'm yours."

What did I really want? To be held? To be told everything would be okay?

"The wake is tomorrow night and the funeral is scheduled for the next day. Can you go with me?"

Jed put his finger under my chin and gently tipped it up. "Of course I can. When do you want to leave?"

I wanted to ignore everything except the amazing sense of warmth and security that was seeping through my body. "Soon. I told Fiona that I'd be there in the morning, and it's an eight-to-nine-hour drive to the mountains." I stepped back, reluctant to put any distance between us.

Jed wiped his face with the hem of his T-shirt. "I need about an hour-and-a-half to make some arrangements. Do you want me to call Sam and tell him what's going on?"

"Sure, that would be great." I wasn't positive I could even be coherent.

Jed touched my face. "Do this one thing a time. And remember, you can lean on me." He kissed the end of my nose. It was a little thing, but it made me feel a whole lot better.

"I'm going home to take a shower, and then I'll take care of my errands. Are you positive you'll be all right?"

I didn't have any tissues, so I took a page from Jed's book and used the hem of my shirt to mop up my tears.

"I'm fine. You do what you need to do, and I'll get packed. Go for casual clothes."

Jed put his hand on the nape of my neck and I thought he was about to kiss me. Instead he dabbed the moisture from under my eyes. "Why don't you take a bubble bath and try to relax. A glass of wine might be a good idea, too."

"Uh-huh." Intelligent response had escaped me.

"Do you want to drive or fly?"

I couldn't stomach the thought of airport hassle. "Drive."

"Okay. You relax. I'll take care of everything."

After he left, I sank back in the couch cushions and looked around at the home I loved.

It had taken me five years of scrimping and saving to have a down payment. For my interior color scheme I'd used a palette that reminded me of Appalachia—the smoky blues of the mountain mist, the green hues of the lush forest and the vivid color splashes of spring flowers.

Daddy had helped me refinish the hardwood floors that gleamed in the multi-faceted light of the

Tiffany lamp that I'd rescued from a garage sale. The Wedding Ring quilt that Granny Bea and her sisters had made as part of her dowry had a place of honor on a handcrafted pine stand by the fireplace. But my favorite piece was the antique rocking chair that had been in the O'Flaherty family for generations. It had its share of dings and nicks, but that made it even more precious.

Being at home was usually like cuddling up in a feather bed on a cold winter night when sleet was beating against the window. It wrapped me in a comfort that I couldn't find anywhere else, but terrible things had wormed their way in.

Enough of that! I had to focus on the here and now, so I packed and took care of all the details associated with an extended trip–stopping the paper, holding the mail, etc.

Jed said he'd be back in an hour-and-a-half, but I was getting antsy after only an hour. And when he showed up I discovered that he'd traded his sleek Porsche for a shiny black SUV.

"Is that your mother's car?"

"I thought it would be more comfortable for traveling and she likes to cruise around in my hot car," he said. "My folks send their condolences. They asked me to tell you that if there's anything they can do, just give them a call."

"That's nice." My impression of Jed's mom had changed after our dinner.

He picked up my suitcase and carried it to the car. "We have a long trip ahead of us, so we'd better get rolling." Jed's statement was meant to be literal, but I was afraid it was applicable in more ways than one.

He didn't realize that an O'Flaherty wake would involve food, drink and a number of stories—some poignant, some funny and others downright ribald. My dad was a man of God, but he'd apparently been a wild child, or at least that's what Uncle Hiram claimed. So no telling what kind of stories would surface in this celebration of Daddy's life. And even more important, I hadn't had a chance to tell him my story. That might prove to be a disastrous example of procrastination.

Jed stowed my suitcase and opened the door for me.

"Ready?"

"As ready as I'll ever be." I sat down and snuggled into the luxurious, heated leather seats. The cold front that had caused the turbulent weather was on its way to the coast, and the night was chilly.

"Are you comfortable?" he asked, pulling onto the Interstate that would take us through Knoxville on the first leg of the trip.

"I'm fine." I'd dressed in a pair of slacks and a cotton sweater, knowing that April in the mountains could be chilly. "Do you mind if I turn on the radio?" Car travel was like a sleeping pill, and when you added the hum of the heater and the muted light of the dashboard, keeping my eyes open would be a challenge. A nap might be exactly what I needed.

"Go ahead." Jed waved toward a console that looked as if it came from the space shuttle. I touched a few dials, but nothing happened.

"I give, how do I turn it on?"

He knew about my aversion to anything techie. "What's your pleasure, talk radio, sports, music?"

Jed's question was one of those *ohmigosh* moments that rarely happened, but when they did they almost knocked your socks off. It dawned on me that although we were engaged–and yes, I will admit it–we'd never discussed music, or listened to the radio, or even watched a chick flick together.

"I think country music is appropriate for this trip."

"You got it." Jed hit the Scan button and on the third station he hit pay dirt with Martina McBride, one of my favorites. For the next hour I sang along with Martina, hummed with Toby Keith, pulled off a perfect harmony with Carrie Underwood, did a fine duet with Josh Turner and mentally drooled over Tim McGraw.

"You have a beautiful voice. I didn't know you sang."

"I guess I never mentioned it." Ditto for the fact I was clairvoyant, but it was not the time or place for that disclosure, so I decided to stick with the easy stuff.

"I started singing in church when I was four. By the time we hit our teens my sisters and I were the divas of the Appalachian gospel circuit."

Jed laughed. "Did that go to your head?"

"Sort of." Truthfully, a lot. "We had quite a following. Daddy used to say that folks came to his services to hear us." Although I was trying to be serious, I spoiled it by laughing.

"We were darned cute."

"I've never been to a revival. Episcopalians are more traditional."

I told him more about our revival meetings, but I neglected–and yes, that was on purpose–to mention the ten-foot mural of Jesus on the bus.

"Daddy liked to do baptisms in creeks and rivers." Just thinking about it gave me a case of the chuckles. "When we were kids we practiced baptizing each other. My little brothers Beau and Bubba usually took it one step further and tried to drown each other. I guess I'd better warn you about the O'Flaherty clan."

Despite the dim lighting, I could see Jed's grin. "Are they serial killers armed with chainsaws?"

His teasing made me feel better. "Nope, we're short on killers, but we can be flamboyant. Some folks in Spirit Hollow think we're eccentric. And the more superstitious people avoid us."

This was the perfect time to tell him about my *gift,* but I didn't want to ruin the moment.

"Eccentric?"

"A couple of my ne'er-do well relatives don't have a lot of respect for the law. To be completely honest, I come from a long line of bootleggers and moonshiners, but that's not out of the ordinary in the mountains."

I could tell that Jed wanted to grin again, instead he responded with a raised eyebrow.

"I do have some kin who line up on the side of the angels."

"That's great. But let's go back to your relatives

who have wants and warrants."

"I didn't say they were wanted, not exactly." Leave it to an officer of the court to assume the worst. "You wouldn't arrest them, would you?"

"You know that I don't arrest people, and even if I did, Virginia isn't in my jurisdiction."

I knew that, but my brain wasn't firing on all cylinders. "When you put it that way, Uncle Hiram used to be a moonshiner, but now he grows pot. And Cousin Jerome is in charge of his...uh, distribution system."

"By distribution system do you mean dealing?"

I took a deep breath, wondering how much to tell him. "They claim it's medical, but I have my doubts."

"Medical?"

I answered with a shrug, realizing that Jed was trying to distract me. "Everyone else is pretty much law abiding."

"What's your definition of pretty much?" His grin negated the seriousness of the question.

"My little brothers Beau and Bubba had their share of tussles with the sheriff when they were kids, but they're now the pillars of the community. I suppose that's the pretty much."

"Are there any horse thieves, train robbers or embezzlers in the clan?"

"I don't think so, at least not in our immediate family."

"That's good." Jed chuckled. "It sounds like your childhood was interesting."

"It was." Actually, it had been was a case of

highs and lows—the highs were a ton of fun, the lows not so much. And those low spots were off-limits for this conversation, at least for the moment.

I didn't verbalize that last thought, but my tone of voice must have given me away. He didn't ask any more questions as we settled into a mutually agreeable silence.

I leaned back and closed my eyes, drifting in and out of that dream-like state where could haves, would haves and should haves floated in and out teasing the edge of my consciousness. It was a place where conversations could be played out in depth, and a tweak here or there could make a world of difference.

In hindsight—and I do realize that's 20/20—I regret that I hadn't told Jed the whole story. But in my defense, I felt as if I had to get my act together before introducing him to the creepy crawlies.

"You don't have to stay awake," Jed said, inter-rupting my mental conversation. "I can find my way using this." He tapped the built-in navscreen.

"Okay," I wadded up my jacket and snuggled down for a nap, but before I slipped into REM sleep I heard my Daddy's voice, punctuated by his infec-tious laugh.

"Let me tell you about the Glory Place," he said adding a familiar chuckle. "I had a sneak peek and it's everything I expected." In my dream he leaned close enough to stroke my face, but before he touched me, he stepped back. "I love you, always remember that. And at least for the near future, I'll be pestering you.

Chapter 13

"Spring, wake up." Somewhere in the deepest part of my consciousness the words registered, but the meaning wasn't quite clear.

"Huh?" It took an effort to drag myself out of the fuzzy part of sleep where logic doesn't quite compute. When I managed to make it from the depths, I looked around trying to figure out where I was, and what I was doing there.

"Believe it or not, I found Spirit Hollow. And that wasn't an easy feat."

While I'd been lolling away in dreamland, Jed was trying to make heads or tails of the back roads of Appalachia. Even in the daylight that could be a daunting task for an outsider, but somehow he'd managed to find my hometown in the dark.

"Oh, okay." That wasn't very articulate, but I was still trying to process Daddy's comment about the Glory Place.

The sun was peeking around the mountain, creating dapples of crimson and gold, a contrast to the misty gloom of early dawn. There was something magical about the way the day started in the mountains. It felt as if the hills enfolded you in their loving arms.

Believe

Jed pulled into the parking lot of the closed Mini-Mart. That meant it wasn't even six o'clock. It was too early to show up at anyone's house, even Mama's, and she was an early bird.

I stretched, trying to work out the kinks. "Would you like a nickel tour of my hometown?" Spirit Hollow, population 946, wasn't exactly an urban area. Calling it a village was something of a stretch, and as for having a Walmart—nope and ditto for a Kroger, a Target or even a Kentucky Fried Chicken.

"That's our Mini-Mart. It's the only place in the county to get gas and a three-day old hot dog. Denby Jenkins is the owner. He lives in an apartment upstairs. If the lights are off, all you have to do is ring the bell. But when he wants to go fishing, he turns over the closed sign and heads off to the creek."

Jed was probably thinking that Spirit Hollow and Atlanta weren't even on the same planet. Actually, the cultural disparities slipped my mind until I came home.

"This is Main Street." I indicated the road we'd come in on. "It's the lifeline to the rest of the county. The city building is that double-wide with the attached metal garage. It's the home of our volunteer fire department, and it's where the deputy hangs out here when he's on duty." The sheriff's deputy who patrolled the mountain was on call twenty-four/seven; however, we didn't see him very often.

"We don't have much of a tax base, at least not of the legal variety. The more profitable cottage industries aren't on speaking terms with the IRS, or the DEA for that matter."

Jed grinned again, knowing exactly what I was referring to.

"About a block that way," I pointed toward the right, "is my first school."

Jed nodded and drove in that direction.

The Stonewall Jackson Elementary School was a square brick building built in the late forties. It was surrounded by a chain link fence and set back in the trees.

"I went from kindergarten through the sixth grade there." The memories of that time were so vivid they almost took me to a place far from reality.

"Anyway, that was where I learned my ABC's. The building across the street is Joe Don's Country Store." I indicated a large white barn surrounded by a gravel parking lot. "It's a bit rough around the edges, but the folks around here don't care what it looks like as long as Joe Don stays in business. The original Joe Don retired several years back. Joe Don, Jr. owns it now. His inventory ranges from fishing worms to hubcaps. The worms are fresh and the hubcaps are probably stolen, but I'm not sure anyone cares." I smiled thinking about my childhood. "He had a hot dog stand, so we'd walk over and spend our lunch money. Mama claimed that Joe Don's wasn't sanitary. It probably was E-coli central, but I loved those chili dogs, the messier the better."

"You like chili dogs, huh?" Jed gave me one of

those looks that made my head spin.

I was tempted to jump his bones; instead I kept up the monologue. "We have two churches in Spirit Hollow." All I needed was an umbrella and bullhorn, and I could get a job as a tour guide.

"The one with the steeple is the Baptist church. When I was a kid I was sure that angels lived in the bell tower." Just the memory merited another smile. "Daddy's church is about a mile down this road. It's called Angel's Heart. Would you like to see it?"

"Sure," he answered.

The village quickly gave way to the rolling green hills of the Shenandoah Valley. "Here it is, on the right." The antebellum building with its adjacent cemetery had been the religious home for generations of valley residents. "It's a nondenominational cross between Anglican and Evangelical." I couldn't resist a chuckle. "Actually our congregation is an interesting mix of hippies and bible thumpers." The tears started to well up, but I beat them back. "Daddy was the heart of this place."

Jed pulled into the circular gravel drive and stopped. "It's beautiful."

My extended family had been going to this little stone church for almost a century, and I'd always taken it for granted, but it was impressive. The rhododendron bushes were in bloom and the array of colors ranged from baby shower pink to prom dress magenta.

"I haven't darkened the door of any church in a very long time," I admitted. "I really miss it." Today seemed to be my time for tell all.

"I abandoned the religion of my youth, too. It would make my mom happy if I returned to the fold. So I know how you feel.

Jed probably did understand. Our relationship reminded me of what I'd had with Tommy, but with Jed there was an adult passion that had been missing with my first love.

That was something to think about later, much later. Just seeing the church of my childhood, a place that held so many fond memories, tempted me to grieve like Ruth in the Old Testament.

"I, u…" The remainder of that sentence was lost in a sob, followed by a flood of tears.

"Oh, honey." Jed came around to the passenger side. He opened the door and helped me out. Then he sat down on the grass and pulled me into his lap, allowing me the luxury of crying as long as I wanted. All he did was rub my back and make soft comforting noises.

I was on the tail-end of my hysteria when I heard Daddy's voice. "Baby, don't mourn for me. Like I said, I'm on my way to the Glory Place. Everything's good."

"Did you hear that?" I needed to know if Jed could hear him.

"What are you talking about?"

"Nothing." I sat up to check out the damage I'd done to my make-up and Jed's clothing. His shirt was splotchy from my tears. My nose was running and my mascara was probably smeared all over my face.

"Do you have any tissues?" I ended my question

163

with a combination hiccup and sniff.

"Let me see." He set me on the grass and got up to rummage through the glove box. "Will this do?" He pulled out a travel pack of Kleenex.

"That's great." Mama said that when I blew my nose I honked like Mother Goose.

"Feeling better?"

"I think so. It's too early to go to the farm, so why don't we head down to Maude's Diner for a cup of coffee?"

"That sounds good." He helped me in the car before strolling around to the driver's side. "Just point me in the right direction."

I wiped off the make-up smears and dabbed on some lip gloss.

Although it was only six-thirty, Maude's parking lot was full of pickups and service vehicles. The diner looked just as it had in my childhood. The 1950s-era café with its aluminum skirt and bright red awning still seemed to be the happening place in Spirit Hollow.

"She opens early to catch the truckers and loggers," I explained as we walked past a pickup with a rifle rack in the back window.

The aromas of fresh-brewed coffee and bacon felt like a welcome home. "Springen O'Flaherty!" Maude exclaimed, bustling over to meet us at the front door. "Girl, you're a sight for sore eyes."

Before I could blink, she had me engulfed in her bountiful bosom. It was akin to being suffocated in a feather bed. I was tall, but Maude was *really* big, and *very* enthusiastic. Her welcome started a fresh flow of tears.

"Oh, honey. I'm so sorry about your daddy. I couldn't believe my ears when I heard about that terrible shooting. You and your young man sit right down." She gave me a gentle push toward a booth with a familiar Formica table and cracked vinyl seats.

"I'll go fetch the coffee pot. Tavish started it brewing bright and early this morning." She pointed at me. "You've got a ring on your finger so this must be your fiancé. When I get back, you introduce me, now ya hear. I'll be back in just a minute." She waddled off, muttering the entire way.

"I think that lady means business." Jed gave me a grin and scooted into one side of the booth, while I took the other.

True to her word, minutes later Maude returned carrying a coffee pot. She flipped the cups over and filled them. Then she started the inquisition.

"So, you two are getting married." Maude plopped her hands on her hips and gave Jed the once over. "Quite nice, indeed," she said, sticking her hand out. "Maude's the name, and yours would be?"

Jed slipped out of the booth and reciprocated Maude's handshake.

"Jed Collinsworth, ma'am. It's a pleasure to make your acquaintance."

"I figured you'd have good manners. Springie wouldn't have put up with anything else. So how did you meet?" That was the first of many questions.

Jed apparently passed the pop quiz because Maude finally pulled her order pad from her apron pocket. "We can do you a full breakfast, or you can wait for the doughnuts. Tavish is back there fryin' em up right this minute."

Jed looked to me for guidance. He'd probably never had a homemade doughnut.

"Go for the doughnuts," I advised. "Tavish Smith makes the best on the planet. The minute you bite into one you'll swear you've died and gone to heaven."

"Doughnuts it is." Jed shot Maude a smile and you could almost see her toes curl.

"You sure do look like one of them movie star fellas." Maude put her finger on her chin. "Or is it that guy in the TV commercials, you know the one who models that underwear or something New Yorky. He's usually half nekkid."

"Calvin Klein?" Jed did look like he should be on a CK billboard, except all grown up.

"Yep, that's it." Maude gave my newly dubbed GQ model a wink before sauntering off.

"I can't believe it! You're blushing." I'd never seen him flustered.

"That's the price I pay for being blond."

"I know the feeling." As a tow-head, I'd certainly had my share of red-faced episodes.

Before we could expand on that topic, Maude returned carrying a plate of hot pastries. The scent of sugar and cinnamon was sinfully delicious.

Jed waited until Maude walked off before saying anything. "There are enough calories on that plate to give Richard Simmons a stroke."

"But he'd die happy." I took a nibble and then quickly devoured the entire doughnut.

"You have powdered sugar on your chin." He pointed out a smear that I quickly wiped off. "Pretty good, huh?"

"The best there is." I grabbed another doughnut and popped it in my mouth.

Jed gave a quick nod. "Here she comes again."

I licked some stray sugar off my fingers.

"Really?"

"Yep."

"You kids take your time. I'll wrap a package of doughnuts for you to take home to your Mama. Tavish says to tell you that he'll be bringing out a mess of fried chicken for the wake." She grinned. "Your folks can go through food like locusts through a wheat field."

"You're right about that," I said.

Maude leaned down to give me a hug and then left to continue her round of tables.

"Do you realize that your accent is changing?"

"No, it isn't!" I'd worked so hard to lose my twang, and now he was telling me that I sounded like a…a…hillbilly. A hillbilly! I hated that word.

"I think it's cute."

Speaking of blushing, I'm sure my face was fire-engine red. "I don't have an accent."

"Oh, yes, you do."

I didn't have time to contemplate the reversion to my childhood before Maude returned carrying a grocery sack full of hot doughnuts.

"Give your mama my condolences. Come back for a meal before you head back to the big city, ya hear."

"Yes, ma'am."

"She's nice," Jed said, after she went back to the kitchen.

"Yes, she is." Being in Spirit Hollow reminded me of the old *Cheers* TV show. It's only human nature to want to be where everyone knows your name.

"We should probably head out to the farm. If we don't show up pretty soon, they'll send out a search party."

Jed scooted out of the booth and waited for me to join him. "Lead the way. I have a feeling this is going to be very interesting."

Chapter 14

Windy Hill Farm has been in my family for four generations, so I knew every landmark on the meandering road leading to the mountain. It wasn't much of a stretch to say that this land has always been a part of my soul.

I seemed to be slipping back into tour guide mode. "What do you know about the Appalachian Mountains?"

"Not much," Jed answered. "I hiked the Appalachian Trail for a week when I was in college, but that's about it."

I didn't want to sound like a history teacher, but I wanted Jed to know why I adored this place.

"Thousands of years ago after the ice sheets receded, this area was an Eden. There were more species of flora, fauna, birds and animals than any other place on earth."

He glanced at me, looking surprised. "I didn't know that."

"The mountains were formed millions of years ago when the continents collided. Now they're soft and welcoming, unlike their upstart brothers, the Rockies."

"Again, I have to plead ignorance," Jed said. "I took Rocks for Jocks, but I must have missed that class."

Thomas Wolfe was famous for saying you can't go home again, but I'm afraid that's what I was trying to do. That thought raced through my brain as we bounced and jostled down the lane leading to my childhood home. The bright green tree canopy was highlighted by a froth of color, courtesy of the wildflowers.

Daddy said that I was his spring, a time of new beginning. Fiona was the fiery fall with her russet coloring, and Maeve was the winter, a peacemaker between the more turbulent personalities of fall and spring.

As we rounded the final curve, my heart almost burst with longing. The house I called home was a rambling family place set among the orchards and fields of Christmas trees. A craggy mountain stood guard in the backyard. The main structure had been built well before the Civil War, and as the years went on it was added to, remodeled and changed so many times that the original builders probably wouldn't recognize it.

"Why are there so many cars?" Jed's question brought me out of my musings. It did resemble a Walmart parking lot at Christmas time.

"It appears my relatives have arrived en masse. And the rest of the cars and trucks belong to well-wishers who are calling to offer condolences."

Jed pulled in beside a candy apple red Corvette.

"Is that the moonshiner's car?"

Actually, he was a pot smuggler. "Yep, that's Cousin Jerome's ride."

"*The* infamous Cousin Jerome?"

"One and the same." I put my hand on Jed's leg. "I gave you the Cliff Note version of what's about to go down, but I think I'd better go for the longer edition. This will be an Irish wake. In the old days they laid the body out in the parlor and everyone would sit up all night eating, drinking and telling stories about the deceased. Since Daddy wanted to be cremated, that won't be the case. We'll just go for the eating, drinking and telling stories part, and I'd better warn you that there'll be a *lot* of whiskey."

Jed turned so he could look me straight in the eye. "In case you're concerned that I'm a prude, I was in a fraternity, so I've seen more than my share of serious drinking." He cocked his head as if trying to decipher a puzzle. "I'm getting a weird feeling, and I'm not sure what to make of it. Are you ashamed of me?"

Why would I be *ashamed* of him? My family put the fun back in dysfunctional.

"Absolutely not! I'm just frazzled. I want you here, believe me I do. But if at any time you're not comfortable, please tell me. I can do this on my own."

"I'll pretend you didn't say that." Jed jumped from the car, marched around the hood, and then jerked the passenger door open.

If looks could kill, Daddy wouldn't be the only person they'd be getting ready to plant.

He took a deep breath and flexed his shoulders. "There are two tall redheaded guys watching us from the porch."

That was when I noticed Beau and Bubba, my little—if you can describe someone who tops 6'3" as little—brothers. The two hooligans were identical, right down to their grins. I'd missed them like crazy, so without further ado, I hopped out of the SUV and ran to greet them.

Bubba, known by Mama as Rufus, came down the stairs and pulled me into a hug that left me breathless.

"You little stinker! It's high-time you got here."

I managed to extricate myself without incurring serious bodily harm, but then Beau repeated the procedure.

"You two stop manhandling your sister. You're gonna kill her. Lord have mercy, I sometimes wonder if you're civilized." That came from Bubba's wife, Sally. She had the voice and presence of a combat commander.

I gasped for air before giving my sister-in-law a squeeze. "Thanks, Sally. You saved me from death by suffocation."

She was tiny, and so pregnant she resembled a butterball, but that didn't keep her from holding my brother on a tight rein.

"This must be your fiancé. Are you going to introduce us?" she asked.

I turned to discover Jed standing behind me. He had my roll-aboard in one hand and Tavish's bag of doughnuts in the other.

"This is Jed Collinsworth. And Jed, this is my sister-in-law Sally. The two ragamuffins are my brothers Beau and Bubba. She's married to Bubba."

That elicited some good-natured poking and jabbing—a natural state of affairs with the O'Flaherty twins. Bubba was the first to remember his upbringing. "Good to meet you." He shook Jed's hand, and then Beau followed suit.

"Actually, I'm the good-looking one," Beau said with a laugh. "And here's another hint. I wear jeans. Old Bubba here thinks he's hot stuff because he works in an office and has a fancy title. I'm just a poor farmer."

Bubba gave his brother another jab.

"Hey!" Sally shot her husband a lethal look. "Spring and Jed want to go in the house."

"Sorry." Bubba nudged a tan hound with big floppy ears out of the way. "Useless, move it." The dog greeted us by thumping his tail.

"Useless has some canine buddies, but they're out chasing rabbits," Beau said. "He figures why hunt when someone provides the kibbles. That's why we call him Useless."

Jed leaned down to ruffle the dog's ears. "Name tags would be really helpful. Or one of you could put a flower in your lapel."

"Sure thing," Bubba agreed. "I'll get some daisics for dork brain. Guess being the ugly one isn't enough." He feinted left to avoid his brother's friendly—or maybe not so friendly—swat.

"Boys, behave yourselves," Mama scolded. I hadn't noticed her standing inside the screen door.

She was in her late sixties, but you couldn't tell it by her looks, although now her normally twinkly blue eyes were sad with grief.

"Spring, baby, come here." She opened her arms, welcoming me as if I had just skinned my knee. "Sweetie," she cooed, all the while rubbing my back.

That pesky stream of tears started again, and there wasn't a darned thing I could do about it, not that I really wanted to. A good cry in Mama's arms was exactly what I needed, and she must have felt the same way.

Once the emotional storm subsided, I managed to remember my manners. "Mama, you remember Jed, don't you."

"Of course I do," she said, wiping her eyes.

"Mrs. O'Flaherty, I'm so sorry."

Until that moment, I hadn't considered how uncomfortable this situation had to be for him.

"Please call me Paloma, or Mama," she said and then opened her arms. "Come here and let me give you a hug. You're one of my kids now." And that steered the conversation back to our *engagement*. Mama took my hand and held it up for inspection. "That's a gorgeous ring. It looks antique."

Jed put his arm around me and gave me a comforting squeeze. "It was my grandmother's," he said and then stepped back and held up the slightly greasy—and now flattened—bag of doughnuts. "What do I do with these?"

I took the sack and handed it to my mom. "Tavish sent the doughnuts. They're fresh. He said to tell you he'll be bringing fried chicken out later."

Mama smiled, obviously aware of my desire to delay a discussion of my relationship with Jed. "Family and friends get you through the troubled times, but enough of that." She opened the paper bag, pulled out a pastry and took a bite. Then she brushed her hands together to dust off the powdered sugar before pulling out the chopsticks that held up my chignon, letting my hair fall to my shoulders.

"Would you do me a favor?"

"Sure."

She placed her hands on my cheeks. They were slightly calloused from farm work and playing the guitar, nevertheless they were comforting.

"You're gorgeous like a princess, but I think everyone would be more comfortable if you changed into something a little more casual. Would you do that for me?"

"Sure, no problem." I hoped that in the confusion of packing I'd thrown in some jeans or shorts, or anything that didn't look like lawyer attire.

"And another thing, I hope you don't mind, but I put you girls up in your old attic room. The husbands and boyfriends are bunking in the barn. I thought the old folks would be more comfortable in the private bedrooms. As for those no-good cousins of yours, they can fend for themselves."

"That's fine." The attic was the bedroom of my youth. It was a dormitory-style room with multiple beds. I was thinking about the fun we'd had as kids, when a crashing noise came from the kitchen.

Mama rolled her eyes. "I'd better go see what's

happening in there." She scurried off, taking the sack of doughnuts with her.

Jed gave me a quizzical look. No doubt he was envisioning sleeping on a hay bale, not that he'd catch too many Z's with the wake lasting well into the night. Nevertheless, I decided to put his mind at ease.

"The barn loft has been converted into an apartment. That's where Bubba and Beau lived when they were in high school. Mama was of the opinion they weren't house-broken. And knowing them, I don't think they minded being banished."

"I'll bet not. When I was a teenager I would have loved to have my own digs," Jed said, adding one of those grins that made my insides go all squishy. "Where does this go?" He indicated my suitcase.

"Come with me." I headed toward the stairs. "I'll take you on a tour of the house while my aunts fix breakfast. I can guarantee that you'll be well fed. All bets are off about anything else."

Chapter 15

Our first stop on the tour was the kitchen, and as expected, it was bustling with activity. "Stick your head in the door and take a quick peek. You don't want to be noticed by any of those ladies. They'll talk your ear off."

Jed did as instructed and then shook his head. "That place is huge."

"Our family meals sometimes felt like a training table, courtesy of my brothers." Just thinking about the copious amounts of food Mama and Pearlie Jean prepared made me grin. "Let's keep going. There are four bedrooms upstairs, but since those rooms are occupied we won't go there. Down here we have the kitchen, the dining room, the living room and the sun porch. There's also a mother-in-law wing. That's where Beau and his wife, Alma live. Eventually they'll take over the main house."

Spirit Hollow homes were handed down through generations of family—no flipping, no real estate speculation and no foreclosures—but, enough on that subject.

"This is our dining room. We use it on special occasions." A white damask tablecloth covered the long cherry table. Mama's china serving pieces were laid out on the sideboard. It was reminiscent of the holidays we'd enjoyed as a family.

"There's a big crowd in the living room, and they're all going to want to meet you. Are you up for this?"

"I'm tough. Let's go for it."

The living room was a gathering spot for the extended O'Flaherty clan. It was a large, but cozy, room dominated by a massive stone fireplace. After I left home, Mama had redecorated, and the sunshine yellow of my childhood had been replaced with a color scheme of soft coral and blue. Regardless of the palette, this was the place where my family had lived, loved, fought and learned to forgive.

I knew that my relatives were dying to meet Jed—my ring had obviously been the subject of family gossip—so I quickly made the introductions, and then hauled him off before the serious questioning could commence. We took the back stairs and were halfway up the steep attic steps when we ran into Fiona.

"Hey, brat," she squealed. That greeting usually meant she was getting ready to bowl me over. Sure enough Fiona grabbed me and we almost took a tumble.

"Cousin Jerome told me you were here with your fiancé." She gave Jed a not-too-subtle once-over.

"For a change Jerome was right, *you* are quite the looker."

At first I thought she was going to shake hands with Jed—atypical for Fiona—but then she went for a classic O'Flaherty hug, otherwise known as an ambush.

I was tempted to smack my sister. "Let go of him."

"Okey-dokey. I can't believe you didn't tell me about this." She picked up my left hand. "I had to hear it from Auntie Aurora." She shot me the same squinty-eyed look she used in junior high school and then she turned to Jed. "Did she bother to tell you that we're best friends? I'm supposed to be her maid of honor."

"Fiona, mind your manners. Jed's probably wishing that he'd never set foot in this madhouse." Her laugh was a wonderfully infectious sound that never failed to put a goofy grin on my face.

"Sorry," she told Jed. "I'm not usually so tact-less."

"Ha!" I couldn't let that lie go unchallenged.

I thought she was going to stick out her tongue, but instead she shot me a saucy grin. "Well, I'm not. It's just a crazy time."

"No problem, I completely understand." Jed put his hands in his pockets.

"When did you get here?" I asked.

"A couple of hours ago," Fiona said. "I hate those red-eye flights. I always feel like roadkill when I finally make it to my destination."

"I know what you mean." Actually I didn't. It wasn't that I was afraid to fly; it was simply that I didn't want to be in a small space with a lot of strangers.

"Is Maeve here?" I wasn't as close to my oldest

sister as I was to Fiona; nevertheless, I loved her.

"According to the twins she showed up last night, but then she went home to collect her *husband*." Fiona accompanied the "H" word with an eloquent sneer.

"Is Tim still up to the same nonsense?"

"That's what Bubba claims. But you know Maeve. She makes you look like a chatterbox."

"He's a smarmy jerk." That was a charitable description of my brother-in-law. Despicable, deplorable, degenerate and a whole litany of "D" words worked better.

"Do you remember what Beau did when he caught Tim and his administrative assistant doing the horizontal boogie?"

"How could I forget? Tim was lucky to get away with his body parts intact. It wouldn't bother me if someone decided to take a two-by-four to his head." I'm not blood-thirsty, but I'd be glad to make an exception in Tim's case. "I don't understand why Maeve stays with him."

Fiona shook her head. "I don't either." she said. "But hey, I'm heading to the kitchen to see if I can help. Come find me when you get through doing…whatever."

I chose to ignore her suggestive comment. "I'm taking my suitcase up to our old room. Then I'm going to show Jed where he's supposed to sleep."

"You'd better make it snappy. Mama said to tell you that she's putting the kettle on and you know what that means."

"A family conversation?"

"Afraid so. Nice meeting you, Jed." And with that, Fiona made her grand exit.

"She doesn't mince her words, does she?" Jed watched as Fi disappeared down the stairs.

"She does have quite a dramatic streak. She's been trying to break into Hollywood for years, but I think she's given up on that dream. Now she's working as an ER nurse in Newport Beach." I shrugged. "I suppose talent will take you only so far."

"I have a hard time relating to show business."

"Me, too. I'm sorry we got wrapped up in that Tim bashing. We were being rude."

"It didn't bother me. He doesn't sound like my kind of guy."

"Absolutely true." I paused, thinking about the differences between Jed and my brother-in-law, and Tim came up on the short end of that stick. "Once I show you the barn, I'll have to leave you to your own devices while I go to the family conference."

"No problem. I'm here to support you," he said. "Let's go check out my new digs."

Fifteen minutes later, I made my way to the kitchen. My brothers were already at the table. Maeve had arrived and was rummaging through the refrigerator, while Fiona poured a cup of coffee. The kitchen hadn't changed much since I was a kid There were new appliances and counter tops, but the wide pine floors, cherry cabinets and long trestle table had remained the same. Ditto for Pearlie Jean. She wasn't our blood kin, but she'd been with our family for well over thirty years. Consequently, she was privy to all our secrets–good, bad and in between. Her black hair was frosted with gray, and at first glance you might take her for a shriveled apple doll, but to us she was beautiful.

Pearlie Jean pinched my cheek, and then placed her hands on the sides of my face.

"Springen O'Flaherty, you little rascal. The minute your mama gets finished doing whatever it is she's doin', you bring your young man down here for me to check out. Maeve didn't let me meet her fella, and you can see how well that worked."

"Yes, ma'am." That had always been our stock answer when dealing with Pearlie Jean.

Apparently appeased, she spoke to Mama. "Paloma, I'm gonna serve the young'uns some breakfast. That is if I can get some of these folks out of the way." She shot Aunt Eleanor the evil eye. "They can't start the day on doughnuts, no matter if that old reprobate Tavish did make them, and everyone else around here seems to be lollygagging."

One of the twins snickered. Only God knew the identity of the culprit.

Maeve sat down next to me. "How are you doing?"

"I'm okay, I guess. I can't seem to stop crying How about you?" She looked like she'd lost a lot of weight.

"A little stressed, but aren't we all?" We both knew that was a rhetorical question. "I've been thinking about visiting you in Atlanta, but something always seems to come up." That was a quick change of subject, but I was willing to let her skate, at least for the time being.

Mama set a plate of brownies on the table. "Let's sit down. Your Aunt Aurora made these. I don't know what she put in them, so be careful."

Auntie was known for adding a secret–and not legal in Virginia—ingredient to her baking. "And I suspect you're going to need this, too." She plunked down a bottle of Jack Daniels.

Things had to be dire for Mama to break out the hard stuff so early in the morning. Bubba and Beau must have been thinking the same thing because they shared one of those twin mind melds that inevitably resulted in matching eye rolls.

"Mom, it's nine o'clock in the morning and we have a house full of company. Do you really think we should be drinking?" Bubba was the only one brave enough to say what we were all thinking.

Mama gave him one of *those* looks. "Rufus Michael O'Flaherty would you like to retract that statement? I'm sure you're not suggesting that your poor addled mother has gone over the edge, are you?" She was using her tough love voice—a sure prelude to someone getting into a ton of trouble.

"Of course not. I was simply suggesting that we practice decorum, not go off half-cocked like we're prone to doing."

"Decorum?" Paloma O'Flaherty had spent her teen years in the rough and tumble world of 1970s rock music, so that *I'm such a sweet southern belle* voice she slipped into didn't fool me, not one little bit.

183

"Did you say we should use decorum?" she repeated.

By that time, Bubba and Mama were going toe to toe. On the surface it would appear that he had the advantage, but faster than a pit viper, Mama reached up, grabbed his ear and twisted it.

"Damn!" Everyone in three counties probably heard him. "That hurts!"

"Is that any way for a public servant to talk," Mama asked, all sweetness and light. However, she didn't let go of his ear.

"No, ma'am."

"Are you going to sit down and listen to what I have to say? And do you plan to share a friendly drink with your brothers and sisters?"

"Yes, ma'am."

"Good answer." She patted her son's face before resuming her seat.

Beau cringed. The twins had endured the ear twisting ordeal so many times it was amazing they both didn't have cauliflower ears.

"Good." Mama picked up her glass. "Darn, I forgot the ice. Spring, the ice bucket is on top of the refrigerator would you fill it, please?"

"Sure." I'd never had my ear twisted, and I didn't intend to start now.

Pearlie Jean plopped a platter of crisp bacon and scrambled eggs on the table. "Here's breakfast. Paloma, these kids don't need to be drinking on an empty stomach. Eat up, you guys," she ordered.

We were too smart to ignore Pearlie Jean, so we obediently filled our plates. The conversation was limited as we ate, but after we finished Mama raised her glass in a toast.

"Here's to your Dad. He was my soul mate and the love of my life, and he was also one of the best fathers ever." Tears were streaming down her cheeks.

"Here, here," we responded in unison.

The liquor burned all the way down resulting in a coughing spasm. So, that's why people sipped the stuff.

Bubba slapped me on the back. "You don't drink much, do you?"

Wheezing was the best I could do under the circumstances. "No, at least not this stuff."

Mama took a delicate sip before placing her glass on the table. "I wanted to talk to you before the wake. There's something you need to know." I could see that she was strengthening her resolve. "Micah doesn't want you to grieve. His greatest wish is that you celebrate his life and his journey to the Glory Place." She took a deep breath. "He knows you'll miss him, and for that he's sorry, but he also realizes it's his time to go." She cocked her head as if listening to someone. "One of these days, we'll all join him."

She was clutching the glass of whiskey as if it held the secrets of the universe. "So here's another toast to your dad." Mama smiled. "I don't know if the Glory Place is prepared for Micah O'Flaherty, but ready or not, he's on his way. This was God's will and He–although I'm a bit more partial to a She—must know what She's doing."

It was obvious that Mama and Daddy had been talking. I dutifully lifted my glass and wondered why God would call home a fine man like my dad, leaving so many scumbags to wreak their havoc. Unfortunately, that thought took me full circle back to my crisis of faith, and my misgivings about how He doled out the special gifts, especially the talent that I wanted to jettison from my life.

Chapter 16

Mama stood and sighed. "That's about it. We have company coming and there's work to be done before the wake. I'd like you boys to entertain our guests while I have a word with the girls."

Bubba tossed back his remaining Jack Daniels. "We can do that, can't we Beau?"

Beau hopped up like he'd been hit with a live wire. "Sure."

I glanced at Fiona, hoping she knew what was going on, but no such luck. I turned to Maeve and realized that she wasn't in the loop, either.

Mama waited until the twins left before continuing. "Your dad and I have been worried about each of you girls. Maeve, I realize you're unhappy in your marriage, and I'm certainly not telling you what to do, but you're the only one who knows what's good for you."

For a moment, I thought Maeve might stalk out, but instead she started to sob.

"Oh, Mama, I don't know what to do. The president of my college frowns on divorce. I'm not sure I can keep my position if I get rid of Tim. Music is all I've ever wanted to do, and I love my job." Maeve's tears were flowing freely.

"I know, baby, I know."

"Our home life is horrible. We're not really married, we're simply co-existing."

"Come here." Mama opened her arms and her eldest daughter went toward that source of comfort.

Maeve was one of the most self-contained people I'd ever known. For her to break down, the situation in the Modrelli household had to be completely out of control. Add that turmoil to Daddy dying, and she must be a wreck.

"Maeve honey," Mama said, pushing a strand of dark hair behind her daughter's ear. "Do what's good for you. God will understand, I promise. And if that stuffed shirt at your school doesn't get it, that's his problem. Remember, God always opens a window when he closes a door."

Maeve gave one last sniff before rubbing her eyes. "Do you really think so?"

Mama touched her daughter's cheek. "I know so."

She then turned her attention to Fiona. "And don't think you're going to get off easy."

"Oh, boy." Fiona flopped back in her chair.

"Your dad and I want you to concentrate on your music, but we also think you should remember your roots."

Fiona looked puzzled. That wasn't the norm for my *damn the torpedoes and full speed ahead* sister.

"What do you mean?"

"Have you considered moving closer to home and family?"

Fiona frowned, but didn't say a word.

"And last, but certainly not least, we have Spring."

Great! Maeve was in the middle of a marital crisis, my middle sibling had just been counseled to pack up and leave Tinsel Town, and now Mama planned to focus on me.

"I'm pleased that you've found a nice young man. I was afraid I'd never see that happen. But you're in desperate need of a nice long chat with God. You won't be happy until you make your peace with Him."

A talk with God! Was she kidding? It had been a long time since we'd been on speaking terms—the short prayer for Daddy notwithstanding. The rift with God was primarily my fault, but holding the person you love as he bleeds out is enough to turn anyone into a cynic. I'd managed to survive that black hole once, but I wasn't sure I could do it again. And frankly, just the thought scared me witless.

Grief was a simple word for something complex and overwhelming. And I suspected that my current grief had a lot to do with Tommy's death and my estrangement with God.

"Oh, Mama," I threw myself into my mother's arms.

"Baby. Don't cry. It won't be today, and it won't be tomorrow, but eventually everything will be okay. I promise."

People tend to make empty promises when they don't know what else to say, but I knew she was right. Everything would be okay, eventually. It might not be easy, and undoubtedly it wouldn't be prettied up with a bow, but somehow, I'd find my way. And that meant I had to solve my problems, before I could get on with the rest of my life. The good news was I was already working on that part of the equation.

"How did you get so smart?" I desperately needed a tissue.

"Don't even think about it." She apparently remembered when I used to wipe my snotty nose on my sleeve. She produced a lavender-scented handkerchief and put it to my nose.

"Blow," she instructed. It was so reminiscent of my childhood that I almost forgot I was a college-educated member of the Bar.

"Good girl." She patted me on the back. "Will you be all right?"

"I think so," I said, and then noticed that my sisters had left. "Where did Fiona and Maeve go?

"They knew we needed some time alone, so they went to make themselves useful."

Members of the O'Flaherty clan were accustomed to displays of emotion—we were Irish—but full-on hysteria was another story.

"I'm looking forward to getting to know Jed." Mama was about to say something else, but was cut short by Aunt Eleanor's strident voice. "Paloma, where are you?"

"We'll continue this later," she whispered. "I need to keep her out of the kitchen. Swear to goodness, that woman can't cook her way out of a paper bag, but she can certainly be disruptive."

Just the thought of Aunt Eleanor's meat surprise casserole gave me a case of the giggles. Her culinary disaster consisted of nothing more than tomato soup, macaroni, hamburger meat and Velveeta cheese–no seasonings, no zip, no nothing.

"Remember to introduce Jed to Pearlie Jean," Mama said. "She'll be piqued if you don't."

In this case, surrender was the better part of valor. "Okay. I think he's getting unpacked."

About that time Pearlie Jean strolled by carrying another pound cake. "Nope, he's in the living room talking to Hiram."

"You'd better rescue him," Mama suggested. "You never know what your uncle Hiram will say, and considering that Jed's a prosecutor..."

She didn't have to finish that sentence. Jed did *not* need to hear the excruciating details of how Uncle Hiram supplemented his Social Security check.

"And after you do that, would you and your sisters run into Harrisonburg to pick up some liquor?"

We should probably just run a pipeline in straight from the distillery for this crowd. "No problem."

"And I have a couple of other errands I'd like you to do."

"Sure. After I take care of Jed, I'll track down Fiona and Maeve. Make a list and we'll get it done." I was looking forward to some girl time with my sisters, even if it was a shopping trip.

I found Jed cornered in the living room by Aunt Emilia and Cousin Jerome. *Mr. Tough as Nails* District Attorney, scourge of criminals all over Fulton

County, looked more like Bambi facing a speeding BMW than a scary prosecutor.

"Hi guys." I hoped they hadn't told him anything terribly incriminating. "Let me steal Jed from you." I didn't wait for an answer before I grabbed his hand and pointed him toward the front door.

"Thanks," he said, once we made it to the front porch.

"I hope they didn't bore you." Or even worse, unearth too many family skeletons.

"I wouldn't characterize it as boring," he said with a grin. "You didn't quite tell me everything."

"What did they say?" Then I had a terrible thought. "You didn't tell them what you do for a living, did you?"

"Nope." He added another of his heart-stopping grins.

"I suppose it's a good thing that we're outside your jurisdiction, right?"

"Yep."

I let out a breath that I hadn't realized I'd been holding. "My mom wants my sisters and me to run some errands. Would you like to go with us, or do you want to stay here?"

"I'm beat, so I think I'll crash. From what I hear, we have a long day and night ahead of us. So if you don't mind I'll grab a couple of hours of sleep."

"Nap as long as you like."

Mama said she wanted us to run a couple of errands. A half-dozen stores and three hours later we made it back with Maeve's minivan loaded down with food, liquor and flowers—you name it and we bought it.

It was mid-afternoon and cars were parked all the way down the lane and across the lawn. It reminded me of Remembrance Sunday at the Baptist church where everyone—including people who hadn't been to church in well over a year—showed up to decorate the family burial plots.

"How many people will be at this wake?" I asked. "I thought it was only for close family and friends."

"It is," Maeve agreed. "Most of these folks are here to pay their respects and drop off their favorite funeral food."

How could I forget that Southern comfort food and funerals were synonymous? The menu might vary, but it almost always included fried chicken, potato salad, Jell-O in all shapes and flavors, casseroles of indeterminate origin and content, green beans with bacon, collard greens, Mac and cheese, scalloped potatoes and ham. And the desserts were to die for—pineapple upside down cake, banana pudding, red cake, pecan pie, lemon squares, coconut cake and sweet potato pie.

"I don't know why Mama sent us to the grocery store. I'll bet the kitchen is full of food." In fact, there were probably enough victuals to feed a fourth-world country.

The kitchen was a beehive of activity. Auntie Aurora was busy finding room for another delivery from the Ladies' Church Guild and Mama was engaged in a discussion with the head deacon.

We made four trips hauling stuff in from the car. Once that was accomplished, I went looking for Jed. My first stop was the barn apartment, but he wasn't there. I had the same result in the living room, the kitchen and every other nook and cranny.

"Aunt Eleanor, do you know where Jed went?"

She rubbed her chin. "Last time I saw him he was heading off with Jerome."

Jerome! Cousin Jerome who'd spent more than one night in the county jail? That Jerome? Good Lord!

"Do you know which way they went?" I squeaked.

"Out behind the tractor shed, I 'spect. You know how it is with them boys. They probably went out for a chaw."

Out for a chaw! The heir to one of the biggest fortunes in Atlanta was out having a chaw? I didn't know whether to snort or scream.

As soon as I got close to the shed, I heard loud laughter. What in the heck was going on? When I rounded the corner, I got my answer.

The hood of Jerome's 1997 Callaway Corvette C7R was standing at attention displaying the super-charged V8, 16 valve 415 cubic-inch engine. What red-blooded American man from preacher to pimp wouldn't admire a machine that could go from zero to sixty in 2.9 seconds and have a top speed of 223 miles per hour? *And* there wasn't a cop car in Appalachia that could outrun that icon to American engineering.

I could understand the car interest, but Jed sitting under the shade tree with cousins Jerome and Hinky (known as Hiram Jr. to his mother) and a bottle of Uncle Hiram's white lightening was an entirely different subject. To make matters worse they were acting like middle-school boys.

"What do you three think you're doing?" I barked.

"Hey, Springie."

Springie? Had Jed just called me Springie? He held up a plastic cup containing a clear liquid. "After the first couple of swallows this stuff isn't half bad."

Isn't half bad? Isn't half bad! My head was about to erupt like Mt. Vesuvius, except this time it would be even more cataclysmic.

I grabbed the cup and poured out the *shine*.

"Do you realize this stuff is 190 proof? A couple of drinks and your liver curdles. A few more and you'll be laid out on a slab."

Jed had on the goofiest grin I'd ever seen. "Guess you love me, huh, Springie."

He came within a gnat's eyelash of giggling. Giggling?

"Good grief! Look what you've done." I whacked Jerome upside the head. "You got him drunk, you idiot. He doesn't know about this stuff. How much has he had?"

"About half a cup. You didn't give us time to get him totally soused," Hinky admitted without a smidgen of apology.

"I'm sure he'll be fine in a couple of hours."

"Fantastic! You two take him back to the barn

and stay with him. And get a lot of coffee down him. Do you hear me?" I screeched.

"Everyone on this side of the mountains heard you, brat."

"Don't call me that, you scuzz. I swear if something bad happens to him I'll cut you up in little pieces and feed you to old man Henderson's sow. Got it?"

"Yep, we got it." Jerome gave Jed a hand up. "Hey, guy, let's go in where it's air conditioned and have some coffee."

Jerome and Hinky appeared to be fairly sober, but they'd been swilling moonshine since they were teens, so they probably had a built-in immunity.

"Pearlie Jean wants to meet Jed, so you two better have him sobered up. If he isn't in good condition, I'll sic her on you. Two hours." I held up two fingers. "Got it?"

Pearlie Jean had had my cousins' number for years, and to say they were scared of her was something of an understatement.

"Got it," Hinky said. He looked a little green around the gills.

Two hours later Jed was ambulatory and had made it to the kitchen. He was a head taller than Pearlie Jean, but that didn't seem to bother the kitchen commander.

"Pearlie Jean, this is Jed."

She responded with a snort. Yep, she was annoyed that I hadn't brought him home earlier.

"And Jed, this is Pearlie Jean. I've told you all about her."

Jed's manners were impeccable, even if he wasn't quite steady on his feet. "I'm pleased to meet you."

My irrepressible, and somewhat tenacious, substitute mom didn't miss a beat before she started her questioning. "What do you do for a living, young man?"

"I'm a lawyer."

"Oh, one of them."

Uh-oh. I'd heard her diatribe on the criminal justice system more than once.

"Criminal or civil?"

"I'm a District Attorney."

Her eyes narrowed. "I had a set-to with a district attorney once upon a time. He threatened to throw me in jail." Her frown was enough to scare even the most stalwart. "I used to be married. That son of a dog hit me one time too many, so I took a straight edge razor to his private parts." This time her grin was devilish. "I didn't hurt him bad, just scared him enough to make him think twice about hurtin' another woman. Got real close to them family jewels, you know what I mean?"

I'd never heard that story before.

"Anyways, Brother Micah talked the judge into letting me come live here. He gave me a job, a home and a family. That man was a saint and I'm gonna miss him like crazy. The way I figure it, the bad times I had with my husband were just a down payment on my good life now."

Jed recovered his composure faster than I did.

"I'll keep what you said in mind when I have a domestic violence case."

Pearlie Jean patted his hand. "You do that. And you be good to my little girl, now ya hear." Apparently satisfied, Pearlie Jean scurried off to referee a disagreement between Auntie Aurora and Aunt Eleanor.

Chapter 17

"I'm starving. Let's grab some food and get out of here," I said. "There's a swing in the orchard that's private."

Jed had a full plate in his hand and was halfway out the door almost before I finished my sentence.

I led him to one of my favorite childhood retreats. "I used to come out here to read and daydream. Even in the hottest part of summer the breeze is cool."

Jed sat down and balanced his plate and a large glass of iced tea on his lap. "I like your family, but I'm not so sure about the white lightening."

I still couldn't believe he'd been out behind the shed with my ne'er-do-well cousins. "Why were you drinking with Jerome and Hinky?"

"I was just being sociable."

"Those two will get you in trouble. They're the spawn of Satan."

"No kidding. I figured that out too late," Jed said with a laugh, but then got serious. "On to a entirely different subject. Would you like to tell me what you and your mom discussed? I'm not trying to pressure you, but I am a good listener."

"I know." He was also good at sharing, not one

of my strong suits. Even as a little kid I'd carefully chosen my confidants, and when Tommy passed, my ability to trust died with him. And speaking of Tommy, I hadn't heard his voice since Atlanta.

"Mama said that I need to have a good chat with God."

Jed waited a second before asking an unusual question. "Did she tell you that she's seen your dad?"

"No, she didn't."

"When my great-grandmother passed, she came to my bedroom the night of the funeral. She told me that she was going to the Glory Place. I remember thinking they were in for quite a surprise. Granny was a feminist before it was accepted in proper Atlanta society."

Did he really say the Glory Place? "That's what Daddy called it." There were coincidences, and then there were COINCIDENCES. This was the perfect opportunity to tell him everything—including the conversations with my dead father, but the words simply wouldn't escape my lips.

"Do you believe there's another plane of existence?" Jed asked.

"Well, yeah, sure. It's just..."

He shrugged. "Okay, I get it. This is another off-limits conversation. So let's talk about the wake."

That sounded like a good idea to me, anything to procrastinate. "You've met Jerome and Hinky, so there's not much more to say about them. My uncles have stocked up on the finest Tennessee bourbon, and my brothers have provided a keg. Don't be surprised by anything that happens tonight."

Jed raised our joined hands and kissed my fingertips. "I'm up for whatever occurs. You look exhausted." He pulled my head onto his shoulder. "Why don't you close your eyes? We have a long day and night ahead of us."

I was so tired I didn't have the energy to argue. One moment I was thinking about how comfortable I was, and then I was out. The combination of a spring breeze, Jed's delicious smell, and the lack of sleep sent me reeling off to dreamland.

It was one of those *am I dreaming or am I awake* situations. Daddy was as real as the last time I saw him, but there was something ethereal about him. We were sitting on the bank of the creek where he used to take us fishing.

"Mama told me that you think I should make up with God. Why would I want to do that?" I asked.

"What are we going to do with you?" His grin went a long way toward minimizing the critical nature of his words, that and his accompanying rumble of a laugh.

"What do you mean?"

He reached out as if to stroke my cheek, but he didn't touch me.

"Of all my children, you're the one who's always questioned everything. That's a good trait for a lawyer. I'm afraid you take after me a little too much." He did one of his self-deprecating half-shrugs. "I know that Tommy's death broke your heart, but have you ever wondered why it happened, in the cosmic scheme of things?"

That thought had been my constant companion throughout college. It wasn't until I was in law school that I'd been able to banish it to my sub-consciousness. "I have, and what I can't accept is that an eighteen-year old kid, someone I loved more than life itself, died in my arms, and there wasn't a thing I could do about it."

I knew I was dreaming, so why did I feel the tears running down my cheeks.

"Tommy's worried about you. He thinks you should embrace your talent. He wanted me to tell you that God needs your help."

"Spring, wake up." The voice sounded like Jed's, but that didn't make sense. I'd been talking to Daddy. "Spring!"

"Don't yell!" I have to admit that I'm crabby when I first wake up. "What do you want?"

"You were crying in your sleep."

I sat up and pushed my hair behind my ears. The dream had been so real.

Jed pulled me closer. "Do you want to talk about it?"

How could I explain something that had such a strangle hold on my mind. "I was dreaming." It was another perfect time to tell him everything—from hearing voices, to seeing auras to being clairvoyant, but again, I hesitated.

My internal conversation must have taken longer than I thought. He gently pushed me away and leaned back.

"This situation is making me nuts," he said, frustration seeping from every word. "I feel, no make that I know, that you have secrets you're not willing to share. That's not fair to me, to you, to us. You know everything there is to know about me." He shook his head, obviously perturbed. "You shut me out, and it's really getting to me." Talking about the situation was Jed's way of dealing with life. "You're a riddle, and like I said, that makes me crazy."

On the surface he appeared to be laid back—and in his personal life that was certainly the case—but there were hundreds of guys and gals in the Georgia penal system who would strenuously disagree. Even the baddest of the bad quaked in their boots when they heard that Jed Collinsworth had them in his sights. Now I knew how they felt.

He was right, and I had to do something about it, soon—but that would have to wait a little while longer. Right now, I needed a nap. I knew from experience that I didn't function well when I was exhausted. And the conversation with Jed had to be done when I was at the top of my game, otherwise, I could really botch it.

"I hate to leave it at this, but I'm not going to be worth anything if I don't get some serious shut-eye."

He stood, signaling the end of this conversation. "Go relax. I can fend for myself. In fact, I can probably talk Uncle Hiram into sharing a couple of drinks."

"No! Why don't you get to know Auntie Aurora, but don't eat any of her brownies. They're more dangerous than the white lightening."

203

It was almost supper-time before I came out of my stupor. I changed my clothes and repaired my make-up wondering what I'd missed while I was asleep.

Bubba ambushed me as I entered the living room. "Hey, brat," he said, and then went for the headlock I remembered from our childhood.

"Stop it," I said, emphasizing my request by jabbing him in the ribs. If I didn't know better, I'd swear that Beau and Bubba were still in middle school.

Bubba put his hands up in surrender. "Hey, that hurt."

"Is that little girl beatin' up on you again?" Beau never had been able to keep his mouth shut.

"I can take you on, too." Bubba gave his brother a *come and get it* sign.

"Did Uncle Hiram bring booze that has a tax seal on it?" Beau asked his twin.

"Yep, there's some mighty fine Tennessee whiskey on the menu for tonight."

"Do you think the story telling is going to get…uh…out of hand?" I asked, even though I didn't want to hear the answer.

Beau and Bubba glanced at each other before breaking into belly laughs. "Are you serious? You're about to learn some things you never wanted to know."

That's what I was afraid of.

"Have you seen Jed?"

"The last time I saw him he was in the sun-room."

Sure enough, I found Jed sitting on the wicker settee looking very comfortable.

"What did you do while I napped?"

"I had a long talk with Pearlie Jean. We're big buds now."

"Don't believe a word she said, especially if it had anything to do with me."

"Right." Jed's answer came a bit too quick for my taste. "I hear that everyone is heading to the dining room for an early supper." He patted his flat stomach. "I don't think I've *ever* seen this much food before."

"We do have some chow-hounds in the O'Flaherty clan. Don't be surprised if we get trampled in the stampede to the table." I put a hand to my ear. "The sound you hear is probably the thundering herd."

Before Jed could reply, Fiona sauntered into the sunroom. "Why are you guys out here? Haven't you heard that supper is on?" Interesting how she'd ditched her West Coast TV accent. "If you're waiting for an engraved invitation you're outta luck."

"We're right behind you." I waited until Fiona turned her back before I shot her an eye-roll and then said to Jed, "As much as I'd like to make a grand escape, that's not an option."

"Just remember, I'm here." His comforting squeeze gave me some much needed courage.

"If it gets too bad, fake a stomach ache."

Mama would never fall for that one.

As expected, it was a gastronomic orgy guaranteed to spike the human cholesterol level into the stratosphere. The dining table was groaning under its load of home-cooking.

Following the gluttony—oh excuse me, I mean supper—a *few drinks* preceded the story telling.

"Now that everyone is full, why don't we adjourn to the living room?" Mama had assumed her preacher's wife persona. On a scale of one to ten, Paloma O'Flaherty fell in the minus category as a stereotypical preacher's wife, but strangely enough it worked for her. That was probably because she was true to herself.

She shepherded the clan into the living room where folks were congregating in front of the fireplace. The spring evening had turned chilly so one of the twins had started a fire. The memories of special events past, present and future were alive in this room.

The chairs and sofas were assembled in a big half-circle with the most comfortable seats reserved for the senior members of the extended family. I spied an out-of-the-way loveseat and pulled Jed in that direction.

"So." Mama took the easy chair that had been Daddy's favorite spot to watch NASCAR, football, baseball and anything else that had a score attached.

She held her hands out in a gesture that almost looked like a supplication. "Would someone like to start off with a few stories about Micah?"

Her request was met with silence.

"I suppose it's up to me." She glanced around the circle. "I'm tempted to send my children from the room before I share this tale. And Mother, you might want to take a potty-break, too."

If I hadn't been watching closely, I wouldn't have noticed that the fabric of her flowing skirt moved higher on her leg. With a squeak she plopped her hand on her knee, and then gave the empty seat next to her a dreamy smile.

"I'm sure most of you have heard that Micah and I met at a coffee shop." There was the smile again. "That's not quite true. We met in a honky-tonk during a bar brawl. For obvious reasons, this is a story we've never told our children, or for that matter our parents and siblings. The only one who has heard it is Aurora."

Her comment was met with chuckles from the people who were quick on the uptake, and blank stares from the not-quite-so-bright crew.

"Mother!" Leave it to Maeve to express what almost everyone else was thinking.

"Would I lie to you?" she asked, adding a laugh. "I was in my Chubby Checker phase."

"Chubby Checker?" I blurted. My blonde, Nordic, blue-eyed mother had a Chubby Checker phase?

"I wanted to be just like Chubby."

"Holy cow!" Fiona exclaimed.

Mama patted her own knee. "I was something of a rebel, and so was Micah."

"Ya got that one right," my grandmother agreed. "She and Aurora 'bout sent me around the bend." Her statement drew nods of agreement from some of the older members of the family.

Amazing! Our mother, the designated disciplinarian, had been a hell raiser.

"When I met Micah I was underage, and as you can imagine, that was a no-no for playing a gig in a beer hall, but the guys in the band claimed I was twenty-one, and the manager didn't really care so..."

"Paloma Bennigan O'Flaherty! I would've whupped your butt up and down the street if I'd a known you were doin' that." Leave it to Granny Bea to add her two-cents worth to the conversation, and knowing her it probably wasn't an idle threat.

"Mother, please." For a second I thought Mama might go for an eye-roll, but resisted the urge.

Everyone was talking at the same time, but with a simple look, she reclaimed our attention.

"Does anyone want to hear the rest of this yarn?"

Was she kidding? We were sitting on pins and needles waiting for the rest of *this* account.

"I was quite a cutie, even if I do say so myself." She was getting into the rhythm of a good story. "Apparently your daddy thought the same thing. He was so handsome he just about took my breath away, and he couldn't keep his eyes off me. Even with the stage lights shining in my eyes, I could see him watching me."

"That is so romantic." Maeve looked like she was about to tear up, and I wasn't far from the waterworks myself.

"That bar was a favorite watering hole for frat boys and jocks, and Micah didn't fit in either category. He looked like what he really was, a bad boy."

Mama rubbed her knee and grinned as if she was sharing a secret. Was Daddy up to some shenanigans with the skirt?

"There was this redneck in the audience. You know the kind—stringy hair, bad teeth and a chaw in his cheek. He was as drunk as a skunk." Mama shook her head and grinned, obviously reliving that time and place. "We were about to take a break when he moseyed up to the edge of the stage and grabbed my ankle. Lord in heaven! I was scared. I jumped backward, but he hung on like a hound on the scent. That was the final straw, so I whapped him with my guitar."

Maeve looked like she was about to stroke out. "Mom!"

Mama ignored her oldest daughter. "That raunchy redneck was bleeding like a stuck pig, but for some reason it didn't slow him down. Whew!" Mama did a mock wipe of her brow. "I'd about knocked him into the next county and he was still coming," she said with a smile. "That's when Micah jerked him off the stage and all heck broke loose."

"Bar fight!" the twins exclaimed.

Bubba gave his brother a high-five. "Our dad was into some good old fashioned whoop-butt."

"Did he win?" Leave it to Beau to cut to the chase.

"Of course. Although when all was said and done, he had a split lip and a world-class shiner."

"Then what happened?" Fiona asked.

Mama grinned.

"When the fight really got to going your Dad tossed me over his shoulder and hauled me out of there. I have to admit that was the first, and only, time I've ever felt tiny."

I could relate to that. I was a carbon copy in body type to my mom—tall and curvy, more voluptuous than skinny.

"Much later, Micah admitted he almost busted a gut hauling me out of the bar. That man could be such a hound-dog."

I couldn't believe that my parents had met at a barroom brawl. I glanced at Jed wondering what he was thinking.

He scooted over close enough to whisper in my ear, eliciting chill bumps. "So far we have Chubby Checker, bar fights and pot growers? What's next?"

That was a good question. What was our next *ohmigosh*?

Chapter 18

"Was it love at first sight?" Maeve asked. She had such a soft-heart. It was a pity she'd married a philandering sleaze.

"Love?" Mama shrugged. "I don't know if I'd call it that. But there was some heavy lusting going on."

Granny Bea's face turned an alarming shade of red. "Paloma Bennigan O'Flaherty!"

"Well, it's true." Paloma shot her mother a glare, and then grinned. "Once the cops left, Micah found me backstage, and do you know what he said?" Her question was obviously rhetorical. "He got down on one knee and asked me to marry him. Can you believe that? He was such a dear soul." Her eyes were sparkling, but her laugh was sad. "Keep in mind that his sleeve was ripped off and he had an impressive black eye, but I'd never seen anyone quite as handsome."

My sisters both sighed.

"Did you say yes?" Maeve asked.

"I was tempted, that is until he opened his mouth and told me that he planned to become a preacher. *That* was a major bummer. I was *so* not suited to be a pastor's wife. But he was a persistent cuss. It took him almost a week to break down my defenses."

"And it all worked out. That is so sweet," Fiona said, adding another sigh.

"I can't believe the old man was a fighter. The time Beau and I got hauled down to the police station, he asked us if we were changelings."

Mama patted her knee in that now familiar way. "If you two hadn't been the spitting image of your uncle Leslie, *I* would have thought the fairies had dumped you on our doorstep."

"Thanks a lot," Beau groused. "Our pranks were all Bubba's idea. I just went along for the ride."

Mama sent her youngest son a knowing smile. "I'm sure you were totally innocent. You were always such a good boy." How could she tell that obvious fib without breaking into a fit of giggles?

"Yeah, whatever," Bubba said. "But I've got a good story. How many of you remember Dickie Wombat's funeral?"

Dickie Wombat's funeral was legend in Sprit Hollow. I was in high school when it happened, but it felt like it was only yesterday.

"Yep, that was a real goat rope." Cousin Jerome's description was colorful, but apt.

Uncle Hiram bit off a chunk of a chicken leg, and then wiped his face on his sleeve. "If you ask me that idiot got the sendoff he deserved. He was as worthless as a tit on a boar hog."

Family legend had it that in the distant past Hiram and Dickie had been best buddies, until Dickie hijacked a load of Hiram's moonshine.

Hey, this *was* Appalachia.

"Dickie Wombat?" Jed whispered.

"Keep listening, this one's priceless."

Granny Bea's hearing aid was making high-pitched squeaky noises. "What's Bubba sayin'?"

Aunt Eleanor leaned over to scream in her ear. "He's talking about Dickie Wombat's funeral."

"That man was a pervert," Granny Bea said, and several family members nodded in agreement. "It ain't natural what he done. And him with a God-fearin' wife."

Jed raised an eyebrow.

"Rumor has it that he died doing what he loved best, if you know what I mean." I whispered.

Beau jumped in to assist his brother in the telling of the saga. "What with the deceased being a purveyor of plentiful cheap liquor, aka moonshine, the church was so full that Daddy recruited us to be ushers. We were only freshmen in high school, but somehow we managed to stuff people in like sardines."

The brothers shared a laugh before Beau continued. "The air conditioner was on the fritz, and it was hot as blue blazes. Sweat was rolling out of my armpits. It got downright pungent in there."

Bubba shot his twin a grin. "Yep, there was some big-time deodorant failure that day.

I knew exactly what my little brothers were up to. They were trying to lighten up the situation.

Bubba glanced at Jed. "We're being rude, so we'll turn the stage over to Auntie Aurora. She can fill in on the details."

"Oh, my." Aurora shook her head. "Good old Dickie Wombat. Now that was a funeral I'll never forget. This was one of Micah's favorite stories, at least after he got over his wrenched back, wasn't it, Paloma?"

"It certainly was. On more than one occasion, he told me that Dickie was not destined for heaven."

Auntie Aurora was off and running with Dickie Wombat's story. "The Wombat family didn't spare any coins when it came to that brass casket. I think spending a lot of money on a funeral is a waste, but that's just me. The flowers were beautiful, even though they were starting to wilt. That old biddy at the florist uses her oldest flowers for funerals. She thinks no one will notice, what with everyone crying and carrying on."

"Aurora!" Mama gave a speed it up hand motion.

"Whatever. I'm pretty sure some folks showed up just to make sure the old devil had really kicked the bucket. He wasn't exactly a paragon of virtue. There was a rumor that he ran a loan shark and bookie operation."

"He was a thief, that's what he was," Hiram muttered.

Great-Aunt Hermione came awake long enough to get involved in the conversation. "You're jealous because he got the best of you in a business deal."

"Dickie Wombat would snatch the fillings right out of your teeth if you didn't watch out," cousin Hinky said.

"You shouldn't be talkin' trash about the dead.

It ain't seemly." Great-Aunt Hermione thumped her cane for emphasis. "He was a church goin' man."

Hiram's snort was eloquent. "So how do you explain Merry Chino Cherry?"

"Well, there was that," she agreed, albeit reluctantly.

Bubba shot Jed a sly grin. "Merry Chino was a person of unknown gender who danced in a club in Charlottesville. Dickie was quite a fan." He exaggerated a wink. "*Quite* a fan, if you get my drift. Much to Mrs. Wombat's consternation, Merry Chino was left a chunk of change in Dickie's will."

"The fun really started after Daddy finished his eulogy." Bubba continued the sorry tale of Dickie Wombat and his love life.

"That's when the congregation was invited to come down to view the body."

Beau resumed their tag team act. "Mrs. Wombat was the first one down the aisle. I thought she was going to throw herself in the casket, and considering the junk in her trunk, she would have had a heck of a time fittin' in with good old Dickie."

"Beauregard O'Flaherty! A little respect, please," Mama said using her best *mother's not pleased* voice.

Bubba came to the aid of his twin. "You have to admit that woman had some meat on her bones."

"Yes, still," Mama conceded.

Auntie Aurora took over the story telling. "So after they got Mrs. Wombat settled down, a long line of mourners wandered down to check out the body. I saw one guy stick a mirror under Dickie's nose to make sure he was dead. I suspect he wasn't the only one who was tempted to do that."

"Aurora, please," Mama said.

"So when Merry Chino sashayed down the aisle wearing a red-sequined gown that looked like sparkly Saran Wrap, the congregation about went nuts," Beau said. He had a decided gleam in his eye, and Bubba, the scoundrel, was also wearing a wicked grin.

"It all hit the fan when Merry Chino leaned in the casket and laid a big smacker on the old dude. That's when Mrs. W. really went ape." It was obvious the twins were having a ball, and thank goodness, this was a celebration of Daddy's life—and what a life he had led.

"Mrs. Dickie bustled over like she was on speed and slammed the lid down on Merry Chino's head. You could have heard the ruckus all the way to North Carolina." Beau was laughing so hard that he couldn't continue, so Bubba took over.

"Then she took to beatin' the whey out of Miss Cherry. Swear to goodness, Miz Wombat's purse should have been registered as a lethal weapon." Both brothers joined in the laugh fest. And my giggles were coming fast and furious.

"So Daddy and Mr. Fauquier, the organist, jumped off the dais and tried to break up the fight," Bubba said. "I suspect Daddy was afraid he'd have to do a eulogy for Merry Chino."

"Anyway, Mrs. Dickie had a lower center of gravity than Merry Chino, and when she went for a tackle she accidentally hit Mr. Fauquier. They went flying into the casket and knocked it off the stand. Daddy ended up under Mr. Wombat and a spray of lilies. It was the funniest thing I've ever seen." Bubba could barely talk for laughing.

"That's not funny." Mama's grin weakened the effect of her scolding. "Micah had a bad back for weeks after that episode. And I still can't look at a spray of lilies without breaking into laughter."

I looked at Jed wondering what he thought of the latest O'Flaherty story. Thank goodness, he was laughing.

"I think we can all use a refill." Mama went to the makeshift bar and held up a cut-glass decanter of Irish whiskey. This time, her tears were from laughter.

Chapter 19

Mama and Auntie Aurora took advantage of the lull in the activities to set up a dessert table that featured an array of baked goods provided by the good ladies of Spirit Hollow.

I was weighing the merits of a glass of Chardonnay versus a shot of Jack Daniels when Jerome wandered by. I almost got high from the fumes that wafted off his clothes. Couldn't he give it a rest, just for this weekend?

I glanced at Jed to see if he noticed that distinct smell. Yep, his jaw was clenched so tight that I could see his cheek twitch. As an officer of the court, he had an obligation to enforce the law, but in this situation his hands were tied.

Fi strolled up. "Come with me to the powder room."

"I don't need to go."

"Oh, yeah, you do." Fiona pranced toward the powder room under the stairs, expecting me to follow.

There should be an expectation of privacy in a one-person loo, but no such luck. Fiona elbowed her way in behind me and locked the door.

"Jed is *so* good looking." Waffling was not part of her make-up.

"Yes, he is. And he's sexy and smart."

"You mentioned you were dating, but you didn't bother to tell me that you were about to get engaged. We're best friends. Best. Friends! That means we share everything." She ended her diatribe by plopping her hands on her hips.

"I'm sorry. At first it felt very private, and then when it got serious, I was in a fog. And now I have a problem."

Fiona looked puzzled. "What kind of problem?"

"I haven't been honest with him."

"About what?"

"About my *gift*."

"How much have you told him?"

"Very little," I said, adding a shrug. "Actually, almost nothing."

"Oh, boy." Her sigh was eloquent. I *had* screwed up.

"Not that it's any of my business, but you'd better get honest with him, real fast. Lots of secrets are going to come out tonight."

"I know, and that's my dilemma. I've been going to a therapist. I wanted to get my head on straight before I had the *talk* with Jed. Now I'm afraid I'm too late. How can I take him aside and hit him with 'Not only can I see dead people, I have conversations with them.' "

"When you put it that way, I can see your predicament."

Before I could say anything, someone started pounding on the door.

"What are you two chicks doing in there?" That voice belonged to cousin Hinky.

Fi jerked the door open. "None of your business."

While she was reaming out our cousin, I took the opportunity to get rid of her, too. "We'll finish this discussion later," I said, pushing her out the door. "I have some business to take care of."

"All right. But remember my advice."

I halfway expected Fiona to still be standing there when I opened the door, but the hall was empty. I hadn't won the skirmish, but when it came to my sister, a draw was as good as a knock-out.

By the time I made it back to the living room, Jed was talking to Auntie Aurora, or to be more accurate, she was doing most of the conversing.

I slipped my hand through Jed's arm. "I'd like to borrow him for a few minutes," I said and then turned to my fiancé. "I don't know about you, but I could use some fresh air."

Jed grinned. "Ma'am, if you'd excuse us, please."

"Go, go." Auntie Aurora made a shooing motion. "You kids don't need to keep us old people company."

Jed and I went out on the porch and sat down on the steps.

"I figured you needed a rescue." I cuddled next him, not only for comfort, but also for his body heat.

"It was quite a conversation. Aurora is something else."

There was no telling what my aunt had told him. "You don't plan to call anyone at the DEA, do you?" I asked, trying to be facetious.

Jed put his hands on my shoulders. "As far as I'm concerned, this is like Las Vegas. Whatever happens in Spirit Hollow stays in Spirit Hollow."

"That's good." There was a soft spring breeze with the fresh scent of newly turned earth. "When I was a kid, I'd sit out here and watch the lightning bugs."

Jed put his arm around me and looked me in the eye. "I know there are things you're not willing to tell me, but I do want you to trust me."

Why was I hesitant to be completely honest with the man I loved? That was easy. I'd learned a hard lesson when I was far too young, and to put it simply, it made me skittish.

In a nutshell, I was different, and different didn't necessarily equate to anything good. When it came right down to it, I was afraid that Jed would be repulsed by my special talent and all its ramifications, but I couldn't procrastinate any longer.

"I have an ability that's hard to explain."

Jed cocked his head.

"What are you talking about?"

"Occasionally when someone touches me, I'll have visions about what they've done and what's going to happen to them in the future."

There was an uncomfortable silence, or at least that's how I perceived it. Was I being paranoid, or was he so grossed out that he couldn't say anything? In his job as a prosecutor he'd surely seen the worst of the worst.

When he got up and stomped down the stairs, I knew the answer. He turned and the look on his face was one I'd never forget.

"We've dated for months and now we're engaged. Or at least that's my take on the situation. I'm not sure what you think." He rubbed his head as if he had a terrible headache. "I can't believe this! Why did you wait so long to tell me something this important?" Jed moved to the other end of the steps, as far away from me as he could get without going back inside.

What could I tell him other than the truth? "I've always been afraid that at some point I wouldn't be able to control my ability." This was the ultimate baring my soul. "My fear was that I'd eventually do something embarrassing, or even worse, crack up totally. Fear has been my constant companion." So that's how it felt to jump in the deep end of a pool without knowing how to dog paddle.

"Is that it?"

"There's a whole lot more. Are you sure you want to hear it?"

"Yes, I do." There wasn't any equivocation in that statement.

I didn't quite start with *I see dead people*, but close. I did, however, explain everything from seeing auras, to my capability to predict death, to Tommy's murder and my subsequent visit to Sister Sarah. I also went into an explanation about retrocognition and precognition.

Jed didn't utter a word, but at least he didn't

cross himself or pull out a clove of garlic. The silence, however, was deafening. I'd heard that term before, but I didn't know how profound it could be.

"Listen, I..."

"No." Jed interrupted before I could finish my thought. "Let me have my say. Before tonight, you haven't shared anything important with me, have you?"

That was a rhetorical question and we both knew it.

"I don't keep secrets from you. I asked you to *marry* me. I gave you a ring. That's as committed as a person can get. So what's with all the secrecy?"

What could I say? Everything he said was true. "I'm sorry."

"Did you think you couldn't trust me?"

"I was…uh…I was afraid."

He looked stunned. "Afraid of what?"

How could I explain? "I was afraid that when you found out how different I was, it would scare you away. That would have devastated me."

"Bull! Do you think I'm really that shallow?" Jed put his hand up in a stop motion. "Don't answer that. Frankly, I don't care if you can leap buildings in a single bound." Then he apparently had an ah-ha moment. "But you thought that if I ran into a really tough case, I'd pressure you into helping me. That's what this is all about, isn't it?"

My first thought was to put my arms around him and make everything go away, but he flinched when I reached out and touched his arm. "Please try to put yourself in my shoes. If someone found out what I can do, you'd be put in an untenable situation. I don't want that for you."

"That wasn't your decision to make, at least not alone. As far as I'm concerned, we're a couple." He got up and started to pace. Then he stopped. "I love you. I'd never ask you to do anything that would make you uncomfortable. I assume that goes both ways. I think we need some time apart," he said, before disappearing into the dark.

So much for revealing my deepest, darkest secrets. The dolt who said honesty's the best policy was obviously deluded.

Chapter 20

I went inside and discovered that folks were slowly returning to the living. Jed wasn't among them.

"What happened?" Fi asked.

"I'll tell you later," I muttered, trying not to break down.

"Okay." She sat down on the love seat with me.

Mama held up her glass. "Here's another toast to Micah. As I said before, and I can't repeat it too many times, he was the love of my life. Lord knows, he wasn't perfect. But he always tried to do the right thing." She swiped at a tear that was trailing down her cheek. "I'll miss him terribly. But I know he'll be waiting for me on the other side when my time comes. Not that I'm planning to take that plunge anytime soon. I have some children to harass and grandbabies to spoil." She gave each of us a significant look.

"And to all my children who have been dragging their heels in providing those babies, I say get on it. Here's to Micah who loved life and lived it to its fullest. He cherished his family and would have done anything for them. And he loved his God."

"Here, here," the family said in response to the toast.

"It's getting late, and I'm sure some folks would like to go to bed." Mama obviously made that suggestion in deference to the older members of the family.

Great Uncle Rufus jumped at the chance. He hoisted his considerable girth out of the easy chair.

"I'm outta here."

"Me, too," Granny Bea concurred before tottering out, followed by her septuagenarian and octogenarian cohorts.

After the older members of the family left, Bubba stood to gain everyone's attention. "I have another story about when we were teens. As you all know, we were hell-raisers, but we didn't intend to harm anyone."

"How about that awful thing you painted on the water tower? It cost the town big bucks to have it repaired." Aunt Eleanor had never forgiven the twins for that slur on Jerome's parentage.

"We said we were sorry, and I'd like to repeat it now. Jerome, dude," Bubba addressed his cousin. "Beau and I would like to apologize."

Typical of a conversation involving the twins, it was like watching a tennis match. "In our defense, Bubba and I paid for that stunt with blood, sweat and tears," Beau added.

True to his smart-aleck nature, Cousin Jerome played an air violin.

"Bite me." Beau couldn't resist a good-natured reply to his cousin's ribbing.

"It was quite a summer, wasn't it?" Jerome asked, but didn't wait for an answer. "As I remember it, you two got sucked into every dirty job in town, including cleaning the Porta-Loos at the park." He started laughing and couldn't seem to quit. "That's what you got for bad-mouthing your relatives."

"It was awful," Bubba admitted. "Dad said we were responsible for reimbursing the town, so we assumed the role of indentured servants. If someone in the city wanted it, we provided it."

"And see how well that worked," Mama said. "I'm very pleased with what you've become, and I know your dad is, too."

Her skirt was making its way up her thigh again, and it looked like there was the imprint of a hand in the fabric.

"Making us work our butts off all summer taught us a lesson I'll never forget. We got in trouble one more time, and that was a doozey."

Bubba glanced at his brother for confirmation. "Yeah."

"That would be your grand-theft auto escapade, right?" Maeve was using the syrupy- sweet voice she'd mastered as a teen—the one that drove Bubba and Beau nuts.

"I was planning to skip over that particular debacle, but whatever," Beau said, somewhat sheepishly.

Uncle Hiram and Cousin Jerome exchanged puzzled looks. Had Daddy really kept Bubba and Beau's night in jail on a need-to-know basis?

"We were seventeen and bored. And in a small town that's a bad combo," Beau said. "We took old man Fechter's tractor out for a joy ride, so I guess that would make it more like grand-theft-tractor. We did doughnuts in the park and tore the grass up something awful."

Bubba then took over the story telling.

"Dummies that we were, when we saw the police car, we ran from the deputies on a tractor geared for planting corn. Obviously we didn't get very far, and those cops were really mad. One of them fell flat on his face in the mud while he was chasing us. Looking back on it, I realize we were lucky they didn't beat the snot out of us and then tell everyone we fell off the tractor. Instead, they handcuffed us and threw us in the back of a cruiser. On the way to the jail they stopped for coffee, giving us plenty of time to stew in our own juices."

"I'll never forget that night," Mama said. "We thought you were in bed, and then we got a call that you were in the county jail." She shook her head. "The county jail! I'd never seen Micah so wigged out. We practically flew to Harrisonburg with him muttering all the way about military schools and boot camp."

"Did he ask the sheriff to keep us in jail overnight?" Bubba asked the question, but Beau was apparently as curious as his brother.

"Yes. He thought you needed to get scared straight. This was much worse than the water tower incident. We were afraid it was a prelude to something truly serious."

Bubba and Beau glanced at each other and grimaced, but it was Bubba who worked up the gumption to continue.

"The deputies tossed us into the drunk tank. We'd heard some nasty stories about that place, so we decided to stay awake all night. We figured we could take on a drunk as long as he couldn't blindside us."

I noticed that Jed was standing across the room. He glanced my way and frowned. This was probably a story he'd heard before, and it usually didn't have a good ending. The saving grace was the fact my parents were willing to do whatever it took to get the twins back on track.

"The long and the short of it was that we were on probation with the juvie system for six months. And then we were grounded for most of our senior year. I believe that Daddy and Mama's tough love is the reason we turned out okay, right bro?"

"Right," Bubba agreed. "And I'm sorry I never took the opportunity to tell Daddy how grateful I am, but I can thank you." Bubba walked over and gave Mama a kiss on the cheek.

"I feel bad about that, too," Beau agreed. "And I also want to tell you how much I appreciate everything you've done for us."

"Amen." Fiona was the first to utter that sentiment, but we all joined in.

Mama smiled and did that now familiar knee patting. "Don't worry, he knows."

"That night at the jail was the only time I ever saw Daddy cry," Bubba said.

Maeve shot her husband a telling look. "Daddy cried the night I told him I was marrying Tim."

I glanced at Maeve and her husband. It was apparent—even to the casual observer—that life in their household was on the downhill slide.

Chapter 21

I was pondering Maeve's marriage when the doorbell chimed. It was ten-thirty. Surely it wasn't round two of the pound-cake brigade. There was enough food in the kitchen to feed the populace of western Virginia.

"I'll get it." I went to the door and discovered a man, a woman and a young girl.

The man was holding the child's hand. "I'm not sure we have the correct address. We've been driving around for hours looking for this place. The lady at the diner told me the family was having a wake for Micah O'Flaherty, but it sounds like a party."

Although they were strangers, their auras assured me that they were good people. "We're telling stories about my dad, and things have gotten a little out of hand. I'm Spring O'Flaherty." I didn't extend my hand, and if he thought that was strange, he handled it graciously.

"We're the Holmes family. I'm Josh, and this is my wife, Heather." He put his arm around a woman who looked barely old enough to vote.

"And this is Gemma, our daughter."

Josh put his hand on the little girl's shoulder.

"May we speak to Mrs. O'Flaherty?"

"Sure, come on in."

"We don't want to intrude."

"Don't worry, it's just the family." I led the way to the living room. "Mama, there's someone here to see you."

Although it was obvious the man was uncomfortable, he didn't let a case of nerves stop him.

"Mrs. O'Flaherty, I'm Josh Holmes." He had taken off his baseball cap and was twisting it. "I, uh, we thought we should come to give you our condolences."

Mama looked as if she was trying to place the name, and the moment she made the connection, her eyes brimmed with tears.

"I'm so glad you're here." She hugged Josh, and then made her way down the line to Gemma.

"Everyone, this is Josh, Heather and Gemma," she announced still holding the little girl's hand. Then she brushed away her tears. "I've never met these folks, but they're our new friends. Heather and Gemma were at the bank during that awful time. They've come to join us in celebrating Micah's life."

The family's reaction varied from gasps to sighs, but Maeve was the first to regain her equilibrium. Always the gracious hostess, she stood and gave each of the visitors a hug.

"We're delighted you could be with us to celebrate Daddy's life. He was a very special man."

"Yes, ma'am. That he was," Josh agreed, tears streaming down his face. "He saved my girls' lives, and for that I'll be grateful until the day I die."

Maeve leaned down to speak to the little cherub with dark brown curls and cocoa-colored eyes. "Would you like a piece of cake or a cookie? That is, if you mom doesn't mind you having a treat."

The child looked to her mother for permission.

"Sure, go ahead."

"Yes, ma'am, I'd like a cookie."

Maeve led Gemma to the dessert table, while Fiona took over the hostess duties. "Can I interest you in something to drink? We have everything from soda to Irish whiskey. What's your pleasure?"

Josh looked to his wife.

"I'll take a soda, but go ahead and have a drink. I'll drive," she said.

"If it's not too much trouble, I'll take you up on the whiskey offer."

"It's no trouble at all." Fiona turned to our family. "Come on over and get to know these folks," she instructed before going to the bar for the drinks.

My brothers recognized a command when they heard it, although they didn't need any coercion. Hospitality's the hallmark of the O'Flaherty family. We welcomed anyone, and everyone, into the fold, as long as they were good people.

Fiona and Maeve plied our guests with food and drink. It was their way of coping with grief and trying to turn an *unusual* situation into something more commonplace.

I stayed in the background. I didn't want to shake hands, or hug, or do anything that would make me uncomfortable. I was afraid the images might be too much, especially when I felt so vulnerable.

Jed came over to stand by me. "Do you want to go outside?"

"No, I'm fine." I wasn't, but I knew something important was about to happen. And I also realized that I had to be an active participant.

Maeve found a place for the young family to sit.

"Heather, would you like to tell us what happened that afternoon?" Mama asked. "We have the police report, but that's so impersonal."

I could tell that Heather was tempted to get up and walk out, but when Josh put his arm around her waist, she nodded. "I was planning to have peach cobbler for supper, but we were out of ice cream and I didn't have any money in my wallet, so Gemma and I stopped at the bank to cash a check. Mr. O'Flaherty was behind us in line. I didn't know his name, but I did notice how good looking he was, for an old guy." She blushed, obviously realizing what she'd said.

"I'm old, too, and he was definitely good looking." Leave it to Mama to make our guest feel comfortable.

"Anyway, we were standing in line for the next teller when two men wearing Halloween masks ran in waving guns." She took a deep breath, clearly reliving that terrifying day.

"I pushed Gemma behind me, praying that I could keep her safe. One of the guys jumped over the counter and was screaming at the teller to fill a duffel bag that he'd thrown at her. I remember he said if she tried to slip in a dye pack, he'd start shooting people. Then he spied Gemma and told his partner to grab her for a hostage. That's when Mr. O'Flaherty tackled the short one and yelled at me to run. Then they shot him. I'm not sure that was their intention, because as soon as he fell it looked like they got scared and ran out of the bank."

Heather's cheeks were wet with tears. "I'm so very sorry. If we..." she didn't complete her sentence before breaking into sobs.

Daddy was a hero to us, and Heather had just validated his status. The twins moved to stand behind Mama. It was their way of comforting her, but we all knew she was a survivor.

"Micah did what he had to do. That's why he's going to the Glory Place. He feels good about the situation." The conviction in Mama's voice was enough to make a believer out of me.

There were tears and hugs all around. Carefully—very carefully—I put my arms around Gemma and realized what this was all about. The bank robbery, the shooting, even Daddy's passing was part of His plan.

After the Holmes family said their good-byes, there was a collective sigh.

"I don't know about anyone else, but I need a little time alone," Mama announced. "Let's reconvene in about an hour." It was past eleven, and it had already been a very long day.

"Would you like a cup of tea, or a glass of wine?" Jed asked.

"Tea, please." That was about the extent of my

communication skills, especially considering that my knees were about to give way.

After Jed came back with my drink, he asked the question I knew was coming. "Why did you hug that little girl?"

"She had the most amazing aura, so I knew that touching her was safe. And I made a wonderful discovery. When Gemma grows up she's going to accomplish something that will change the world. I'm positive Daddy knew that, too."

"Did you see what He has planned for her?"

"Not quite, but when we're old and gray we'll open the paper and discover that her research has helped medical knowledge take a quantum leap. That's why the angels weren't ready to take her. She's a true child of God."

Jed nodded. He didn't touch me, or really say much. The fact that he hadn't left for Atlanta was encouraging.

It was almost midnight before everyone made their way back to the living room. All the aunts and uncles—with the exception of Aurora—had called it a night. Maeve's husband was also gone, so we were down to our core family, including Jed and the sisters-in-law.

"I'm the newcomer to this group. Are you sure you want me to stay?" Jed asked. That was the first ray of hope that he might forgive me.

"Yes, please stay." I had a feeling that something disturbing might happen.

Mama reached for her drink and patted the cushion next to her. "Spring, I'd like you to come here."

I'd barely had time to sit down before she blindsided me.

"I want you to help the police catch these killers. Now that they have a taste for blood, they'll do it again. And the next time it'll be much worse."

I didn't have to ask her where she got that information, I already knew. But helping the police was something I wasn't willing to do. I'd been there and done that, and my life had been changed forever.

"What's she talking about?" Bubba asked. Only a small circle of people knew the true extent of my abilities, and that didn't include my brothers. I suspect my parents had thought the twins were too loose-lipped to be trusted. My sisters and Auntie Aurora were in on the secret.

"Spring wasn't at the bank. How can she help?" Beau asked.

He knew that I'd assisted the police in solving Tommy's murder, but he probably thought I'd identified the guy from a picture. Fifteen-year-olds were notoriously oblivious to anything not in their line of sight.

Mama ignored the questions and went straight for the guilt card. "Please, think about it. This is something your dad really wants you to do."

That wasn't a news flash. Daddy and Tommy had been saying the same thing.

"Brat, we're dying of curiosity," Bubba said and his brother nodded.

Thank goodness Jed was already in the loop.

I shook my head, contemplating a myriad of complications. "I have some unique abilities that I used to help find Tommy's killer." I ignored my brothers' blank stares. "It all started when I was very young." And from there I revealed everything.

Bubba, Beau and their wives were gaping at me as if I'd grown another head.

Mama ignored her children's reaction. "That was a horrible time in your life, and I would give anything if I didn't have to put you through that again, but it's imperative the police catch those awful men. They're enjoying the killing, and the next time it'll be a bloodbath."

I was tempted to run from the room, but I was trapped by guilt, by love, by whatever you wanted to call it. "Oh, Mama. I can't."

"Don't you mean you won't?"

"No, I mean, I can't conjure up a vision. I have to touch someone."

"That's the thing. They have a person of interest."

Oh, please God, not again.

"No!" I shook my head so hard I was about to give myself a headache. "I won't do it!" As childish as it was, I ran out. I was halfway up the stairs before I heard Daddy's voice.

"God needs your help."

I dropped down on one of the risers and put my head in my hands. Anguish filled my soul. I was confused and exasperated. If God needed my help, did that mean I had to make peace with Him? And could I really accomplish that?

I was wallowing in self-pity and doubt when Jed sat down and put his arm around me. "This doesn't mean I'm not still mad, but like I said before, I'll always be here for you."

I intended to ask his forgiveness, but when I opened my mouth something entirely different came out. It was a secret I'd been keeping for years, and it was screaming for release.

"After Tommy died, and the whole debacle with the press happened, I stopped talking to God. I was so angry that I lost my faith." Ironically, this was the first time I'd talked about my feelings.

"And now?"

"And now I don't know. Mama seems to think I'll never be completely happy until I get my relationship with God back on track. Even Daddy has been nagging me about it. He's also a big advocate of helping the police solve this case."

"Have you been talking to your dad?"

"Yes."

"That's fascinating. Do you think he's right?"

"I do."

That answer came as a surprise to me.

"Then you don't have a choice, do you?"

"No, I suppose not."

More than anything, I wanted him to hold me. Instead, I continued the conversation.

"I do trust you, and I love you more than I can even say," I said, hoping my words would sway his decision. "It would kill me to lose you. I'm so sorry that I didn't tell you everything. I want us to have a future."

"I know." Jed dropped his head and then said, "I need some time to think."

239

Believe

My greatest fear was coming true. I'd told the truth and lost the man I loved.

"We'll talk in the morning," he said before walking off, leaving me with a broken heart.

Part 3

A Celebration of Life

Chapter 22

Sunlight peeking through the slats of the blinds provided the first harbinger of dawn. At first I didn't know where I was, but then rational thought prevailed. This wasn't a bad dream. I was sharing a bedroom with my sisters, and we were here to commemorate Daddy's death.

"Are you awake?" Maeve asked from across the room.

"I am now." I put my arm over my eyes, hoping this day would magically disappear.

Maeve tiptoed over and sat on the edge of my bed, trying not to wake Fiona. "I'm so sorry about what happened with Tommy," she whispered. "I knew everything was a big mess, but I was so caught up in my own drama, that I didn't give much thought as to how the trial and everything was affecting you."

She grabbed a pillow and scooted me over, making herself at home against the headboard. "I wondered why you went on that mission to Mexico. I never figured you for the type."

"I'm not, not really. God and I weren't even on speaking terms. But it was a good life, sort of slow-paced and gracious. It gave me time to get my bearings and decide what I wanted to do with the rest of my life."

"Have you been able to control your psychic ability all this time?"

"It's been touch and go. In college, I had a bad episode with a blind date. Let's just say he wasn't a nice guy, and the moment he touched my arm I went nuts. Thinking back on it, I suppose socking him the nose wasn't such a good idea, but in my defense, I was acting on pure instinct."

The look on Maeve's face was enough to give me a case of the chuckles.

"It was only by the grace of God that I didn't get arrested. I gave the guy a black eye."

"Did he call the cops?"

"No."

"Why not?"

"I suspect it was one of two things. Either he was embarrassed that a girl could get the best of him, or he didn't want the police to get wind of his seduction method, which was unpleasant, to say the least. He was a pretty-boy on campus so the word spread like wildfire. After that I was dateless in At-lanta."

"I suppose that would do it, especially if the whole story wasn't told." Maeve said, plumping the pillow. "I really do like Jed. You'd better hold on to him with both hands. He's one of the good guys. I had my chance and blew it."

This was the first time I'd had a serious discussion with my oldest sister. Did she have a first love?

"Do you mean you had a serious boyfriend before Tim?"

Even in the dim light I could see that she was smiling.

"He was a…" she paused. "Let's just say everyone thought he was a bad boy. A really bad boy, but that wasn't true. We had ourselves a very hot summer. No pun intended."

I wanted to clap my hands over my ears. There are some things you simply don't want to hear.

"What are you two whispering about," Fiona muttered. "If you're telling secrets, don't say another word until I get over there."

"Love is special, just remember that." Maeve didn't have a chance to say anything else before Fiona bounced on the bed, almost gutting me in the process.

"I have a question, two actually. First, do either of you have a stash of chocolate?"

Maeve and I looked at each other and simultaneously responded, "I do."

"Great," Fiona said with a grin. "What kind?"

"Snicker's mini-bars." Maeve was a made-in-America kind of gal.

"Lindt Truffles."

"Lindt Truffles? Only a city slicker would admit to packing Lindt Truffles." Fiona stuck her hand out. "Give!"

"They're in my suitcase on the chair. Scoot your rump over there and grab them. I feel a chocolate attack coming on myself."

Half a bag later, we'd satisfied our cravings.

"I guess we'd better get going," Maeve said. "Mama's going to need our help." She wadded up the colorful candy wrappers and made a three-point shot at the trash can.

Fi flopped back on the bed. "I'm dreading this. I wouldn't mind taking a pass on this day."

"Me. too. What do you think the guys are doing?" I was wondering whether Jed was still at the farm?

"I don't know about mine, but I do know that when I went downstairs last night for a glass of milk, Jed and Mama were sitting at the kitchen table having quite a conversation," Maeve said. "When they spied me their discussion came to a halt."

"Jed and Mama were in the kitchen together, in the middle of the night?" That sounded ominous. "Did you hear what they were talking about?"

Maeve shook her head. "No."

"Would you tell me if you did?"

She shrugged. "If I thought it was something you needed to know, I'd tell you. On the other hand, if I was sure it would hurt, I wouldn't. But I really didn't hear a thing."

I suspected that Jed and my mother were colluding in persuading me to help the police. That was a bummer, but I'd have to stew on that later. Today was Daddy's day.

By the time we made it downstairs Jed was having a kaffeeklatsch with Mama and Pearlie Jean.

Our housekeeper was the first to notice us. "Lordy mercy, the sleepy heads are up."

"Funny," Fi muttered, heading straight to the coffee.

Jed was dressed for the services in a exquisitely tailored dark blue suit, starched white shirt and burgundy silk tie. His coat was hanging on the back of his chair and his sleeves were rolled up. Not many guys could look that good in business gear.

"Good morning ladies," he said, giving me the once over.

"Is it hot in here?" The moment those words came out of my mouth, I knew I'd made a mistake.

Fi and Maeve both giggled.

"Well, I'm hot." Oops, another blooper. I lifted the window over the sink to let cool air flood in.

"Spring, grab a cup of coffee and go out on the front porch with me?" Jed's invitation sounded innocent but—

"Okay." I picked up a sticky bun and followed him out the door.

Jed sat down and casually rested his arm across the back of the swing. He looked like a man who had come to terms with a nagging problem. "I'm leaving for Atlanta late this afternoon. I had a long talk with your mother, and we came to the conclusion that I need to go home and do some research." He leaned forward and propped his elbows on his knees.

"Regardless of what you decide to do about helping the police, I want to make sure that we have all the facts. I have some contacts in the FBI who are bank robbery experts. I'm going to call them to see what they know. Your safety is very important to me."

It had taken me a long time to decide what to do in Tommy's case, and that had turned into a debacle. "I haven't decided what to do about helping the police."

"I'll support you in whatever you want. Right this minute, I need another cup of coffee." Without saying anything else, he got up and left. Had he made his mind up about us, and didn't want to tell me? It appeared the universe was conspiring to drive me crazy.

"Why doesn't someone tell me what to do?"

"I think I have been." Daddy was at it again. I loved him dearly, but I really wanted him to hush, just for a little while.

"That's a good man you have." Tommy had returned and they were playing another duo act. "I'm glad you found him."

"Me, too," I muttered. "I hope I can keep him. Now, I'm going inside and don't follow me. I mean it."

For once my celestial visitors listened, because the next voice I heard was Fiona's.

"What did you guys talk about?"

"Stuff. Has anyone thought about how we're getting to the church?" I asked, hoping to change the subject.

Bubba had wandered into the kitchen and joined the conversation. "Mama's taken care of everything. You're not gonna believe it."

I soon discovered the truth of that statement. My first clue was a backfire that sounded like a gas-line explosion. When I glanced out the window to check for damage, I laughed until I got a stitch in my side.

It was the revival bus in all its Elvis glory. Where was the dignified limousine everyone else used for funerals? I would have even taken an understated station wagon or an over-the-top SUV.

"Mom," Maeve moaned, and Fiona joined in.

"It's time to get loaded. Grab your wives, kids and whatever." Pearlie Jean appeared to be orchestrating this soiree. "Let's get this show on the road." She grabbed Bubba when he tried to sneak out. "Rufus," Pearlie Jean was also allowed to use his given name. "Run to the family room and grab a couple of guitars. We're gonna have a sing-along."

Fiona rolled her eyes, making sure our surrogate mom didn't notice. "Let's go," she said, locking arms with me. "Where's that handsome man of yours?"

"I don't know."

"He's already on the bus." Mama shot me a wink. "He and Beau are setting up folding chairs so everyone will have a place to sit. And Pearlie Jean is right. We have to get rolling. I'd like to be there before our guests show up. I think there'll probably be a huge crowd. And yes, missy, you are riding on the bus."

Mama had always been able to read my mind. My unusual abilities *had* come from her side of the family.

Although at times she seemed like a fairy sprite, Mama could morph into a softer, more feminine version of General Patton. As kids, we'd frequently seen that side of her personality.

"Let's get going." Having said her piece, Mama marched out the front door, her gossamer skirt of orange, red and yellow silk floating in the breeze. On anyone else that would be inappropriate funeral attire, but for her it worked.

Family members trudged across the lawn in varying degrees of grumpiness, directly related to the amount of alcohol they'd consumed. Hiram and Jerome were sniping at each other, and Aunt Eleanor was giving both of them a tongue-lashing.

"Hurry it up, Hiram," Eleanor yelled, hefting her ample derriere up the steps. "We don't want to be late."

Mama was obviously not happy with the loading process, so she started directing traffic. "Mother, let me help you." She put her hands on my grandmother's rear and pushed. Once Granny Bea was aboard, Mama started issuing seating instructions.

"Mother, I'd like for you to sit over with Hiram and Eleanor on the padded benches. And Hiram, make sure the older folks all have comfy places. The youngsters can take the folding chairs."

That task accomplished, she stepped back and whispered to Auntie Aurora. "I don't want Hiram to sue me if he falls off a chair. That old reprobate would steal from a beggar."

"Right on to that," Aurora agreed.

My family was nothing if not entertaining, and if Jed's grin was any indication, he was thinking the same thing.

When everyone was finally situated, Bubba brought the requested guitars on board, handed one to Mama and then settled in behind the wheel.

She turned her captain's chair around to face us and started tuning her guitar. "Maeve, would you come and help me, please?"

"Sure." Maeve walked forward and picked up the other guitar. My siblings and I had learned to read music before we tackled the Dick and Jane books, but Maeve was the most talented member of our family.

"Fiona, where are you?" Mama asked, glancing around. The bus was getting more and more crowded.

Fiona stood and waved. "Back by the loo."

"Would you please lead us in singing?"

"Sure."

I'd been spared.

"What would you like to sing?" Fiona threw it open to the family for suggestions.

I was about to raise my hand, but Mama beat me to it.

"We're going to do 'The Wheels on the Bus Go Round and Round.'"

"You have to be kidding!" Maeve squealed, and then slapped a hand over her mouth. Mama didn't take well to back-talking.

"That's what I want to do, and I don't want to hear any arguments."

"Ooh-kay. I'd better hear everyone singing, especially my sisters," Fiona said. "Here goes, on three. One, two and three."

"The wheels on the bus go round and round, round and round. The wheels on the bus go round and round, all through the town," Fiona belted out the first verse and then put her hand to her ear. "I don't hear you. If I'm going to make a fool of myself, I demand full audience participation."

When she put it that way, I was game, but it was hard to ignore the snickering. Daddy was in the middle of a full-on belly laugh, and I'm sure God was getting quite a chuckle out of this rolling freak show.

We went straight from the kindergarten tune to rousing renditions of "The Rock of Ages, Onward Christian Soldiers, Jesus Loves the Little Children, So High" and as a finale, "The Battle Hymn of the Republic." They were the songs of our childhood that we loved dearly. As kitschy as it was, it seemed to be the perfect way to celebrate Daddy's life.

Chapter 23

God had to be riding shotgun with the O'Flaherty Travelling Circus. And speaking of God, He must have consulted Monet when he designed Daddy's send-off day. The sun was shining, the birds were singing and there was a fragrance of honeysuckle in the air.

Mama had wanted to beat the crowd, but by the time we arrived at the church there were people everywhere. Realizing it would probably be standing room only folks had arrived early in order to claim a seat. Our family church wasn't big enough so we'd arranged for the services to be held at the much larger Baptist Church.

"Oh dear," Mama fretted. "I wanted to greet everyone, but never mind, we'll make do. Rufus, drop me off at the front door. And girls, why don't you come with me. Except you, Spring. I don't think you should be in a receiving line."

I wouldn't even consider touching that many people.

Bubba stopped to let Mama, Maeve and Fiona off. Then he parked at the end of the circular drive. Needless to say, our mode of arrival had turned more than a few heads. Our family was known for our eccentricities, but the bus ride was over the top, even for us.

The flowers that lined the brick walkway weren't the somber blossoms of a funeral. They were the wildflowers that God had whimsically tossed throughout the mountain meadows.

"Let's see if we can find a backdoor," Jed whispered.

"I know where it is." I steered him toward the rear of the building, hoping it would be unlocked. When we walked in, the familiar smell of old hymnals and fresh flowers brought on memories of my childhood.

Brother Josiah, Daddy's revival buddy, rushed over to give me a hug. "Child, it's been a long time!"

It wasn't until that moment that I realized how much I'd missed the rotund preacher with the booming voice. In fact, I'd missed all of this, the music, the church, the sense of security, and…even God.

"Brother Josiah, it's really good to see you." I gave him an embrace that I generally reserved for cherished members of my family.

He stepped back, putting his hands on my shoulders. "I can't tell you how sorry I am about Micah. That man was like a brother to me. I pray they catch the men who did this, and soon. No tellin' what they'll do next."

Did he know about my psychic ability? That question was answered when he gave me a knowing grin. Daddy had confided in him.

"I know it would please Micah if you helped the authorities."

"I'm thinking about it."

"You do that, child, you do that. A little praying' wouldn't hurt none. I'm sure God has an opinion he'd like to share." His smile gave me a sense of peace.

"Oh, and by the way, your mom wants you to sing the "Battle Hymn of the Republic" accompanied by my choir." There was that wink again. "She knew that if I asked you, you wouldn't be able to refuse."

"I'd love to, and I think Fiona and Maeve should also be involved."

His chuckle came all the way from the tips of his toes. "They're gonna be. Your mama can be a mighty persuasive lady."

Jed cleared his throat, reminding me it was time for my manners to kick in. "Brother Josiah, this is my fiancé, Jed Collinsworth."

"It's right nice to meet you, Brother Jed." The men shook hands and then Brother Josiah turned his attention back to me.

"Your Daddy told me that you'd met a nice young man."

"Jed's a city boy, so this is all new to him." I waved my hands to encompass the flower bedecked sanctuary. "He's from Atlanta."

"I have kin in Atlanta, but most folks in the South have someone living' in that big city." The preacher grinned, welcoming Jed into the fold. "I guess we'd better get down to business. Spring, I'd like you to meet our choir director. It's been a spell since you were at our church, so you probably don't know him." He summoned a wiry little man with skin the color of a Starbuck's latte.

"Brother Ezekiel, this is Brother Micah's youngest daughter, Springen. She's a lawyer in Atlanta. And this here's her fiancé, Jed Collinsworth." Brother Josiah made the introductions. "Ezekiel Jefferson here is a genius. He keeps our choir on their toes and in tune."

"Right on!" That spontaneous response came from a group of musicians who were setting up enough instruments for a small rock band.

Brother Josiah noticed my interest in the set-up. "Your mom wants this to be a party. She said that's what Micah would want, and knowing him as well as I did, I agree wholeheartedly. I can tell you it's not going to be your run-of-the-mill funeral."

"Amen!" That sentiment came from the only person in the room who resided on another plane. Daddy was back.

"Where did that monstrosity come from?" he asked. Daddy was referring to an eleven by fourteen photo that sat in a place of honor next to his ashes. It had been taken during his early Elvis phase, and yes, he had a pompadour.

"I look like a dork," he groused.

"Puleeze!" I was fairly adept at not responding verbally, but I couldn't let that one go by. Who would have thought that spirits could be vain?

"What?" Jed gave me one of those *what's up* looks.

"Nothing," I whispered. "Brother Ezekiel, would you like to run through a couple of choruses? Or should we simply decide on a key and go from there?"

"How about this? You sing the first stanza and the choir will come in on the chorus? Pick any key you like."

"I need a piano accompaniment."

"You got it," the choir director agreed before wandering off.

"'The Battle Hymn' is one of my favorite songs. I'm glad you're going to sing it," Daddy said.

Brother Josiah's next words took me back to the logistics of the ceremony. "Your sisters will be doing a couple of pieces after the eulogies, and your song will finish up the service."

I gave him another hug. "I know you have things to do, so we'll leave you to it. We'll sit down before the crowds come pouring in."

Jed and the preacher exchanged another round of handshakes. "Nice meeting you, sir."

"You, too. Take good care of my girl."

"I'll do that, or at least as much as she'll let me," Jed said with a wink. On our way to the front pew we had to side-step the bank of flowers that formed a semicircle behind Daddy's picture and extended the length of the church on both sides. Arrangements had come from around the state in remembrance of a man who had influenced people from all walks of life.

We were the first to find a seat. The rest of the family members were in the receiving line.

Jed put his arm around my shoulders. "You're doing great."

"I'm trying. Daddy was talking to me."

"What did he say?"

"He doesn't like that picture up front."

"He doesn't like the picture?" I could tell that Jed was trying not to laugh. "I wish I had gotten to know him better."

"Me, too. He was an incredibly nice person. But he seems to have an opinion about everything." I shrugged. "I suppose if I was having my last fling on earth, I'd be obnoxious, too."

Come to think of it, Tommy had been equally annoying. It wasn't surprising they were best friends in the hereafter.

Chapter 24

The church was packed to the rafters. There wasn't a seat or a space left empty, and according to Bubba there were equally as many people outside listening to the service being broadcast on loudspeakers.

And like Mama—and Daddy—had wanted it to have the feel and tempo of a party. The choir, accompanied by the band, was rocking out to the gospel music that was so much a part of the country churches of the South. Choruses of hallelujah, amen, and glory-be echoed to the roof.

But it wasn't until Pearlie Jean stepped into the aisle and started to dance that the party really took off. Folks who couldn't get into the aisles, danced in place to upbeat gospel songs like "So High" and "Joshua Fit the Battle of Jericho."

I even got into the spirit. After all, I'd been the princess of the gospel rock scene.

The choir in their white robes took me back to a place that I'd almost forgotten. It was a time of innocence and belief—a respite preceding my cynicism and doubt. I could almost feel my Humpty-Dumpty life coming back together again.

And I didn't need all the king's horses and all the king's men to make that happen.

I was so immersed in my own thoughts I didn't notice that some of Daddy's Elvis buddies had taken the stage. The trio consisted of two middle-aged guys in white jumpsuits and a dark-haired, sloe-eyed man dressed in jeans and a white T-shirt.

Why did he look so familiar? Then it hit me. No way. No way!

"You guessed, didn't you?" Leave it to Daddy to read my mind.

"How did you pull that off?" I whispered, trying not to move my lips.

"I have connections." Daddy's chuckle said it all. He did have friends in heavenly places. No doubt about it, that man would give St. Peter a run for his money.

After the Elvis wannabes and the young man from Tupelo—and I quickly discovered I was the only one who could see him—finished singing, Beau continued the service with a beautiful eulogy.

He had inherited his beautiful voice from Daddy, and when he spoke you'd swear that everything would be A-okay.

"And speaking for my family and our dad, we want you to know how much we appreciate you coming to celebrate his life. He'd get a kick out of his farewell party. As you all know he was a man who loved his music."

Beau waited until the chorus of amens died down before he extended a hand in invitation. "Pearlie Jean, would you please join me?"

Our surrogate mom's choice of attire—a swirly skirt, ruffled peasant and multiple silver bracelets—was somewhat strange for a funeral, but she'd apparently taken her fashion guidance from Mama and Auntie Aurora.

"Pearlie Jean has been a member of our family since I was a little kid," Beau said. "If there are any secrets about our dad, I'm sure she'll be glad to share." He reached down to help her to the podium.

"Before I relinquish the microphone, let me make some announcements. After Pearlie Jean finishes we'll have an open mike. If you want to speak, line up on either side of the church. I can't guarantee we'll get to everyone, but we'll try. So please keep your comments short. Here you go, Pearlie Jean," Beau said and then stepped aside. "Keep it clean."

"Hi." The microphone squealed and she jumped.

"Step back about a foot," Beau prompted.

"Oh, okay. Like Beau here said, I'm Pearlie Jean Renfro. I met Brother Micah when he rescued my bony butt from the hoosegow."

The entire church erupted in laughter. From there, she explained about Daddy's interest in helping victims of domestic violence, and told how many women and kids he had assisted.

"So, to conclude, I'm pretty darned sure that Micah and Hiram threatened to cut my old man's nuts off, and that's why I never saw him again. For that, Brother Micah, I praise ya."

"Did you really do that?" I whispered.

"You bet, and I'd do it again," Daddy said with

a chuckle. "It worked, didn't it? Sometimes you just have to go with what works."

Although I couldn't condone the tactic, it was funny. And if the ripples of laughter were any indication, most of the members of the congregation were of the same opinion—although a couple of men did place a protective hand over their privates.

"Look at all these people. It's amazing," Daddy said. The line to speak snaked around the church and then doubled back. It was a wonderful testament to how much he'd done for the community.

It took a couple of windbags for Beau to realize he had to take charge of the situation. "Friends, I know all of you want to say something, but we have more music and the good ladies of the Church Guild have prepared a picnic for us. So we're going to limit the testimonials to the next ten people. Then my sisters will finish the service with more music."

Once the testimonials were over, Maeve spoke briefly to the pianist and then made her way to the podium.

"Here's a song that my dad loved. I'm sure you'll recognize it."

Maeve had an understated beauty that didn't strike you until you looked past her quiet demeanor. Today she was dressed in a white dress that emphasized her raven black hair and those clear-blue O'Flaherty eyes. How that lying, scum-bag husband of hers could cheat on someone who looked like she belonged on a cloud with a lute was beyond me.

This was not the time for negative thoughts. That could wait until later because—good, bad or indifferent—I was going to encourage her to ditch her deadbeat, philandering husband. She deserved better, but as I said, that was for another time and place.

All bad thoughts were vanquished when Maeve started singing. Her clear contralto voice was guaranteed to bring goose bumps.

"Take my hand precious Lord, lead me on, let me stand. I am tired, I am weak, I am worn." When she finished there wasn't a dry eye in the chapel. It was a song that had been sung throughout the ages and had provided comfort to countless people in need.

Fiona joined her sister on the podium. They were a visual contrast between dark and light. Not only did Fi's red hair seem like a beacon, she enhanced the illusion by wearing a crimson dress.

Fi gave her sister a hug before taking the microphone. "Let's get a little more up tempo with this one. Give me a second to check with the musicians. And please feel free to dance or sing along." She stepped down from the dais to confer with the lead guitarist. The way he beamed, I knew we were in for a treat.

From the moment she started her rousing rendition of "Rock a' My Soul In the Bosom of_Abraham" with the exuberant accompaniment of the band the congregation went wild. There was dancing in the aisles and a chorus of 'hallelujahs.'

Fiona had one of those smoky voices perfect for country/western songs.

"Good going. Daddy's so pleased," she said after an encore.

"Now I think we'll do 'That Old Time Religion.' Mr. Foster, can I talk you guys into playing that one?"

"You bet," he replied, and off they went.

Fiona had the place a-rockin'. "Whew! That was so cool. Now my little sis, Spring, will close this party with the 'Battle Hymn of the Republic.' And just a reminder, there's a picnic on the church grounds to follow the close of this ceremony." Fiona held her hand out to me. "Spring."

I'd performed in front of hundreds of audiences, but I had to admit that I was nervous. Music was a part of my soul that had been absent for a long time.

When I was packing for the trip I'd tossed in a black sheath with a pencil-thin skirt, black pumps and a string of pearls. Looking out on the sea of color—multi-hued auras, pastel spring dresses and the occasional splash of red, orange and turquoise—I realized I'd made a fashion faux pas.

The ceremony of death and the process of grieving was different in Spirit Hollow. It was more like a celebration than an occasion for sadness. And Daddy would be the first to tell you that most of his flock had made their peace with God.

"They know all about the Glory Place," Daddy whispered. "That's why this is a party."

"Hush," I mumbled.

"Make me proud," he said.

The choir director and I had decided I would do

the first stanza a cappella with the choir joining me on the chorus. I took a deep breath and went to that place where the music was everything.

"Mine eyes have seen the glory of the coming of the Lord: He is trampling out the vintage where the grapes of wrath are stored:

He hath loosed the fateful lightning of His terrible swift sword:
His truth is marching on."

After the first stanza, I realized that the church was almost unnaturally quiet—no rustle of clothing, no children whispering, no coughing.

On the chorus the choir joined me in celebration.

"Glory, glory, hallelujah!
Glory, glory, hallelujah!
Glory, glory, hallelujah
His truth is marching on."

When we finished there was utter silence. One person started to clap, and then another and another. Seconds later the congregation erupted in applause.

That's the way mountain folks said good-bye. They didn't go silently into that good night. They did it with a bang.

Chapter 25

Following the service, the congregants were ushered out pew by pew, including Jed and the members of our extended family. Mama wanted to talk to us after everyone left, so my siblings and I remained seated.

"I'm proud of you all," she said. "And you girls were unbelievable." Tears pooled in her eyes and a single drop fell onto her cheek. "Your daddy is tickled pink."

The present tense of that sentence didn't escape me. I glanced at Fiona, wondering if she'd been talking to Daddy, too. She grinned and I knew that indeed she had. How about Maeve? The twins never stayed still long enough to listen to anyone.

"Boys, I'd like you to entertain our guests. I'll join you in a minute, but first I want to thank Brother Josiah and the choir."

"Don't worry, Mom, we're on it." Bubba stepped into the aisle and held his hand out to his wife. "Let's go greet our guests."

"Sally and I are right behind you," Beau said. "That barbecue I've been smelling has my tummy rumbling." He patted his abs. "I'll find Jed and introduce him to the guy who won the BBQ championship in Memphis. His baby back ribs are enough to make a grown man cry."

I caught my brother's eye and said, "Thanks." My relationship with Jed was rocky, so any help I could get would be welcome.

"Tim, you should probably go with the guys, too." Maeve's suggestion was more of a command than a request.

"Sure thing." He was up and out of the church so fast it looked like someone had goosed him.

Fiona muttered something incomprehensible, and knowing her, it was probably profane. Disdain for our brother-in-law appeared to be a common denominator in our family.

Mama watched her son-in-law disappear out the front door. "Oh, well." She plastered a smile on her face. "Let's tell these nice folks how much we appreciated their glorious music."

The musicians were stowing their gear while the choir members were busy folding their robes and chatting.

"Brother Josiah, the music was wonderful. Thank you, thank you all." Mama opened her arms to encompass the entire group. "Please join us at the picnic."

"My friend would haunt me for the rest of my natural life if I didn't." Brother Josiah's grin was both toothy and infectious. "A couple of our folks have other commitments, but everyone else is planning to eat, drink and be merry, because that's what Brother Micah would want."

Mama squeezed his hand. "He'd be pleased."

266

She turned to us and smiled. "Come on, girls. It's time to assume our hostess duties."

The broad expanse of lawn looked more like the site of a county fair than a post-memorial reception. Kids were playing hide and seek, old folks had settled themselves in lawn chairs under the shade, and the Elvis guys were paying homage to the keg.

The church ladies of Spirit Hollow had put on a spread worthy of a Southern Living magazine photo shoot. It was country cuisine at its best, including a Southern Comfort cake liberally doused with the potent liquor.

I looked for Jed and found him getting tips from the BBQ champion.

"Is Henry revealing the secrets of his sauce?" I asked in an attempt to break the ice.

Jed held up a half-eaten rib. "Not quite, but he's feeding me some of the best ribs I've ever put in my mouth."

"Henry Davis, I haven't seen you in forever." Henry had been one of Daddy's oldest friends. "How have you been?"

"Been better, Miss Spring. I've been better. I'll miss that old buzzard something fierce."

"We will, too."

At the last second I remembered that Henry talked with his hands, and he *was* holding a sauce mop dripping in red sauce. I backed up, pulling Jed with me, and not a moment too soon.

"Those son-of-a-bucks better not show their faces around here, not with most of us owning a .12

gauge." Henry was referring to an old-fashioned put-down that most of the folks in Spirit Hollow would appreciate. "We have our own way of dispensing justice." Barbecue sauce went flying in every direction.

It was a toss-up as to whether Jed's flinch was a result of his near-miss with the red stuff, or Henry's threat of vigilantism.

"I'm sure the sheriff is working hard on the case," I said. "And the FBI is involved, so I'm confident the case will be resolved quickly." That wasn't exactly a lie, but it was pretty darned close.

"The proper authorities are on the job." Although Jed was trying to be optimistic, he didn't sound confident.

"Keep the faith, Henry. Keep the faith." That was wimpy, but it was the best I could do.

"It sounds like the people of Spirit Hollow are getting antsy. That worries me," Daddy said, mirroring my concern.

"Um-huh."

"Have you given any more thought to helping the police?" Tommy asked.

"Hush." As much as I loved the heavenly men in my life, I really wanted them to be quiet.

"What did you say?" Jed asked.

"I was talking to myself."

I was considering the wisdom of getting involved with the police when I noticed a man with a muddy brown aura that looked suspicious. And he was lurking around the fringes of the picnic.

I was transported back to the time and place

when I'd discovered the color of evil. I tried to speak, but my voice came out sounding like the squeaking of an old screen door.

"Are you okay?" Jed seemed to be saying that a lot.

"Look, look over there," I croaked.

He glanced in the direction I was pointing. "What about him?"

"He's…he's, uh not right. Do you think he could be one of the guys who killed my dad? Criminals sometimes attend the funerals of their victims."

Jed looked around for back-up. "Bubba, Beau! Come here." It wasn't like Mr. Cool, Calm and Professional to get so excited, but it was nice to know that he believed me.

Beau trotted over with Bubba right behind him.

"What's up?" Bubba asked.

A subtle head tilt was all it took to focus the twins' attention. "Spring thinks that guy could be the killer."

Bubba and Beau didn't move, other than to glance in the right direction.

"That isn't exactly what I said."

"Do you know him?" Beau asked his brother.

"Nope, I've never seen him before. What do you think we should do?" Bubba asked.

"I don't know." I was beginning to have some doubts. If I was wrong, I'd look like a fool. "Perhaps we should call the detective that Mama's been talking to."

"Good idea." Jed pulled a phone from his pocket and handed it to me. "Call 411 and get the number for the sheriff's office. We'll keep an eye on the guy until we get some help."

"Before you do that, I have an idea," Bubba said. "This place is crawling with cops. I'll find one and see if he recognizes the guy." He scanned the crowd. "There's a deputy I know. I'll talk to him."

I was feeling like Alice after she fell down the rabbit hole. How could I explain any of this to the constabulary? Under the best of circumstances, they didn't take well to the concept of extrasensory perception.

A few minutes later, Bubba returned with a tall blond with a badge.

"Ms. O'Flaherty, I'm Deputy Sheriff Cooper. Your brother tells me that something going down. How about telling me what's happening?"

Now I really felt stupid. But I'd started this, so I'd better see it through. "See the man in the gray suit, over by the food table?"

The deputy glanced at the man. "What's he done?"

This was where things got dicey. How could I explain an aura to a guy who looked barely old enough to buy booze? "My brothers and I don't know him," I said, my confidence was eroding by the second.

He held his hands up as if looking for guidance. "And?"

"And...uh, he looks suspicious." This was déjà vu of my last police debacle.

He gave me one of those *are you some kind of weirdo* looks. "Tell you what. I'll have a chat with

270

him and see what I can find out." The deputy's aura was as bright as a spring day.

He didn't believe me, but that wasn't surprising. Skepticism regarding anything otherworldly was typical. And that was exactly why I'd been hesitant to go to the cops. Add in the problem of the paparazzi, and it was definitely a no-win situation.

Jed put his arm around my waist and pulled me close. "It'll be all right," he whispered.

That was debatable, especially if I was wrong, or even more so if I was right. I didn't know which option I preferred, but it didn't take long to figure it out. Deputy Cooper returned, accompanied by the man with the evil aura.

"Ms. O'Flaherty, this is David Armbruster, he's new in the prosecuting attorney's office." Terrific, the man I'd fingered as a murderer was an officer of the court. That didn't, however, make him one of the good guys. On the contrary, there was something off about him.

Jed obviously picked up on my tension and stepped forward to greet the newcomer. "Hi, I'm the Fulton County District Attorney down Atlanta way. We're in the same business." It took a couple *good old boy* sentences for the tension to ease.

Armbruster shook hands with Jed, but he ignored me. "I understand Ms. O'Flaherty thinks I'm a suspicious character."

"There's been a misunderstanding." Jed clapped the man on the back. "I hope there aren't any hard feelings."

"None," he said. "I thought I'd pay my respects

and get a lay of the land since I'm new to the area."

"That's a good idea," Jed agreed. "I would have done the same thing."

Had Armbruster's aura been destroyed by something he'd done, or by something he'd seen?

Chapter 26

Once the brouhaha subsided, Jed and I retired to an out of the way picnic table.

"What happened?" he asked.

"His aura was all messed up, and I...I don't know. I guess I just wanted this thing to be finished. I'm tired of being pressed to do something that's out of my comfort zone."

Jed didn't take me in his arms, which would have been my preference. Instead he patted my hand. At least he was talking to me.

"I can see why you're not thrilled about talking to the police. We haven't dealt with anything like this in our office, at least not that I've known about, but I understand why you're hesitant to get involved. Uh-oh. It looks like someone is about to join us," Jed warned.

The man approaching had cop written all over him, from his bad suit to his jaded aura.

"Do you mind if I sit?" He didn't wait for permission before he plopped down on the bench. "I'm Detective Smithfield and I'm handling your dad's case," he said, producing a gold shield. "I understand you fingered one of our esteemed prosecuting attorneys."

His cough sounded suspiciously like a chortle.

"That's right."

"The sheriff tells me that your track record is good. That works for me." He didn't wait for my reaction before continuing. "Have you decided to help us with the investigation?"

"Obviously my mother has been talking to you."

"Yes, ma'am. I don't know if she mentioned it, but we've identified a person of interest. We haven't picked him up because we don't have any hard evidence. Your mom thinks you can help us, but she said it's strictly up to you."

"Oh, boy." Both of my parents were poking at me, from different places. And I was having a crisis of confidence. Could things get any worse?

"What exactly do you want me to do?"

"Do you have to touch someone to get a read on him?"

"That depends." Explaining an aura to a bureaucrat, even one who seemed to have an open mind, felt like a waste of time.

"Good enough for me. If I go out on a limb and pick him up, would you come down to the police station to take a look?"

This was a moment I'd dreaded for a long time. "I...uh... I will."

Jed put his hand on my shoulder. He must have understood the angst involved.

"Are you sticking around for a couple more days?"

"I'll be here as long as you need me." I wanted to get this over with. Perhaps then everyone—

including Mama, Daddy and Tommy—would leave me alone.

"I'll be in touch," he said before turning to leave.

I was mulling over this turn of events when Mama and Auntie Aurora strolled up.

"I see you've been talking to Detective Smithfield. Are you considering helping him?"

"I suppose so."

Mama took my hand. "I know I've been pressuring you, but I'm having second thoughts."

"As you know, this wouldn't be my first choice, but I'm beginning to think it's the right thing to do."

"I'm proud of you." She kissed my cheek and stepped back. Then she looked to a point above her shoulder and mouthed "I love you." Tears were streaming down her cheeks.

That's when I knew Daddy was leaving. I wouldn't be hearing his beautiful voice, or delight in his laughter, or be sustained by his wisdom anymore. I'd miss him like crazy, but I knew he was following his destiny. Although that knowledge was comforting, it didn't eliminate the terrible void I felt growing in my heart.

Aurora put her arm around Mama's shoulder.

"I don't know how I'm going to make it," Mama's words were meant for Aurora, but I heard them.

"Spring, would you and Jed go check on the picnic, please?" Aurora asked.

"Certainly." I wanted to be with my mother, but she needed her sister and best friend.

It wasn't until the keg ran dry, and the church ladies had packed away the goodies, that our job was over. Mama personally thanked our guests and we boarded the bus for the trip home. This time there was no singing or chatting. Everyone seemed to be involved in their own introspection.

It was late afternoon before we returned to the farm. Jed had originally planned to go back to Atlanta, but I was worried about him travelling at night. "Why don't you stay over and get an early start in the morning?"

He shook his head. "I need to get back to Atlanta. There are some things that I have to take care of."

Although I hated to ask the question, I had to have the answer. "Do we have a chance to make it as a couple?"

Jed's frown didn't bolster my mood. "I hope so." He covered my left hand with his own. "I love you. Otherwise you wouldn't be wearing my grandmother's ring. But for now, I have to get used to the fact you weren't honest. You said this to me before, but now I'm the one who needs some time."

How could I dispute my own words? "I understand." Could I repair this situation? "I apologize for everything, from not trusting you, to hesitating about a commitment. If you do decide you want me in your life, I pledge to tell you everything."

Jed grinned, showing promise of forgiveness. "So you promise to tell me everything?"

Was that a trick question? "Uh…yeah, I think so. Do I have to confess about splurging at a shoe sale?"

When he shrugged, I knew that absolution was one step closer.

"Don't you already have a closet full of shoes?"

"A girl can't have too many shoes."

"That's true," he admitted and then stood to leave. "I'll call you tomorrow. Do you want me to come back in a few days to pick you up?"

"I don't know how long I'll have to stay," I said. What I wouldn't give to get in the car with Jed and head back to Atlanta, and safety. "It depends on my interview with the police. I think I'll fly back."

"Okay. Let me know your plans."

"I need to call Sam and let him know what's happening." Thinking about my mentor made me smile. "I won't tell him everything, but he does deserve an explanation. I don't think there'll be a problem with me taking some vacation time."

"Do you want me to talk to him?"

"No. I'll handle it, but thanks."

"Take care. If you need anything, let me know. I'm only a phone call away." He leaned over to give me a soft kiss. "I love you," he said before walking off.

Chapter 27

The next morning I was snuggled down in the covers, trying to ignore the upcoming day. My heart and head were engaged in a spirited disagreement. Talking to the police was so far down my *want to do list* that it didn't even make the top hundred. I felt as if I was trapped in a remake of the *Groundhog Day* movie where a day occurred over and over, with no resolution. Just the thought of talking to the police made me queasy, but logic told me I had a responsibility to take the bad guys off the street.

I stumbled to the kitchen for caffeine and a snack and found Maeve and Fiona already dressed and as chipper as a couple of magpies. Frisky was *not* what I needed.

"You look crabby," Fiona said as she handed me a cup of coffee.

"Up yours," I replied before taking my first sip. "I didn't get much sleep last night." To be more accurate, I didn't get any sleep. It was roll here, roll there, punch the pillow, take a drink of water, on and on ad infinitum.

"Fiona and I decided to go with you to the police station."

Maeve was wearing her *don't give me a hard time* look.

I was tempted to get stubborn, but having my sisters come along sounded good. It went back to the misery loves company axiom.

"Okay."

"Have some cake." Maeve cut a piece and handed it to me. "Chocolate will cure what ails you, and even better, Mrs. Harper made it. She's the diva of Coca Cola cakes." She leaned forward as if to impart a secret. "I think she puts a special ingredient in it, just like Uncle Hiram and Auntie Aurora."

That took in a wide spectrum of illegal and potentially dangerous products, but so what? I took a huge bite and quickly decided it was heaven on a fork.

"Oh, good, you're up. The girls said you were sound asleep."

Mama came in and sat down at the table. "I wanted to talk to you before you went to the courthouse. I was awake all night wondering if this is a good idea. I feel guilty about talking you into doing something that makes you unhappy."

"Oh, Mama, there's nothing to feel guilty about. As much as I hate to say it, this is the right decision. I'm older and wiser, and I'm sure I can handle anything that comes my way."

"Are you absolutely positive?"

"Uh-uh."

She patted my hand. "I'm very proud of you. Now, where is the rest of the cake? I can use something sweet."

Pearlie Jean scurried over. "I'll make you pancakes. Chocolate cake isn't any kind of proper breakfast."

The sheriff's office was housed in the basement of the county courthouse. It was a maze of cubicles, exposed ceiling pipes and windowless rooms. The building was typical nineteenth-century Southern architecture. The halls were marble, the facilities were antiquated and the ambiance was post-Civil War.

Fiona shuddered. "Has a castle in Transylvania lost its dungeon?"

Maeve apparently agreed with Fi's assessment. Her frown reminded me of a tyrannical headmistress.

"It smells like mold," she said with a sniff. "I hope it's not toxic."

I looked around and checked out the auras that ranged from dark brown to prison grey. But the one that really surprised me was a man with a graphite black with streaks of crimson, purple and fluorescent green. Was he a cop or a felon?

Maeve pushed me toward the reception desk where a chubby female deputy held court, denying or admitting entrance to the bowels of the cop shop.

"I'm here to see Detective Smithfield."

She gave us a visual inspection before speaking. "He's waiting for you. Go through the door and then all the way to the end of the hall. The conference room is on your left."

"Thanks." She wasn't exactly a friendly gatekeeper, but this wasn't a tony law office.

Fiona clutched my arm. Phones were ringing, people were talking and shouting. Pandemonium seemed to be the order of the day.

Several men were already seated in the conference. The detective stood when he saw me standing in the door.

"Please come in. Ms. O'Flaherty, I was in the department years ago when you helped us solve the Herndon case."

Thank goodness, someone might believe me. However, I did have to let him know there was a limitation to my abilities. "I'm not sure I can help you."

"We'll worry about that later. Let me introduce our task force." The group included representatives of the FBI, the Virginia State Police and the Sheriff's office. "Ms. O'Flaherty, I've briefed everyone on what we want to accomplish today and they're all on board. So let me tell you what we've talked about, and see if you approve."

I was tempted to run, instead I said, "All right."

"Good. Everyone, please sit down. I'll brief our visitors." The detective had an unhealthy aura that was probably the result of rubbing shoulders with too many criminals. One of the younger policemen was a nice cobalt blue. What would he look like in five years?

My attention was jerked back to the subject at hand when Detective Smithfield accidentally bumped my chair. "So, there you have it," he said with a nod.

I'd apparently missed something important. "Would you mind repeating that?" I hated feeling like a dope, but if they had a job for me, I needed to know what it was.

Concentrate. Concentrate. Concentrate.

He sighed, probably wishing he didn't have to deal with civilians.

"We're temporarily detaining a person of interest for a convenience store robbery. A witness saw him at the Shop and Stop shortly before it was robbed last week. He has a prior for an aborted robbery at a credit union, and his description matches what we have from witnesses at the bank where your dad was killed."

"What do you want me to do?"

Smithfield glanced at his teammates. "We'd like you to have physical contact with him. See if you can find out anything we can use."

"You want me to touch him?" He had to be kidding! "Is the man in jail?"

"He's in an interview room. One of my officers is keeping him company. All I have to do is give my pal a ring and he'll walk the perp down the hall. Your job will be to step out and bump into him." He gave me one of his unreadable cop looks. "Are you willing?"

I chewed on my bottom lip. It was one of the worst ideas I'd ever heard, but if that's what it took. "Okay. I'm in."

"Wonderful." Detective Smithfield pulled his cell from a holder on his belt and punched in a number. After he made the arrangements, he said,

"We're good to go." He glanced at his watch. "Three minutes." He walked to the door and motioned me to join him.

"I can do it, I can do it, I can do it," I muttered under my breath.

"Here they come. Just step out in the hall and touch him. It'll be a piece of cake."

That was easy for him to say. He didn't realize how much this would take out of me, both mentally and physically.

I heard the footsteps and knew it was show time. I took a deep breath and opened the door. A nice bump and run was the goal. Instead—and this was totally accidental—I tripped him and we went down in a pile of arms and legs.

"I'm so sorry." I clambered to my feet and helped him up, handcuffs and all.

"Bitch," he mumbled before he was hauled off.

Detective Smithfield was immediately at my side. "Are you okay?"

I straightened my skirt. "I'm fine. But he's not your man. I'm sorry." And I really was, even more than I could express. I'd have to do something similar again, and again, and...

"Seriously?" The policeman looked like someone had just taken away his favorite toy.

"Seriously. But if you want to pin the 7-11 robbery in Charlottesville on him, you'll find the cash and receipts in a box hidden in his attic. And there's a witness to that one, a homeless guy who was sitting on the sidewalk. He ran away before the cops showed up."

"Do you have a name?"

"No. But I can give you a description."

"Good. I'll have the sketch artist call you for an appointment."

"I plan to stay for a few days. Let me know when you want me to come back."

Detective Smithfield nodded. "We'll work with your schedule. I appreciate you coming down to talk to us."

"I'm glad I could be of assistance." That was a stretch, but my Southern manners had made an unexpected appearance.

I was halfway down the hall when I heard the voice. "Don't worry. You'll get him next time." Tommy had returned.

"I thought you left when Daddy did," I muttered under my breath.

Maeve gave me that now familiar *are you nuts* look. "Did you say something?"

"No. I was talking to myself."

"Oh." She shot me another look, but didn't call me on my lie.

"Good save." Great—now I had a dead person giving me kudos.

"I need to run to the girls' room. Go on to the car, I'll catch up with you in a minute." I waited until my sisters were gone before I continued my conversation with Tommy.

"How long are you planning to stay around?"

"Until we get these suckers. I have a new job as your angel guide."

That was *not* what I needed when I was trying to

mend fences with Jed. And I needed to be in Atlanta to accomplish that.

Chapter 28

Later that morning, we stopped at Sandy Sue's Tea Room for lunch. Fiona was into California cuisine so sprouts and cucumber sandwiches were the order of the day. We'd barely taken our seats when my phone chirped.

"What happened?" Mama was on the other end of the line.

"He's not the right guy. The man they have in custody has been robbing convenience stores, not banks. And he doesn't have a partner. But I was able to give them information that should help put him away. Hopefully, he won't be shopping at a 7-11 anytime soon."

"Was it terrible?" Mama knew how much this cost me in terms of peace of mind.

"It wasn't fun, but I did manage to throw him to the ground." I told her about the mishap, and before I finished, we were both laughing. "We're having lunch, but we'll be back to the farm in a couple of hours."

"Good, a lot of people have been dropping by. They all want to see you girls."

Once the call was finished, I inquired about my sisters' plans.

"I understand that Auntie Aurora's moving in for the time being," Maeve said. "That'll help Mama get oriented to her new life. I think I'll stay for at least a couple of days, maybe more."

"I'd better head back if I want to keep my job," Fi said. "How about you?" she addressed her question to me.

"I don't know." I sighed. "I can't stay around indefinitely. My first objective is to make peace with Jed."

"Group hug." Fiona beat me to the punch with her suggestion. "And let's have a glass of wine. We can toast our sisterhood."

"I'm driving so I'll limit myself to one," Maeve said with a laugh. "But you guys can go for it."

"After the day I've had, I deserve a good Chardonnay. You wouldn't believe how slimy that guy was." I desperately needed a hot shower.

Mama and Auntie Aurora were waiting for us on the front porch. They were both holding frosty glasses of some unknown brew—tea perhaps, but knowing Auntie Aurora that could be an iffy assumption.

Maeve gave Mama and then Auntie Aurora a hug. "What are y'all doing?" She sat down on the swing and Fiona jumped up on the porch railing. I had enjoyed three glasses of wine, so I opted for the steps.

"Is that iced tea?" I asked.

Auntie Aurora grinned. "It's Long Island Iced Tea."

"Doesn't that have a lot of booze in it?" Maeve asked.

Mama gave Aurora a look that was worth a thousand words. "Uh-huh. There's a full pitcher on the kitchen table. Help yourselves."

"I don't think so," I said. "I had a couple of glasses of wine a lunch."

Maeve raised an eyebrow. "A couple?"

"Yeah, a couple." Too bad, I wasn't close enough to smack her.

"I think I'll have one." Fiona stood. "Maeve, are you game?"

"A stiff drink sounds like a good idea."

After Fiona passed around the refreshments, Mama broached the subject we'd all been anticipating, and dreading."

"So we're back to square one with the bank robbers, right?"

"Right."

"Do you think the law enforcement guys believed you?"

"I do. Detective Smithfield and the task force members were very polite and respectful. In that way, it was a different experience from the Tommy debacle."

Mama visibly let out a breath. "Thank the good Lord."

"Amen," Auntie Aurora said.

"I regret dragging you into this," Mama said. "You don't have to do anything else, you know."

"I'm committed to it now." I didn't tell her that Tommy had reappeared. "As it is, they don't have anyone for me to vet, but if they come up with another suspect, all they have to do is call and I'll go back. The task force they've assembled is quite impressive. They really want to catch these guys."

"I know in my soul that the people responsible will end up in jail," Mama said. Her level of conviction was comforting.

The combination of stress and liquor must have taken its toll on Fiona. She plopped on the porch and fanned her face. "That iced tea was deadly."

Thank goodness, she wasn't still on the railing.

Maeve was slumped halfway on, halfway off the swing. "I'm not sure I can stand up."

Three glasses of wine and half a glass of the brew had wiped me out, but for some reason the Long Island Iced Tea hadn't fazed Mama or Auntie Aurora. They were in the kitchen putting out leftovers for supper and chatting like magpies.

Before I knew what happened, I was flat on my back next to Fiona. It was either that or slide down the steps—and all things considered, I preferred the former.

"You know what?" Fiona was slurring her words.

"What?" Maeve sounded fairly sober, but she certainly didn't look it.

"I think I have a stalker."

"What!" I sat up so fast I thought my head was going to blow sky-high. "What?" That was better.

"Explain," Maeve demanded in her best big- sister voice. "And I want specifics."

"I dated a guy three, maybe four times, and now

I can't get rid of him. I suspect he's been doing some creepy stuff, but I can't catch him, or prove it." She shook her head. "He's good, really good."

"That's not specific enough. What do you mean by creepy?" Maeve asked.

Fiona put her arm over her eyes. "I see him everywhere, and I do mean everywhere. He parks out front of my house in the middle of the night. And I've been getting scary phone calls. There's heavy breathing and sometimes he calls me lewd names."

She sat up and sighed. "And I think he's been in my house." Her admission was accompanied by a shudder. "My underwear drawer isn't in the right order."

"Good God!" I squealed. "Why don't you call the police?"

"That's the problem. He's a homicide detective."

"Shit!" Maeve spewed expletive, but it mirrored my sentiment.

"Where did you meet this character?" I asked.

"He pulled me over for a traffic stop. I'm positive I didn't do anything wrong, at least not that time."

"And then he took your name, phone number and address, right?" Maeve might not be as innocent as she looked.

"That's exactly what he did."

"Jed knows all about criminals. I'll pick his brain, but let's discuss this when we're sober."

"Don't tell Mama. I don't want her to worry."

I nodded. "Okay."

"Maeve?"

"Sure. But don't think I'll let you off easy on this one. The situation sounds dangerous. We'll help you come up with a solution." Tipsy or not, Maeve appeared ready to do battle.

It felt good to have someone else take charge. I was surprised that it was Snow White—aka my big sister—who was ready to don the armor.

Chapter 29

It was day four of the O'Flaherty sisters' self-imposed sabbatical. We'd spent most of the week eating, sleeping, talking and enjoying each other's company. We cussed and discussed Fiona's stalker, and despite coming up with half a dozen ideas, we still didn't have a viable plan. The corrupt cop scenario seemed insurmountable.

And Maeve's situation wasn't a whole lot better. She wasn't exactly forthcoming, so it was really hard to come up with a strategy.

I was sitting on the porch swing sipping Pearlie Jean's sweet tea—and no, it wasn't the Long Island version—but it was cold enough to flash freeze my brain.

Fiona sat down next to me. "Whatcha' doing'?"

"Drinking tea." The condensation running down the sides of my glass reminded me of summers past.

"That sounds good." She held up a two-pound bag of M&M's. "Do you want some candy? I found it in the pantry. It was probably left over from the church Easter egg hunt.

She held up a lavender piece. "Why do you suppose they make these things in purple and blue?"

"It's probably in keeping with the season," I said. "I'm not a fan of blue and purple food, but I'll make an exception this time. Chocolate's chocolate, and I'm feeling the need."

Fiona answered by picking out a handful of blue M&Ms and popping them, one by one, in her mouth.

The sunny morning had turned into one of those muggy spring days that usually preceded an impressive show of thunder and lightning.

"I'll bet we have a storm this afternoon," Fiona observed. "What do you think?"

"I believe you're right." A turbulent thunderstorm would mirror my mood.

"Did Daisy Duke leave those shorts the last time she was here?" Fiona's question was accompanied by a snort.

"Funny, very amusing. They were in the back of my old closet."

"Is this a private party?" Maeve asked.

"Come, sit down." I patted the place next to me. "Have an M&M." What better way to say I love you than with chocolate, even if it wasn't Godiva?

Maeve munched one piece of candy at a time. "Do you think Mama's getting tired of us?"

We'd decided to stay until she settled into her new life, but she seemed to be doing most of the comforting.

"It's not that I want you girls to leave, but I think you should go home." I hadn't noticed that Pearlie Jean was sitting in her favorite rocking chair.

"Paloma needs some time alone, and you girls just ain't givin' her none. I know you mean good, but yep, I think you should pack and giddy-yup." Pearlie Jean had never been known for her diplomacy.

Maeve started twisting her wedding ring. "I need to go home to take care of some things." She didn't elaborate on the chores she wanted to accomplish.

Mama strolled out and sat down next to Pearlie Jean. "What things?"

"Well, uh." By that time, Maeve was turning her ring so fast I was afraid it would fly off her finger. "I don't have Spring's powers, but I do have a strong sense of intuition. And I know that you've all been trying to keep Tim's cheating a secret, but I've known about his affairs for a long time."

We looked at each other wondering what to say, but she didn't give us time to comment.

"He spent the night before our wedding with an old girlfriend, but I was afraid to call the wedding off." Her expression revealed her disgust.

Mama gasped. "Maeve. You should have told us. We would have done anything you wanted, including returning that ugly china to Aunt Eleanor."

"But I didn't, and after the deed was done, I was committed. But I've decided to do something constructive about my failed marriage. I took the money I had stashed away and hired some help."

I couldn't resist staring. *Who* had taken over my sister's body?

"I have a lawyer, an accountant and a private

detective on my payroll. It appears we've hit pay dirt. Tim has had a mistress for years. They even have a child." She shook her head. "What hurts the most is that he said he didn't want children, at least not with me. The time I've spent here has given me an incentive to go home and disassemble my life. It'll be the hardest thing I've ever done, but everyone, including my boss, will simply have to understand."

"Maeve, baby. Come here and let me give you some luvin'" Mama opened her arms. "Everything will be fine." She patted Maeve's back. "I promise."

I glanced at Fiona, and then Pearlie Jean for guidance, but we were all speechless.

"Do you remember how that old hound Bruno used to chase Tim back to his car?" Mama asked, apparently trying to interject some humor into the topic. Bruno was a stray the size of a Newfoundland, with the grin of a Golden Retriever, and best of all, he hated Tim. "We should have listened to him," Mama said.

Maeve took a deep breath. "Actually, I noticed, but I was too oblivious to realize what it meant."

We withdrew into our own thoughts. Mama and Pearlie Jean rocked while Maeve tapped her toe in time with a song that only she could hear.

"I love having you girls here, it's like old times. But I agree with Pearlie Jean. You need to get back to your lives. And Maeve, you know we're here for you. Whatever you need, it's yours."

I scooted over to give my big sis a hug. Fiona did the same from the other side. She was the bologna in our sandwich, the peanut butter on our crackers, the marshmallow in our S'mores—she was our sister and come heck or high water, we loved her.

"I'm planning to leave tomorrow. When Tim left, he said he was going to Orlando on business. That's where his girlfriend lives. He won't be home for two weeks, and that gives me time to get everything started."

Maeve took a deep breath before continuing. "I have an appointment with a divorce attorney day after tomorrow and the CPA the same afternoon. I've already set up some bank accounts and credit cards in my name. I know he'll try to pull something sneaky, and I plan to thwart him. He'll be shocked at my initiative."

Fiona gave her a high-five. "Good for you."

"Take that sleaze for everything you can get," Pearlie Jean advised.

"Pearlie!" Mama was trying for decorum, but then grinned.

"Damned straight, that's what she should do." Pearlie Jean emphasized her opinion with a huff. "If my old man had had a pot to pee in, and I'd been smart, I'd have made that sucker cough it up." She huffed again. "I never did cotton to that Tim fella."

"I don't like him either," Maeve admitted. "I want this to be as civil as possible, but I'm fairly sure he'll put up a fuss. I don't know what my college administration will think, or do, but my private life is none of their business. At least it isn't as long as I'm not doing anything illegal or immoral. Unfortunately, they may not see it that way.

Chapter 30

"As long as we're discussing our itinerary, I made a plane reservation for tomorrow," Fiona announced. "I have to get back to California and figure out what to do about my little problem."

Mama was suddenly all ears. "What little problem?"

"You left yourself open for that one," I muttered. "You'd better tell her the whole story." Mama wouldn't stop until she had all the relevant information.

Fiona hesitated, but finally told her everything.

"Is he dangerous?" Mama asked.

"I…I don't know."

"What do you think?"

"I think it's a possibility." Fiona glanced at me. "I wish you could read his aura. I'd bet two month's salary that it's a nasty color."

That was a given; stalkers were insidiously evil.

"If you ever need a place to get away, I own a house over in the Northern Neck," Mama said.

"*You* have a *house* in eastern Virginia?" Maeve shook her head. "I have to play journalist and ask who, what, where and when? We want the details—

lots and lots of facts."

"It's called the Willows. My great-aunt Cassandra left it to me. I didn't know what to do with it, so I hired a caretaker. I've also leased the land for farming." She turned to Pearlie Jean, "You remember Cassandra, don't you? She came to visit before the twins were born."

"You mean that crotchety old lady who harangued me about my bunions?"

"One and the same," Mama said with a smile. "You should have let her look at them. Family rumor has it that she was a healer."

"She showed up when you were having trouble carrying them twins, didn't she?"

"Yes, she did. I believe that she was the only reason I was able to carry them to full term. But back to Fiona's situation."

"Thanks for the offer, Mom, but I don't think I'll be heading to the Willows anytime soon," Fiona said. "I do, however, have to decide how to proceed."

"Just say the word and it's yours. Another family legend is that there's a pond on the land that people have been going to for years for healing."

"This gets weirder and weirder," Maeve proclaimed. "I used to think we were a fairly normal family, but that's clearly not the case."

Fiona ignored her sister and asked, "Spring, when do you plan to leave?"

"I want to go home and see Jed. Plus, I haven't heard a word from Detective Smithfield, so it's goodbye for me, too."

That night we had a thunderstorm of biblical proportions. It wasn't a plague of locusts, or the annihilation of a population, but it came close. The sky turned a bilious shade of green that was smeared with splotches of purple, and the cloud bank looked like fudge boiling in a pot, rolling, tumbling and crashing.

Lightning arced across the sky in a light show before hail came crashing down, beating on the tin roof, layering the yard in a blanket of white. That wasn't unusual for the South when a cold weather system swooped out of the Midwest and collided with the warm, humid air of the Gulf. I just hoped that it wasn't a harbinger of things to come.

The next day dawned sunny and beautiful. Maeve's suitcases were stacked in the front hall, but she seemed reluctant to pack her car. She was dressed and ready to go, but instead of leaving, she joined us in the attic room.

"What time is your plane," she asked Fiona.

"Three-thirty." Fiona's answer was muffled as she rummaged under the bed for a missing shoe. "Where is that darned thing? I had it on yesterday." She stood and looked around as if the missing footwear would magically appear.

The travel plans as they stood included Fiona leaving by plane, Maeve driving home and me flying out tomorrow.

"We should probably leave for the airport around noon." I'd borrowed Mama's minivan to make the hour trip to the Charlottesville airport.

Maeve sat down on Fiona's bed. "I might go with you guys to the airport."

"Are you procrastinating about going home?" I asked.

"Guilty as charged. I changed my appointments so I could tell you guys a proper goodbye," Maeve said. "But on to more important things. Rumor has it that Pearlie Jean is making fried chicken for lunch." She licked her lips. "I've used every recipe I can find to replicate her chicken and it never turns out right. That's another reason I'm sticking around."

"And speaking of hungry," I said listening to my stomach rumble, "let's go down and see what's on the menu for breakfast. If I don't go home soon I'm going to be waddling."

Fiona and Maeve nodded in agreement.

There was one constant at Windy Hill Farm— the chances of going hungry were slim and none. The minute I stepped in the kitchen I knew we were in for a treat. The table was almost collapsing from the weight of the breakfast feast.

"I don't know about you, but I'm planning to pig out." Fiona said, and Maeve nodded in agreement.

"Omigod!" Fi exclaimed when we polished off the last of the pancakes. "How much do you think we'd weigh if we lived here?" She emphasized her point by unbuttoning her jeans.

I chuckled at the mental image of my underwear catching fire because my thighs were chafing together—and believe me, that didn't have a thing to do with precognition. "I suspect the newness would wear off and we'd go back to eating like normal people."

"You think so?" Maeve asked, checking the waistband of her slacks. "I think I've gone up a size."

Considering that she started at a four, a couple of sizes wouldn't be a tragedy.

Regardless of our good intentions, three hours later we polished off a fried chicken lunch. "I think we'd better get going," Fiona said. "I don't want to miss my plane."

"We don't need to use Mama's car, I'll drive," Maeve offered. "It's gassed up and ready to go."

There was a flurry of hugs and tears before we made it out of the driveway. The trip was made with a minimal amount of conversation. So much had transpired that we were lost in our own thoughts.

I was the first to break the silence. "Fi, have you ever thought about leaving California?"

"Actually, a move is looking better and better."

"That would be one way to solve the cop problem," Maeve said.

"You see awful stuff on television about stalkers, and that's part of the equation." Fiona shook her head. "But I've also discovered that making it in Hollywood was a pipe dream. Everyone needs nurses, and it would be nice to be closer to family."

Living near my sisters would be wonderful.

"If you lived on the East Coast we could do weekends together."

"And if my boss makes trouble, I might be changing jobs, too."

Maeve tried for a sassy grin, but it fell flat.

Fiona gave her a high-five. "Good girl," she said and then asked me, "Are you're planning to stay in Atlanta?"

"I'm established and I can't see any reason to go anywhere."

Fiona pointed at a road sign. "There's the cutoff for the airport."

"Got it." Maeve clicked on the turn signal.

Instead of dropping Fiona off at the departure area we parked in the short term lot.

"You don't have to come in." Fiona indicated her small bag. "I can roll this puppy in by myself."

"We want to spend as much time with you as possible," I said. "And we don't want you to get lost."

"Sure," she snickered. "Maybe you should come with me to LAX to make sure I find the baggage claim."

It was reminiscent of the good-natured sniping we'd perfected in high school.

"I love you," I said, hoping I wouldn't tear up.

"I love you, too, even if you used to be a pain in the butt."

My phone rang as we were standing in the check-in line. It was Sam with a question about one of my clients. Even though I was busy answering him, I did manage to catch snippets of my sisters' conversation concerning two men ahead of us in the queue.

"Do you think they're straight?" Fiona asked. "A lot of the good-looking men in California are gay. It's embarrassing to flirt with someone who's not at all interested."

"Can't say that I've had that experience," Maeve said. "But I do think those two are hetero-sexual."

I could envision Fiona giving them her squinty-eyed look. "It doesn't matter. We're not planning to pick them up. I just mentioned that they're cute."

"Ma'am, you're next." The airline employee directed Fiona toward an empty computer terminal at the other end of the counter.

"Thanks." She wheeled her bag over and set it on the scale.

"Hey, Sam. I'll call you back in a few minutes," I said. "It's getting busy around here."

The customer service agent handed Fiona her claim check and boarding pass. "The gates are down on your left."

When Fiona leaned over to pick up her carry-on, I stepped back to give her room. That's when one of the men brushed my arm and everything went nuts.

It was that time preceding a cataclysm when you realize that ducking for cover is your only chance for survival. The blackness that surrounded him oozed with evil, like a nest of vipers waiting to strike.

I'd been so caught up in my phone call that I hadn't noticed the ominous colors swirling around the two men. It felt like a replay of my experience with the predator preacher.

My reprieve from evil had apparently come to an end. A mere touch and I was tossed back into the maelstrom of wickedness, and I knew that this man had killed my dad.

Images ran through my brain in a haze of vivid red. Blood from Daddy's severed artery was smeared on everything—the floor, the desks and the walls.

The most devastating picture of all was Heather Holmes holding her hand over his wound, telling him to hang on. She was saying that everything would be okay. But it wasn't, and it never would be again.

All of a sudden I was slammed into another scenario where two women, one young and one old, were huddled in a bank vault. Just when it looked like they might survive, the man returned and shot each of them in the back of the head. Although Daddy's murder was a mistake, it *was* the beginning of the blood lust.

I bit my lip to keep from screaming. Even in my addled condition I realized that making a fuss in an airport wasn't prudent. My heart told me to chase down the sucker and beat him senseless. My knees, however, put the nix on that idea. So instead I dropped like a rock.

"Spring! Springen, what's wrong?"

Fiona was kneeling beside me while Maeve stood back, wringing her hands. I gripped my head in an effort to get rid of the residual wickedness that coated everything like black slime.

"We have to catch that man," I mumbled.

"What man?"

"Him," I croaked. We'd made such a ruckus that

everyone was watching us, including the two men. On the surface they were attractive; but that didn't negate the fact their souls were hideous.

"Why?"

"That's them."

"What do you mean that's them?" Maeve asked.

"Daddy's killers." That's all I had to say. Logically, they should have questioned me, but sisterly love obviously had issued different instructions.

Fiona popped to her feet and screeched. "Stop those men! They're killers!" She looked like an adorable, but demented, Jack in the Box.

Two security guards ran in our direction, their guns drawn.

Should I throw up my hands and hope to goodness they didn't shoot first and ask questions later? That would have been the most intelligent course of action, but considering my black rage, and the amount of adrenaline rushing through my system, all caution flew out the window.

Fiona was several steps ahead of me in our footrace to snag the men. That girl was tiny, but fast. When she came to a screeching halt Maeve and I almost mowed her down.

"What the..."

Then I saw why she'd stopped. They'd gone in separate directions. The one who touched me was running flat-out through the airport knocking down innocent bystanders. The other man had whipped a ninety-degree turn and scrambled out the front door.

"What do we do now?" Fiona looked frantic.

That was a conundrum. The cops were behind

us–waving guns—and the bad guys were running off in two different ways. "I don't know," I wheezed.

"I'm taking the one who's still in the building," Maeve yelled as she jetted off.

Not to be outdone by my hundred-and-ten-pound sister, I followed with Fiona right on my heels.

Maeve managed to tackle him. By the time the airport cops arrived we'd snagged both the bad guy and a huge mess of trouble.

Chapter 31

A wise pundit once said that discretion was the better part of valor. He'd evidently never encountered a killer in an airport. Considering that my sisters and I were now languishing in a windowless cubicle barely large enough to qualify as a closet, perhaps we should have tried another tactic.

"The other guy is probably at Starbucks having a vente double macchiato," Fiona groused.

"You have to admit we're a good team. Too bad there wasn't a movie crew around," I said.

"Yeah, this could have been my big break. As it is, we'll probably have to plan a jail break. All that running made me thirsty. I could use a Coke," Fiona said and then apparently had another thought. "What do you think they'll do with my luggage?"

"I'm sure it never got on the plane, especially not since they think we're terrorists." Maeve had always been the practical sister.

"We could end up in the federal pen," I blurted, even though I didn't want to express *that* thought.

Collectively, we were mulling over that horrendous possibility when a man in his thirties strolled in. He looked fairly ordinary in a pair of khakis and a button-down collar shirt with the sleeves rolled up, but that's where the commonplace ended. A couple of things popped him out of the everyday category—the huge gun nestled in his shoulder holster and his impressive gold badge.. This guy was no deputy-dog or even a private security dude. He was a law enforcement officer.

"Ladies, I'm Detective Paul Hanson from the Charlottesville PD." He turned one of the metal chairs around and straddled it. "Let's start from the beginning." His smile seemed sincere, but he was probably doing the good cop routine. "What's your story?"

Lucky me, I got the first question. Men tend to be skeptical of things in the paranormal realm, so I was reluctant to start off with *I talk to dead people.* But in the end I told him everything.

He listened quietly and sighed when I finished. "That's quite an interesting tale." He turned his attention to Maeve. "What would you like add?"

"Not much other than I was the first to tackle him. I'd do it again in a New York minute."

He made a zipper motion across his mouth. "Mrs. Modrelli, I suggest that you shut it."

She put on her best headmistress face. "If you insist."

He then addressed Fiona. "Miss O'Flaherty, do you have anything to say?"

"Nope." She raised her hands. "Sure don't."

"Okay." He put away the notebook that he'd been scribbling in. "I'm going to interview the man you assaulted. I'd like you ladies to stay right where you are. Can I get you anything before I go?"

"A Coke would be good," Fiona said.

"May I make a phone call?" I asked. In the melee I'd lost my purse and my cell. I desperately wanted to call Jed.

"I'll see what I can do about both requests." After making that concession he walked out, leaving us to study the stains on the floor.

Maeve was nibbling on her fingernail. "What do you think will happen?"

"Personally, I want to ignore it all," I answered, adding a heartfelt shudder.

Fiona didn't say a word. She simply shook her head.

Ten minutes later a young airport policemen knocked on the door. He was carrying three soft drinks. "I brought you some refreshments."

"Good. I'm parched." Fiona took one of the drinks. "Thanks."

"Do you know if someone turned in my purse?" I asked.

"Oh, that's right." He smacked his head. "Detective Hanson asked me to give you this." He pulled my phone from his pocket and handed it to me.

"Thank you." I was tempted to ask him what was happening in the outside world—the other room of this holding facility—but managed to keep my mouth shut.

"Who do you plan to call?" Maeve asked.

"You don't want to tell Mama. And do we know anyone who could bail us out?"

"I know a district attorney in Atlanta." I punched in Jed's office number and within seconds we were connected.

"My administrative assistant said this is an emergency." He sounded distracted.

Just the sound of his voice made me tear up. "I'm in jail," I said, adding a sniff.

"Good Lord!" His expletive made me wonder whether he was at the end of his rope with me and my problems.

"Fiona was supposed to go back to LA today, so Maeve and I drove her to the airport, but when we were at the check-in desk a man brushed against me, and all of a sudden I realized that he was the guy who'd murdered Daddy." I took a breath, but I didn't wait for him to reply. "So we chased him through the airport and Maeve tackled him. That's how we ended up in jail. Except it's not really a jail, it's more like someone's office, but a detective from the Charlottesville police department has been in to talk to us, and he said something about the man we assaulted. And I'm almost positive that if we tried to leave they'd stop us, so it's sort of like jail." About that time I ran out of steam.

He paused for a second before saying anything. "What do you want me to do?"

What did I want him to do? How about hold me and tell me everything would be okay? Yep, that was exactly what I wanted.

"I thought you might know a lawyer here."

"Do you think they'll let you keep your cell phone?"

"I don't know, I guess so."

"Good. I'll call around and see what I can find out. I'll ring you back shortly." Then there was a click. No "I love you." No "I hope you're doing okay." No nothing. Well, shoot!

"What did he say?"

"Not much, other than he'd call some people. I think he's annoyed." From there we went back to sipping our soft drinks, and hoping that someone wouldn't show up to read us our rights.

My cell chirped and it was Jed.

"Since there's a possibility he could be involved in a bank robbery, I called a friend in the Atlanta FBI office. He got me in touch with someone in Virginia and an agent is coming to talk to you. Right away, I hope."

"Do you think he believes us? Or is he simply doing this as a favor?"

"I don't know," Jed admitted. "Is the guy you took down still in custody?"

"Beats me. They're not telling us anything."

Jed sighed again. "I'm sorry I was so short with you. We have a nasty case going, but I plan to leave here in about fifteen minutes to catch a plane to Charlottesville. Don't talk to anyone other than the FBI agent before I get there."

"Okay." Before I could finish the rest of my sentence, he was gone.

"Was that Jed?" Fiona asked.

"Uh-huh."

"What did he say?"

"He told me not to say anything until he got here."

"He's coming here?" Maeve let out a sigh. "I don't know about you guys, but that makes me feel a ton better. I've been thinking about what kind of sentence we could get for assault, and far as I'm concerned, thirty minutes is way too long."

Chapter 32

I checked my watch and noticed we'd been it that tiny room for two hours. Two hours? It felt like days.

Fiona and Maeve were on their thirty-ninth game of Hang Man when the door opened and two men strolled in. One was Detective Hanson. As for the other man, there weren't enough words to describe him, other than the angels had to have been singing when he was born. He was beautiful in that way of Greek gods and poets.

With dark hair just long enough to curl over his collar and a body that would make Michelangelo's David jealous, he was jaw-dropping handsome. And Fiona had obviously noticed the same thing.

"Close your mouth," I whispered.

"Huh?"

"Your mouth." I tapped the bottom of my chin. She turned a bright shade of crimson that clashed with her hair.

It wasn't until the good-looking guy whipped out a gold FBI badge that my sister popped to attention.

"It would seem that you ladies have friends in high places." He pulled out a chair and sat down at

313

the table with us. "I'm Special Agent Remy
Thibodeaux. You've already met Detective Hanson.
My boss is driving over from Richmond. I just
talked to him and he said he'd be here in an hour or
so. In the meantime, why don't you tell me your
story, and don't leave any out any details."

His voice was so compelling that I was tempted
to confess to something, anything, just to have him
talk to me. What was the protocol of meeting a fee-
bie—otherwise known as an FBI agent? Since I
didn't have a clue, I went for a simple introduction.

"I'm Springen O'Flaherty and these are my sisters Fiona O'Flaherty and Maeve Modrelli."

"Ladies." He nodded in a charmingly old-
fashioned way.

"So, Ms. O'Flaherty, where would you like to
start?"

"Why don't you call me Spring?"

"Spring, it is." He glanced at the paper in his
hand. "According to airport security you and your
sisters got in a wrestling match with a man in front
of the United counter and then chased him through
the airport." He looked up and gave me one of *those*
looks. "After 9/11 we tend to take airport events
quite seriously. Homeland Security can be touchy."

The question was how much should I tell him?
If I went for the full meal deal, he'd likely call in
the guys in the white coats, but truth was the only
thing that made any sense. So I laid out it all out–
from Daddy's murder, to my psychic ability, to our
chase with the murderer.

After I finished, he watched me with his chin

cupped in his hands. "That's...uh, different."

Maeve seemed to be pondering the possibility of prison jumpsuits and communal toilets.

"I don't place much store in woo-woo stuff, but my boss obviously does. That's why he's on his way. And your friend, the Atlanta D.A., is also en route. Everyone seems to think this has something to do with our bank robbers. That's why we're involved."

I certainly hoped they hadn't let that guy go. I'd been worrying about that ever since they slammed us in the hoosegow—okay, I'm exaggerating, it's not quite a hoosegow, but close.

"In case you're interested, the person you assaulted is an accountant named Justin Caruthers."

"We didn't assault him," Maeve protested. That was the first thing she'd said since Agent Thibodeaux appeared on the scene.

I was glad she'd come out of her coma, but this was not the time to start arguing semantics, especially not with a lawman.

"Mr. Caruthers might beg to differ," he said. "You ladies gave him a black eye and a possible concussion."

Maeve shrugged. "There is that."

"At any rate, Mr. Caruthers is in the emergency room getting checked out. They can keep him for a while, but not very long. Personally, I'm having a hard time putting this all together."

"Most people would feel the same way," I admitted.

Agent Thibodeaux seemed mired in his own

thoughts. "If you ladies would excuse me, I have a call to make," he said aloud and then muttered, "or two."

"What do you think that was all about?" Maeve asked once she could manage a coherent sentence.

"I don't know. I guess we'll find out pretty soon."

"Damn, that guy was good looking, and no wedding ring." Fiona never missed a chance to check out a handsome man. "But what do I care, I'm on my way to California, hopefully." She held up the pad of paper. "Does anyone want to play more Hang Man?"

"How about Tic-Tac-Do?" I asked.

Two hours, and what seemed like a thousand games later, Remy Thibodeaux returned. This time he was accompanied by man in full bureaucratic attire—boring suit, wing tips and a cartoon tie. A Bugs Bunny tie?

"I'm Greg Garrison, the Special Agent in Charge at the Richmond office," he said by way of introduction. "I've had a chance to chat with my agents and District Attorney Collinsworth."

I didn't want to interrupt him, but I had to know. "Is Jed here?"

"Right outside."

"Is it all right if he joins us?"

The two lawmen looked at each other, and Agent Garrison smiled. "Sure, why not? I suspect he's about to beat down the door, anyway."

Seconds later Jed was holding my hand.

Then the FBI SAC turned to me. "I understand you're Spring O'Flaherty?"

"Yes."

"Was your father Micah O'Flaherty, the preacher?"

That was a strange question. "Yes."

"I thought so." He cocked his head and gave me a look that I couldn't decipher. "Why don't you tell me the entire story? You can begin anywhere you want, but I definitely want you to include anything you know about the bank robbery where your dad was killed. And don't leave out any detail. Does that work for you?"

"Sure." If he was game, I could oblige.

After I finished with my narrative, he asked the most extraordinary question.

"Does Parker's Corner sound familiar?" What did that have to do with us assaulting—and I put mental quotation marks around that word—the infamous, nefarious, but presumably innocent scumbag, Mr. Caruthers.

"That sounds really familiar, but I can't quite place it."

"Jill Garrison was my cousin, but we were as close as any brother and sister. She was murdered by our preacher when she was fifteen."

"Oh my God," I squeaked. "Oh…My…God!" It was good thing I was sitting down or I'd have ended up flat on my face. Parker's Corner was the place I'd had the vision of the dead teenager with the clown make-up. It was where my life had gone tops-turvy. How could I have forgotten *that* name?

"I was at the service that night. I was only fourteen, but I remember it like it was yesterday." His eyes were telling me that he understood everything.

God was in his heaven, and this was just another one of his convenient coincidences.

"My aunt collapsed when she realized it was Jill's name you were screaming."

"I don't remember saying anything."

"You did. That's why I believe every word you're telling me now. The question is how do we use it?" He turned to Agent Thibodeaux.

Mr. Gorgeous was leaning against the wall looking perplexed, so Agent Garrison filled him in on everything, including my meltdown and the preacher's ultimate arrest and imprisonment.

"We have a gold mine with Ms. O'Flaherty. We just have to figure out how to take what she knows and turn it into legal evidence. That is if she'll agree to help us."

Remy sat down and put his head on his hand in a classic Rodin pose, then he turned to me.

"Did you know that there was another bank robbery in a small town out in southwestern Virginia?"

I shook my head. "What with the funeral and everything, I haven't been watching the news."

Agent Thibodeaux looked pained, but he continued. "We have the same description as before; two males, average build, average height, average weight and wearing masks. This time they killed two clerks and a security guard execution style." That was the image I'd had of the women in the bank vault.

"How can I help?" I asked. I could feel the noose of destiny tightening around my neck, and for once Tommy wasn't around to exacerbate the situation.

"Do you see things in a snippet, or is it like a rewind of a movie?" Agent Garrison asked.

That was a good question. Too bad there wasn't an easy answer. "Sometimes I only get bits and pieces, but occasionally I see full scenes."

The two agents looked at each other, but Agent Thibodeaux was the first to speak. "We need to figure out some way for you to touch our boy again. But he knows who you are, so that'll be tricky."

"Why would I need to touch him? As you know, I've already had full body contact with the SOB."

That wasn't a good way for a daughter of a preacher and a member of the Bar Association to talk, but so what? There had been so much confusion during the airport altercation that I hadn't seen any clear pictures, but that didn't mean they weren't lurking in my mind. The problem was I didn't know how to retrieve them.

"Perhaps I can get something from his aura. It's never worked that way before, but it wouldn't hurt to try."

Agent Garrison rubbed his chin. "I'm thinking we should put him in an interrogation room with a low key environment, someplace where he'll be at ease. That way you can observe him." He addressed his next question to me. "Do you think that would work?"

"I don't know." His guess was as good as mine.

"It's worth a try."

"That's good enough for me. Agent Thibodeaux, would you please coordinate this with the Charlottesville PD?"

"Yes, sir, I'm on it." Although he said all the right words, it was apparent that he was baffled by this turn of events.

An hour later we were standing in front of the vending machines at the police station.

Fiona was rummaging through her purse searching for change. "Do you want a candy bar?" She'd already downed a bag of chips and a Coke.

"No, thanks." The thought of food turned my stomach.

"What do you think they're doing?"

"Beats me." I'd barely finished my sentence when I heard familiar voices in the hall.

"We won't keep you much longer, Mr. Caruthers. You'll be out of here in no time."

They were heading in our direction. Agent Garrison had left us in an out-of-the way cubicle and I'd made the mistake of following Fi to the candy machine.

"He's coming this way," she squeaked. "He'll see us and go ballistic."

Sure enough, when he spotted us he went apoplectic. "Those two assaulted me. Arrest them!" He lunged, spittle went flying in every direction.

"Mr. Caruthers, please." Agent Thibodeaux grabbed the man's arm. "Calm down. We're taking care of everything." His words fell on deaf ears. It took two police to drag the suspect down the corridor, kicking and screaming the entire way.

Maeve waited until they disappeared before she showed her face. "Agent Garrison wants us to join him in the conference room. He has on his game face, but I don't think he's very happy."

Fiona was so distressed that she made another detour to the candy machine. She held up her super-sized Snickers. "I can face anything now."

That was good, especially since we were about to confront an irritated federal agent. I had to give it to Agent Garrison, he wasn't frothing at the mouth, but he wasn't smiling.

"Please have a seat. Unless you know something I don't, I presume we're back where we started. If that's the case, we'll have to let him go."

It took a few moments for me to realize that the man had grazed my hand. "I've touched him twice and I had a previous vision of that robbery. Maybe I can put all those images together and come up with something. Give me a few seconds to think it over."

Agent Garrison finally smiled. "Whatever you need, just name it. Agent Thibodeaux will be out in the hall. When you're ready just let him know. He'll come and get me."

I spent the next hour trying to make sense of the thoughts roiling through my brain, but one thing came through loud and clear. The man had to be stopped. Every stride I took toward the door felt as if it was one step closer to my destiny.

"Agent Thibodeaux, please tell your boss that I'd like to talk to him."

My sisters were waiting with Jed in the hall.

"What do you have?" Agent Garrison asked after he joined me in the conference room.

"Although his thoughts are disjointed, I do know that killing has become a sexual pleasure for him." How about that for a conversation stopper?

"Is there any way you can go back in time and consolidate your impressions?" Agent Thibodeaux asked.

"I've never tried it before." Recalling a vision, especially in gory detail, wasn't high on my list, but if it helped catch Daddy's killers, I was game. "I don't know anything about self-hypnotism, but perhaps if I get totally relaxed I can make some sense of his thoughts."

Agent Garrison looked happy enough to dance.

"Good. The Carrolton robbery was his last one, so that might the place to start. Are you ready now, or do you want more time?"

"Let's do it."

"What do you need?"

How about a blindfold and a last cigarette? "I, uh, I don't know. I'm out of my league on this one."

"We all are," Agent Garrison agreed. "Believe me, we all are."

My primary fear about this self-hypnosis scheme was that I wouldn't be able to come out of it, so I asked Jed to stay with me. If I got in too far, he could call for help.

Privacy was at a premium, so our options were limited to an interrogation room and the employee lounge—and considering my recent brush with incarceration I opted for the break room.

The furnishings were austere, but serviceable, with a dingy couch, a chrome dining table stacked with pamphlets, a tiny kitchen, a Mr. Coffee and a soft drink machine.

Although it was fairly quiet, I could hear the murmur of voices. Fiona and Maeve were outside the door along with Agents Garrison and Thibodeaux.

I patted the couch cushion for Jed to join me.

"Sit with me and hold my hand. If you think I'm getting too agitated or strung out, just snap your fingers, or shake me, or something. You have my permission to go for a slap if necessary."

Although Jed looked uneasy, he nodded.

"Here goes nothing." I leaned back, and starting with my toes I relaxed every muscle in my body. Before long I felt like bowl of Jell-O. Then I visualized walking down a golden staircase step by step. A soft spring breeze was ruffling my hair. I was young and free, and then it happened...

Chapter 33

Carrolton, North Carolina

I opened my eyes and I was in the backseat of a minivan. A small Tupperware bowl of Goldfish in the baby seat was next to a My Pretty Pony figure. I picked up a couple of stray Jelly Belly's and popped one in my mouth—tropical fruit, my favorite. You could feed a family of four on the food debris in this backseat.

It wasn't until I heard one of the men speak, that I knew where I was, and what I was doing. My spirit, if not my body, was in a stolen minivan spying on two murderers.

"Are you positive you got the right information?" the driver, Jason Caruthers asked.

"I told you. The armored car delivers bags on Tuesdays and Thursdays after four o'clock. They've already been here, so as soon as the woman in the Buick leaves, we'll go in." That answer was delivered by the guy from the airport who got away. I hadn't touched him, so I wasn't sure how he fit in the scheme of things.

I leaned between the seats, knowing they couldn't see me. There were two Halloween masks on the floorboard, and beside the masks were two deadly looking guns.

Dear God! I was about to see something that would haunt me forever.

We were sitting in front of a bank that reminded me of a manufactured home on a commercial scale—not quite permanent, but not exactly temporary.

"The security guard is at least a hundred, so he won't be a problem. The other employees are women. Remember, we're not getting caught and you know what that means. If you can't hack it, tell me now." Caruthers was obviously in charge. I suspected he was the one with the blood lust.

The one I'd dubbed the Runner paused for a second before he grabbed his gun. "I'm good. Let's do it."

They waited until an elderly lady wandered out to her Buick, got in and puttered off. "I thought the old bat would never leave. It's time to get this show on the road." Caruthers's grin was straight from hell. "Are you sure you're ready?"

Like an obedient sidekick, the Runner nodded before slipping on his mask.

It was high noon, and for a small town the traffic was heavy. Everyone was rushing to beat the lunch crowd. There weren't any other cars in the parking lot, and no one seemed to notice the two men—one masquerading as Bill Clinton and the other sporting a George Bush mask—strolling to the front door of the bank.

I was nothing more than a vapor on the wind, a

product of someone's celestial imagination, and as such, I was powerless. I couldn't call the police. I couldn't warn the future victims. And even more annoying, I couldn't jam Mr. *Scumbag* Caruthers's private parts up to his nasal cavity.

My role in this debacle was to watch and to remember. The devil's in the details, and that's generally where the bad guys generally screw up. And speaking of Satan, Caruthers' aura was ink black. The Runner's was more of a dark brown, but that didn't mean he was a good guy.

The interior of the bank was as nondescript as the exterior. A pudgy security guard was tipped back in a wooden chair catching a few winks. He looked like someone's grandpa. It broke my heart to realize that he wouldn't see his grandkids grow up. He wouldn't be able to play Santa at the church program. He wouldn't...

I was so lost in thought that I almost forgot Agent Garrison's instructions—remember everything, literally everything. Maintaining a laser focus was the key to success.

The two teller's cages were up front and the manager's desk was set back in a corner. Pictures colored by school children decorated a bulletin board near the front door. This was the kind of establishment where patrons were welcomed by name.

The tellers were too engrossed in discussing a new recipe they didn't notice the men, but one of them finally looked up. I could tell by her eyes that she realized what was about to happen. She reached under the counter, but it was too late.

"Don't do it," the Runner ordered, shoving a gun in her face. He slammed a canvas bag on the counter. "Fill it up and don't consider throwing in a dye bag."

"What?" The security guard had awakened and thumped his chair to the ground. That was the last thing he ever did. When Caruthers shot him in the chest blood sprayed over the walls, the floor and door.

The tellers fell to the floor, but I knew that wouldn't save them. They were huddled on the floor, praying. I wanted to tell them about the Glory Place, but I didn't have any substance.

And then I saw the man dressed in white, wearing the most beautiful smile. He folded them in His arms and they knew He was there to take them home. It didn't matter what happened in this realm, because in the end, everything would be fine.

I was mesmerized by the scene. It was everything that Tommy and Daddy had told me.

The most important thing now was my assignment. What evidence could I find that would place Caruthers and the Runner at the scene? I was scanning the area for something, anything.

Then with God's help I saw it. In the chaos of herding the women into the vault, Caruthers dropped his gum and it got pushed under the edge of a tier of safety deposit boxes.

We had his DNA! We had him!

That didn't prove he killed Daddy, but somehow, some way I'd make sure the authorities had the evidence to tie him to my father's murder.

When I came back to my senses I was squeezing Jed's hand and he looked worried.

"How are you feeling?" he asked. "For a few seconds I thought you were in trouble." The way he was leaning over me, I suspected he was ready to do CPR, or the Heimlich, or something.

I shook my head in an effort to clear the haze. Then it hit me. I was ravenous. This psychic thing was more debilitating, or invigorating, than I had expected.

"I have something important to tell Agent Garrison. We can nail Caruthers." I extended my hand for a high five, and Jed obliged.

"I'll tell him you're ready."

Fiona and Maeve rushed in followed by the FBI agents.

"I hear you have something interesting to tell me." Agent Garrison's smile was hopeful.

"Here's what I discovered." From there I delivered my good news

"That's fabulous." He pulled a cell phone from his pocket and punched in some numbers.

"If you'll hang with me for about thirty more minutes, I'll have someone take you back to your car."

"Could you help me get my luggage back?" Fiona asked Agent Thibodeaux. "I'm sure they didn't put my bag on the plane, but I don't know where it is."

"Sure, let me see what I can do." He moved to the corner and had a lengthy conversation on his cell. He finished his conversation with a grin.

"People who think we're too bureaucratic haven't dealt with the Transportation Safety Administration. But it's done. Go by the airport on your way home. They'll have your bag in the airport manager's office. As upset as they are with you, I'm surprised they didn't let the bomb squad blow it up. A word to the wise, you might rethink flying out of Charlottesville. I don't think you're welcome at their airport."

"I've been banned from the airport?" Fiona asked, adding on a pout.

"Not officially, but still..." Agent Thibodeaux gave her one of those *what can I say* looks.

"He's right," Jed agreed. "I think your best bet would be to re-book out of another airport."

"Oh, all right." Fiona let out a huff. "I've had enough of this whole mess."

Agent Garrison returned and joined the conversation. "You're free to go."

"Thank goodness." I wanted to head back to Atlanta, but I had some unfinished business here.

"I need to talk to Jed. Why don't you guys go find the car? I'll catch up with you."

The moment we were alone he took me in his arms.

"Thank you for dropping everything to come to my rescue."

"You're very welcome," Jed said as he kissed the top of my head.

"I hate that you had to do this. But I'm glad you were able to give them enough information to nail the sucker. I hope it wasn't too hard on you."

I snuggled as close as I could get, craving the feel of his body. "I love you," I mumbled. Considering my face was almost buried in his chest that probably didn't come out quite as clear as I wanted.

"What was that?"

"I said I love you."

The grin on his face said it all "I heard you. I just wanted you to say it again."

"You dog!" That deserved a jab in the ribs.

"I love you, too." He pulled me closer. "The thought of losing you was killing me. I realized that I don't care if you can see auras, or catch criminals by touching them, or brew up spells. That is if you promise not to hex me," he said with a laugh. "I'm going back to Atlanta to do some research on who the other perp might be. When you get home, we'll figure out the rest of our lives. A short engagement, a long engagement, whatever you want is yours. As long as you're in my life I'm happy."

"That's wonderful." It also sounded like a solid step toward taking charge of my future. "But..."

"No buts."

"This is important. You really need to consider how my talent will impact you."

Jed put his hands up in the universal sign for surrender.

"You're not listening. As long as you don't turn me into a frog or do something untoward with my privates, I'm good."

That warranted a smile.

"Something untoward with your privates?"

"Guys are funny that way."

"Hush." I snuggled closer. "I'm serious."

"I am, too," he said. "So what are our immediate plans?"

"First, I have to sit down. I'm not positive I can stand up much longer."

He led me to the couch. "You're in shock. You need some caffeine and sugar. Don't move."

I wasn't going anywhere, at least not any time soon. "Okay."

Two minutes later he returned with a cold can of Coke. He popped the top and handed it to me.

"Drink this." I took a sip and realized it was exactly what I needed. Watching a murder up close and personal, even if I wasn't actually there, was enough to zap the starch out of me.

"You're right. This hits the spot." I closed my eyes, letting the cola make its way through my body. "I'm going back to Windy Hill to let Mama know what's happening. But, there's something else."

"What?" He looked baffled.

"I've decided to use the talent God gave me. I can help the police, but first I have to figure out what that entails."

"Do you want me to go to the farm with you?"

"No, it's something I need to do by myself."

"Are you sure?"

I wasn't positive about anything. "Sort of," I said, and then had second thoughts. Now was not the time for white lies.

"Not really, but I do want you to go back to Atlanta. I'll call you every day. I promise. I need to talk to Auntie Aurora, and that means going home for a few days."

Chapter 34

Two hours later, Jed was on his way home, we'd retrieved Fiona's suitcase, and we were on our way back to Windy Hill Farm.

Maeve smacked the steering wheel. "We should call Mama and give her at least an abridged version of what happened."

I pulled my cell from my purse. "Who's brave enough to do it?"

"I'm driving. You're the lawyer. You can talk your way out of anything."

"Oh, all right." Hopefully they'd be at the church, or at the Dew Drop Inn, or...

No such luck. Auntie Aurora picked up on the first ring.

"Where are you?" We were definitely in trouble. "We expected you a couple of hours ago."

"It's a long story. I'll explain everything when we get home. But I will tell you that Fiona didn't go home, Maeve isn't leaving any time soon, and we ended up in jail."

The silence on the other end of the line was almost toxic.

"It wasn't really jail," I continued, " it was more

like detention." I realized I wasn't making any sense, but it was that kind of situation.

"We saw the bank robbers at the airport and we tackled one of them, but the other guy got away. Then I did some self-hypnosis and watched them robbing the Carrolton bank."

"The Carrolton bank?" Aurora squealed.

"Tell Mama we'll be home in about an hour." Before I could finish my story, the cell service died.

"I lost her. She didn't sound happy, but we can explain everything when we get home."

Maeve was driving, Fiona was riding shotgun and I had settled in the backseat. Before we left Charlottesville we'd gone through a fast-food drive-thru and with the combination of a full stomach, a nose dive in my adrenaline level, and a cool car, I was out like a light and didn't wake up until we pulled into the driveway at Windy Hill Farm.

"Are we here already?" I asked, throwing in a yawn and a stretch.

Maeve eyed me in the rear view mirror. "Yes, and I have a car full of sleepy-heads."

That's when I noticed that Fiona had drifted off, too. "I'm sorry we didn't stay awake to keep you company."

"That wasn't a problem. I'm so wired I could illuminate a house if I put my finger in a light socket. Today was one of a kind."

That was an understatement, but before I could express that sentiment, the front door flew open and the ladies of the house poured out.

The rest of the evening—or rather what was left of it—was caught up in explanations, hugs and praise sent heavenward.

"I feel sure that once they get him on the Carrolton job, it won't be long before they find something incriminating for the robbery at Daddy's bank." Mama's proclamation rang with authority.

The irony was that Tommy had told me the exact same thing before I took my car nap.

"What about the man who ran away? If Jason Caruthers doesn't offer his name, how will the police be able to identify him?" Auntie Aurora asked.

"They'll investigate friends, family, known acquaintances and anyone who's ever had dealings with him. Plus, they'll research Caruthers's bank records, e-mail accounts and his computer," Maeve said.

"How do you know all that?" Fiona asked, adding her trademark giggle.

"I watch *Law and Order*, so sue me," she snapped.

"What if there isn't a trail?" Mama asked. That question had been at the back of my mind, too.

It was then that I realized I'd missed something important. The men didn't act like they were friends. As a matter of fact, they didn't seem to know each other very well.

The Runner was clean cut enough to be comfortable in a law office or a brokerage firm. So if he wasn't a career criminal, he was probably flying so far below the radar that no one would suspect him. I knew what I had to do.

"Aurora, I need your help."

"What with?"

"I want to go see Sister Sarah, but I don't know where she lives. She's the only one who can teach me how to maximize my talent." It was the first time I'd really thought of my ability as a talent. In the past I'd mentally referred to it as a curse, or even worse.

"Sister Sarah?"

"You know, the healer. The woman you took me to when I was a little girl and then later after Tommy was killed." How could she forget Sister Sarah? Aurora wasn't old enough to be getting addled. "It's really important that I talk to her."

Auntie Aurora was one of the most confident people I had ever met, but something about this conversation was making her uncomfortable.

"She doesn't live on the mountain anymore. I...uh, I think she's gone home."

Sister Sarah was gone? She couldn't have left. I needed to understand my abilities, or at least that's what Tommy said—over, and over, and over again. And yes, Tommy was still nattering.

"Do you know where she went?"

"I'm not positive. I've heard some rumors, but..." she shrugged.

"Can you get in touch with her to tell her what's happening?"

"No."

This was the most important favor I had ever asked, and my favorite aunt had said no.

"This is out of my league, but I do have a suggestion," my aunt said. "And I'm not sure you'll like it."

When she put it that way, I was sure I wouldn't. But Sister Sarah had disappeared. So what were my options?

Aurora grabbed her enormous purse and started rummaging through it. "I have a lake cottage about an hour from here, courtesy of my third husband. With everything else going on, I haven't been there in a couple of years. I have a housekeeper so it's in great shape." She pulled out a huge key ring. "Here the key to the front door."

"Are you planning a trip?"

"No, but I suspect you might be."

I pointed at my chest. "Me? No, no way." Atlanta was the only place I wanted to go.

"Tell you what, let's take a walk," Aurora suggested.

"Oh, all right."

"That's my girl." Tommy was back.

"You're annoying me," I muttered, hoping Aurora hadn't heard me.

"Talking to *yourself* again?" Aurora asked with a chuckle.

"Yeah." Not to mention having a conversation with a pesky spirit who didn't know when to shut up.

We headed toward the orchard, well out of listening distance for anyone, except Tommy.

"Your mom is worried about you, spiritually."

"I know." I was doing my best to get that relationship under control, but I wasn't having much luck. I suspected that I didn't want to concede control to anyone, even the Big Guy.

She stopped and took my hand. "Here's my suggestion. Why don't you go to my place and spend the weekend meditating and getting in touch with your spiritual side. Forget about what's happening here, forget about the search for the killer, forget everything. Simply clear your mind and see what happens. You might find exactly what you need."

On the surface that sounded good, but I was the ultimate pragmatist.

Aurora continued her persuasive argument. "It can't hurt, can it? All you'll be out is a restful weekend in an amazing setting."

I sighed, realizing that I'd lost the battle. "Okay."

And that's how I ended up sleeping on Egyptian cotton sheets and eating gourmet meals. Aurora had neglected to tell me that her little cottage was a mansion, and the housekeeper was an amazing cook. I took long walks around the lake wondering how I could get my act together.

All I wanted was a quiet life with the man I loved and a houseful of kids. But I needed to make a difference.

Could I do both? And how did God fit in the equation? He was, after all, the one who'd given me my psychic ability.

Sunday morning was beautiful in the way that could only be found in the mountains. The breeze was as fresh as flowers in bloom. Sunlight sparkled through the trees and the water reflected like a mirror.

I sat on a rock, closed my eyes, cleared my mind and talked to God like I'd never done before. I think I was expecting Daddy or Tommy to say something; instead there was blessed silence. Then a calmness that was otherworldly spread over me. There was no way to explain my sense of well-being, other than it was heavenly.

I realized it was imperative that I follow my instinct and use the talent I'd been given. I had a man who loved me—warts and all—and a family that I adored. The difference was that now I was willing to use my abilities. One might call it a force for good. I preferred to think of it as kick-in-the-butt for the evil doers.

I also had the epiphany that I had to live my life to the fullest, and that meant Jed, kids, dogs and maybe even a bunny. My life wouldn't be without challenges, but that's not what He promised, nor was it something I could realistically expect.

Chapter 35

My sense of serenity was so overwhelming that I sang the entire way to the farm. Music had made its way back into my life. I was so caught up in my thoughts that my brain went on auto-pilot.

Auntie Aurora was standing on the front porch to greet me. "How did it go?"

"Wonderful," I said, giving her a hug. "I'll explain everything when we're all together."

"That's fair enough." She patted my hand. "Fiona's making us nuts. Let's go put them out of their misery."

My experience had been surreal, and explaining would be difficult, but my family deserved an explanation. "Let's do it."

Before I could make it to the door Maeve, Mama, Fiona and Pearlie Jean surrounded me.

"What happened?" Fiona asked.

Maeve asked what everyone else was wondering. "Did you decide anything?"

Mama was more interested in the personal stuff. "Are you all right?"

The questions were coming fast.

Thank goodness for Pearlie Jean. "Let the child catch her breath. Now scoot on inside. Shoo. Shoo." She made that familiar flapping motion with her hands.

"Did you stop for supper?" Mama asked.

"Why would I want a Big Mac when I knew Pearlie Jean was fixing supper?"

"She's making chicken fried steak, mashed potatoes and cornbread. And," Mama went for a classic eyebrow wiggle, "she's whipped up a coconut cream pie for dessert."

"I'm going to be so chubby I'll have to fast for a week," Fiona groused.

I was curious about what had happened while I was gone; plus, I was trying to keep it casual until I found the perfect moment to bare my soul. "Fiona, have you made a new plane reservation?"

"Maeve changed her appointments and she's going to drive us to Atlanta. I'll fly from there." She obviously hadn't told Mama that she was a persona non grata at the Charlottesville airport.

"Okay." That solved the problem of getting home. "When is all this going to take place?" It was easier to let them work out the logistics, and simply go along for the ride.

"My reservation is for day after tomorrow. So we thought we'd leave in the morning."

"Not too early, I hope. I'm wiped out."

"We'll leave after breakfast," Maeve said. "We're thinking about spending the night at your house, if you don't mind."

"That's no problem."

Pearlie Jean hit the dinner gong that in the old days had been used to call folks in from the fields. "Supper's ready, come and get it."

"We don't want Pearlie Jean to get impatient, so let's go enjoy the wonderful supper she's made,"

341

Mama said.

She waited until we finished eating before she asked, "Are you comfortable telling us what happened?"

It wasn't a matter of wanting to; it was more a case of how to say it.

"It's all a bit fuzzy, sort of like one of those dreams you can remember when you first wake up, but the longer you're awake, the more you forget."

I told them about the serenity I'd discovered that day at the lake, and Mama nodded.

"I know exactly what you mean. If that's the Glory Place, we don't have anything to fear about passing."

She was right. That sense of well-being was beyond description. But when I told her about my desire to work with law enforcement, she had an unusual reaction.

"Are you positive you want to do that?"

Wasn't she the one who wanted me to catch bad guys?

"It's what I have to do to make my life complete. My entire adult life I've run from who I am. That cowardice stifled all my relationships and almost turned me into a recluse. But I'm a changed woman, and I'm excited about my new life."

"Right on!" Pearlie Jean exclaimed. "Angels are up there singing as we speak."

I wasn't sure about angels in general, but I did know Tommy was tickled.

"I called Jed from the road and told him I was thinking about wearing spandex and a cape. He laughed. I don't think it's that funny," I said with mock exasperation.

"How do you plan to handle the media?" Maeve asked.

That was a good question. "I'm hoping to re-main anonymous. People want a lawyer who's pragmatic, and they might be uncomfortable with a psychic. But who knows?"

In truth, I was hoping to get some celestial guid-ance. "And the police might not want my help."

Chapter 36

It was almost noon before we hit the road. I looked out the back window until I could no longer see my family. I knew I'd miss Windy Hill Farm, but now that I'd tamed my demons, I planned to come back as often as possible.

We sang and talked until I was almost hoarse. It was late in the afternoon before we reached the suburbs of Atlanta.

"Would you go through a drive-thru ATM for me?" Fiona asked from the back seat. "I'm out of cash and I hate to travel without any money."

I was beat—both physically and emotionally—and I was ready to get home. But when a girl needed cash, a girl needed cash.

Fiona handed Maeve her card and when she inserted it, the machine ate it. All she got was a flapping noise—no money, no receipt and no card.

"What!" Fiona screeched. She'd always been a drama queen. "That piece of garbage ate my debit card. I'm going in and give someone an earful."

"Please don't. Remember the airport," Maeve admonished. "We're probably on some kind of watch list. You just never know."

Fi wasn't listening, so I hopped out and ran after my fiery-tempered sister. If she pitched a hissy, we might get arrested. I pointed at an empty spot across the lot. "Park over there and come in," I yelled to Maeve and then managed to snag Fiona before she made it to the door. "Let me do the talking."

She sputtered, but finally acquiesced. "All right. Do your lawyer thing."

We were getting in the line for the teller when I saw him.

The Runner was at one of the desks. This was either a bad dream, or it was the first test of my crime fighting skills.

I pulled Fiona behind a potted palm, hoping he hadn't seen us. It wasn't a great hiding place, but it was out of his line of sight.

"Hide your hair." She was wearing a light-weight sweat suit with a hood. "The color is a dead giveaway."

"Have you lost your mind?"

"The Runner is over there. Take a peek through the leaves and tell me what you think."

His aura was enough to convince me, but I wanted her impression.

Fiona leaned around the foliage to check him out. "That's him! He's in this bank." I was afraid she might faint. "What's going on?"

"I don't know."

Fiona sneaked another glance, apparently hoping that she was wrong. "Jesus, Mary and Joseph," she muttered. "You're right." She took a deep breath, obviously trying to gather her thoughts.

"Do you think he's robbing the place?"

I hadn't considered that possibility, but it didn't look like anything out of the ordinary was occurring. The tellers didn't appear to be stressed, the people at the other desks were working on their computers, and he looked like he belonged.

"I think he works here. Who would know more about a bank than someone who's employed in one?"

"That makes sense," she whispered. "What do we do now?"

"Let's walk out and hope he doesn't notice us. We have to get out of here before Maeve barrels in."

Things were going okay, until I tripped over a trash can and did a pratfall.

Fiona was out the door before I could pick myself up. The twit left me behind. By the time I made it to the car she was hunched down in the front seat.

"Did he see us?"

She was hyperventilating. I was feeling a mite tetchy myself.

"What in the heck is happening?" Maeve asked. She was about to get seriously irritated.

I hit the automatic locks. "The Runner works in that bank."

"The Runner! Do you mean our Runner?"

"One and the same."

"Oh, dear me. Do you think he'll come out here and shoot us?"

I hoped not, but I wouldn't bet on it.

Without saying another word, Maeve started the car and backed out of the parking spot. "We're not going to be sitting ducks."

"Stop!"

She hit the brakes so hard that Fiona was almost impaled on the dashboard.

"Pull in behind that dumpster," I instructed. "We have to call the police and wait until they get here. We can watch the doors from over there."

"If he recognized us, he'll try to get away. And he'll want to get rid of us before he goes." Fiona tossed the contents of her purse on the floor. "Where are my sunglasses?"

"Maeve, do you have a sunhat, or a scarf or anything that Spring can use as a disguise?"

"I don't think so." Maeve sounded like she was about to melt down.

I grabbed my cell. "I'm calling Jed. He'll have more clout than I do. Maybe he can get a SWAT team out here."

He answered on the second ring. "Collinsworth here."

I took a deep breath. This was no time to hyperventilate. "We're sitting behind a dumpster at the First Federal Bank off the interstate in Dunwoody? The Runner works here."

"What are you talking about?"

"We were on our way to the airport and Fiona needed some cash, and then the ATM ate her debit card, so we went in, and there he was."

"Who's the Runner?"

My calm, crime fighting demeanor evaporated. One scary situation and I started babbling. I took a deep breath. "He's the other guy from the airport, Caruthers's accomplice."

"Did he see you?" Leave it to Jed to ask the

most pertinent question.

"I don't know."

"What do you mean, you don't know?"

"I fell flat of my face in the lobby, so yes, he probably noticed me."

There was a moment of silence before Jed said anything. "I'm calling the Atlanta police chief. He'll help us, or he'll find someone who can. Stay where you are and lock the doors. And *do not* do anything brave, or dumb." He didn't give me a chance to answer. "I'm on my way. It'll take me about twenty minutes to get there." I could hear a bell ding in the distance. "I'm getting in an elevator, so I'll probably lose you. Be careful! And I mean it. Do not, hear me, do not do anything silly."

"What did he say?" Maeve was scrunched so far down in the seat that only the top of her head was visible.

"He's getting us some backup, and he's on his way."

"Thank God," she muttered. It sounded like she was digging for something in her purse. "Here."

Maeve pulled a card from her wallet and popped up long enough to give it to me. "That's Agent Thibodeaux's number."

Agent Thibodeaux?

What was she doing with Agent Thibodeaux's card? And why was there a phone number written on the back? I punched in the number and he answered on the second ring.

"Special Agent Thibodeaux speaking."

When I finished my story there was another one

348

of those silences men were so prone to do. "Are you certain?"

Why did everyone keep asking me that? "Yes, I'm sure."

"Stay on the line. I'm calling the Atlanta office."

He switched to a land-line because I could hear his side of the conversation. To his credit, he didn't say that we were escapees from Bedlam.

A few moments later he was back. "They're sending a couple of agents. Have you called 911?"

"Even better, I called the D.A."

"Oh, that's right. I forgot. Hang on the line with me until someone gets there."

"If it wouldn't be too much trouble, I'd like for you to vouch for us when your bureau friends arrive. They might think we're kooks."

Agent Thibodeaux paused before answering. "All right."

"And would you please let Agent Garrison know what's happening."

"If I didn't, I'd be in a lot of trouble. In fact, you'll probably be seeing both of us in a couple of hours."

"Perfect." I was amazed at how calm I felt. My stomach was jittery, but at least I wasn't about to throw up. Perhaps I really could pull this off this crime-fighting gig. However, I hadn't touched the perp. *That* would be the real test of my resolve.

"Do you think he'll try to leave the bank? And if he does, what should we do?" Maeve asked.

"I hope to goodness he stays where he is," Fiona

mumbled. "I've had enough excitement to last a lifetime."

I was at a loss as to what we should do, so I merely gnawed my fingernail.

"Stop that," Maeve said.

How could she see me from where she was sitting? "You can't make me." That slipped out before my brain could get in gear.

Fiona sat up and looked at us like we were both crazy. Then she burst into laughter. It was a great tension breaker.

"Look!" Fiona pointed at the back door. The Runner was glancing around as if searching for something, or someone. Then he stepped out.

Maeve gasped. "What should we do? And where are you going?"

I was out of the car and sprinting across the lawn almost before she finished her question. He spied me as I vaulted the curb and hauled butt like a running back heading for the end zone.

Fiona and Maeve were right behind me. Please God, he didn't have a gun.

The Big Guy must have been listening because all of a sudden the Runner tripped and went flying, landing on his face in an azalea bush. He somersaulted one way and the small black bag he was holding sailed in another.

Not one to miss an opportunity, I lunged and landed on him full force. His breath whooshed out and he went limp. I'm not a lightweight, but please I'm not *that* big. I was almost afraid to get up, and even more terrified not to. What if I was crushing him, or even worse, what if I had killed him?

Fiona was on her hands and knees patting him down. "Do you think he's dead?"

His aura hadn't gone to white, but that didn't mean it wasn't on its way out. "Check his pulse."

She gave me a dirty look, but complied. "He's alive."

Thank goodness. I couldn't go for the classic Twinkie defense—that I'd killed him during a sugar high. In my case it would be more like death by Butterfinger Blizzard.

"The cops are here," Maeve yelled. And sure enough an unmarked car pulled into the parking lot and disgorged two men in dark suits. They were either undertakers or FBI agents, preferably the latter. Then an armored SWAT vehicle showed up and dumped out a crew of heavily armed men.

How embarrassing. I'd knocked a guy out with nothing more lethal than my butt.

Fiona picked up the black bag and was about to open it. "What do you think this is?"

"Ladies, please raise your hands, and you," the older of the two FBI agents pointed at Fiona, "give me the bag."

"Okay." She threw him the duffel. "Do you mind not pointing that cannon at me?"

He obliged by swinging the gun toward me.

"And lady," he nodded at me, "get up."

I managed to get on my knees without killing the Runner—at least I hoped that was the case.

With as much dignity as I could muster, considering the circumstances—grass stained knees, twigs in my hair, a semi-comatose bad guy at my feet, and a phalanx of cops holding guns aimed in my direction–I stood and raised my hands.

Where was my District Attorney when I needed him? Right on cue, Jed came running up.

He flipped out his ID. "I'm Jed Collinsworth, the D.A. for Fulton County."

"Special Agent Henry Smith." The man in the dark suit reciprocated with an equally impressive FBI badge. "SAC Garrison from Richmond asked us to check out the situation."

He opened the black bag and poured out a handful of diamonds. "Well, well. What do we have here?"

All of a sudden, I had another of those moments that came straight from the recesses of my brain. "He used the money from the Brinks robbery to buy diamonds. Check his pocket. He has a plane ticket to Brazil."

"An armored car heist?" the FBI agent looked like someone had smacked him. "Where did this alleged crime take place?"

"In Kentucky." That was another revelation, even to me.

Jed shrugged. "She's almost always right." He was being careful in what he said. He was saved from further explanation when the Police Chief of Dunwoody strolled up and gave the stand-down order to his troops.

"Hey, Jed. I hear we have something important going down here." He shot the Runner a glance.

"Looks like you have it in hand." He stuck his

hand out to shake with the FBI agents. "I'm Chief Hendricks from Dunwoody PD."

"I'm Special Agent Smith and this is my colleague Special Agent Diaz."

"FBI? This really is something important, huh? So who took him down?"

Jed and the feds turned to look at us. "The ladies did," Agent Smith said, adding a reluctant grin.

"Impressive. Looks like he's a little worse for the wear," the police chief said.

"Would you put him in your cruiser until I can make a few phone calls?" Agent Smith requested.

"Sure. What do we have on him?"

"I'll let you know in a few minutes."

"I think you might also want to know that the weapon he used in the murder of the armored car guard and the bank robberies is in a box under the floor boards of his closet," I said, ignoring the astounded looks.

Jed shrugged. "You'd better believe her. Agent Garrison will vouch for her when he gets here."

Two Hours Later

By the time Agent Garrison finished telling his story even Police Chief Hendricks was a believer.

And yes, there had been an armored car robbery in Kentucky. The guard was killed and the bad guys had walked off with a hundred thousand dollars.

The proper authorities followed all the rules of interrogation, and after they obtained a search warrant, they hit pay dirt. I later discovered that the Runner was Sean Smith, a mild-mannered banker/

murderer who happened to be knee-deep in debt.

I was tempted to pat myself on the back for a job well done. That was before I had second thoughts. Sean was well on his way to escaping before he tripped. How had that happened? Did I have a crime-fighting sidekick?

We were in the police station parking waiting for a patrolman to bring our car around. "I'm going to miss my plane again," Fiona said. "I wonder how long they'll keep my job open?"

I hadn't thought about Fiona's work situation. Sam would cover for me as long as I needed, and Maeve worked for a college, so she was probably okay, but Fiona had been away from her hospital for almost two weeks.

"How long is your bereavement leave?"

"I don't know. The last time I talked to my supervisor, she said they were having to do extra duty to cover my shift."

"We'll get you on a plane tomorrow," I assured her.

She grinned. "Now that that's settled, let's go eat."

"There's a good Mexican place close by," Jed said.

"I'm ravenous," I said. "Crime fighting gives me quite an appetite.

Later that evening Jed and I were sitting on my front porch swing. "When you called, I almost had a coronary." He put his arm around me and pulled me close.

I sat up to look him in the eye. "But you know what?" I didn't expect an answer. "I'm happy that I've finally come to grips with my abilities. I never thought I'd be able to say this, but I know what I'm supposed to do with my life. Right after I brought that guy down, Tommy told me goodbye. He said I was going to have a great life."

Jed ran his fingers through my hair before pulling me close for a lingering kiss.

"So Tommy's gone?" he asked after we came up for air.

"I'll miss him, but he's where he belongs."

Jed was silent for a second, and then grinned. "I have a sneaking suspicion that life with you will be one adventure after the other," he said. "And if I'm really lucky, our little ones will take after you."

A lone tear escaped, and others soon followed. I'd spent my entire life trying to fit in, and worrying about what other people thought. In my determination to be ordinary, I'd missed the obvious—being unique could be a good thing, especially when destiny was involved.

And now I could have it all—a husband that I loved beyond reason, and a new-found relationship with God. What more could a girl want?

"I'm so proud of you." The whisper didn't come from Daddy, or even Tommy, and it definitely wasn't from this world.

Epilogue

One Week Later

"Have you heard from Fiona?" This was the fourth phone call I'd had from Maeve regarding the same subject. And no, I hadn't heard from our sister since her first night back in Los Angeles. She called me from the airport to tell me she was on her way home, but since then she hadn't answered her land-line or her cell.

"No, and I'm thinking about flying out there to see what's happening."

"I'm really worried," Maeve admitted.

I was frantic. I supposedly had all these powers, and I wasn't getting even slightest vibe from my sister.

"What do you think we should do?"

"Jed said he'd call someone in LA to see what he can find out."

"I'm afraid something bad has happened."

"So am I." I'd called her work only to discover that she'd never returned. But the most interesting–or should I say terrifying–aspect of this situation was that she'd told them she needed an extended leave of absence.

What was going on? I had a terrible feeling that it had something to do with her stalker, but with God as my sidekick we'd figure it out.

Fiona's Story

When the Magnolia Blooms

will be available in the Spring of 2015

Reading Group Questions and Topics for Discussion

1. Spring always knew that she was different, and those differences social handicapped her. Have you had situations in your life that set you apart from your peers? If so, how did you handle them?

2. The halo was frequently used in early Renaissance art. What did those artists see/or believe that encouraged them to feature the halo of light–or electricity–around the heads of their subjects?

3. As an attorney, Spring lived in a world of laws and logic. That was antithetical to her personal abilities of precognition and retro-cognition. Have you experienced anything in your professional life that was contrary to your personal beliefs?

4. Funeral traditions vary throughout the world. In the South, funeral foods–comfort foods–are an integral part of the grieving process. Are there customs that you'd like to share?

5. Spring could talk to dead people, and that's cer-
    tainly not the norm. However, it's not out of the
    ordinary for people to have that second sense, or
    to have experienced something otherworldly.
    Have you encountered any wee beasties that go
    bump in the night?

6. Tent revivals have been around since the colo-
    nial times. Early in our history, preachers were
    circuit riders and travelling evangelists were
    welcomed with open arms. I grew up in a
    Southern Baptist church in South Texas. We
    had tent revivals, pounding of the preacher and
    baptisms in the river. Have you had similar ex-
    periences?

Enjoy a funny, fast-paced story from
Ann DeFee!

Lucy's Got a Lot of
'Splaining to

BELLASTORIA PRESS
Books that nurture the soul

Annaliese Darr/Ann DeFee is an award winning author of thirteen novels and one novella.

Her hobbies–when she's not dreaming up stories–include tennis, bowling and exploring Colonial and Civil War historic sites on the East Coast. Please check out her website at www. ann-defee. com. She can also be contacted at adefee@cox.net and by snail mail at P.O. Box 266, Lightfoot, VA 23090-0266.

WITHDRAWN
BY
WILLIAMSBURG REGIONAL LIBRARY

9 781942 209027